男たちの
ヒロシマ

ついに沈黙は破られた

創価学会広島平和委員会 編

第三文明社

被爆1カ月後の広島：Hiroshima one month after the atomic bombing

現在の広島市街：Hiroshima today

男たちのヒロシマ――ついに沈黙は破られた

はじめに

　三十八回目となる二〇一三年一月二十六日の「SGI（創価学会インタナショナル）の日」に、池田大作SGI会長は、「二〇三〇年へ　平和と共生の大潮流」と題する記念提言を発表しました。『核兵器のない世界』のための拡大首脳会議」を広島や長崎で開催することを提案する内容です。広島、長崎で核廃絶サミットを、と訴えた二〇一〇年の提言をより具体化したもので、各界から多くの感動と賛同の声が寄せられました。

　本年二〇一四年の提言でも重ねて、各国の青年を巻き込んでの取り組みに触れています。

　これまでの「SGI提言」では、平和と共生の地球社会を実現していくための精神的基軸として一貫して「生命の尊厳」を提示しています。これは私どもの平和運動の原点といえる戸田城聖第二代会長の「原水爆禁止宣言」以来、一貫して揺るがない信念です。半世紀以上も前の一九五七年（昭和三十二年）九月、東西冷戦下で核開発競争が激化するなかで、戸田第二代会長は、核兵器の保有にひそむ「生命の尊厳」への重大な冒瀆（ぼうとく）を許さず、その徹底的な打破を叫ばれました。「核あるいは原子爆弾の実験禁止運動が、いま、世界に起こっているが、私はその奥に隠されているところの

爪をもぎ取りたいと思う」と述べ、問題の本質的な解決には、核兵器の保有を必要悪として容認する思想の根を絶つ以外にないことを強調されたのです。

恩師の遺訓であるこの思いを実現するため、池田SGI会長が長年にわたり多くの提言を発表し、世界の識者と対話と行動を重ねるたびに、繰り返し広島、長崎に言及されるのは「生命」の持つ無限の可能性、未来、そして尊厳が最も傷つけられた地であり、平和原点の地として、核兵器廃絶、世界平和へ大きな使命を持つからにほかなりません。

二〇〇九年十二月、創価学会広島平和会議のなかに、これまでは設置されることのなかった壮年世代による広島平和委員会が全国で初めて結成されました。そして、久保泰郎広島平和会議議長を中心に、月一回の定例会を重ねるなか、二〇一五年の被爆七十年という節目に向けて私たちがいかに取り組むべきかを論議してきました。核時代に終止符を打つには、さらに大きく国際世論を高めなくてはなりません。しかし、これまで国内外の賓客を広島平和記念公園等に案内するたび、広島で起きたこと、いまも続く被爆者の苦悩が、世界はおろか日本のなかでさえ十分に伝わっていないという現実に驚くことが少なからずありました。核兵器廃絶への大潮流をつくるために、国際世論喚起の一助として、被爆後七十年近くを生き抜いてきた男たちの被爆体験証言集を、私たち広島平和委員会の手でつくろうではないかとの構想が生まれました。

まず委員会メンバーが証言を提供していただける方をリストアップし、協力をお願いし、インタビューさせていただきました。私たちにとっても新しい発見に驚き、それぞれの人生を通じて語られる被爆の体験は鮮烈であり、真の世界平和への願いを新たにするものでもありました。被爆の事実そして体験が歳月とともに風化しつつある昨今の感もあります。次の世代にこの被爆体験を伝え

ていく大きな意義と深い使命を感じつつ、私たちはこの証言集を編みました。本書を世界中の一人でも多くの方々にお読みいただき、非人道性の観点から、核兵器の惨劇をなくす挑戦にそれぞれの立場で取り組む手がかりにしていただければ、これにまさる喜びはありません。

二〇一四年三月

創価学会広島平和委員会委員長　塩出大作

目次　男たちのヒロシマ——ついに沈黙は破られた

はじめに……3

広島被爆地図‥証言者の被爆地点……8

証言1　ローマ、フィレンツェで被爆スピーチ　　野々山茂……10

証言2　福島原発事故報道を見て放射能の怖（こわ）さを語る　　下井勝幸……20

証言3　誰（だれ）が被爆を伝えるん？　妻の一言で告白　　河合宣三……32

証言4　命の恩人のためにも語らねばならぬ　　西村一則……45

証言5　平和利用の核ならよい、というのは嘘（うそ）だ　　山田和邦……56

証言6　あの原爆を忘れさせてなるものか　　木原　正……67

証言7	人間の宿命を感じつつ、平和のために尽くしたい	中村良治……75
証言8	毎年、八月六日に韓国人原爆犠牲者慰霊碑へ	森本俊雄……84
証言9	いつか中国語で被爆体験を話したい	谷口宏淳……92
証言10	世界平和への使命と信じて真実を語りたい	橋本 薫……103
証言11	八十歳を前に「ヒロシマの心」の継承(けいしょう)を決意	平野隆信……110
証言12	原爆孤児(こじ)を二度と出さないために	川本省三……121
証言13	子どもの笑い声が永遠に続くように	伊藤 皎……132
証言14	母の一言「戦争だきゃ絶対しちゃいけん」	田島忠美……139

むすびにかえて……147

口絵写真 ©Bettmann/CORBIS /amanaimages（被爆1カ月後の広島）
©progress993 / PIXTA（ピクスタ）（現在の広島市街）

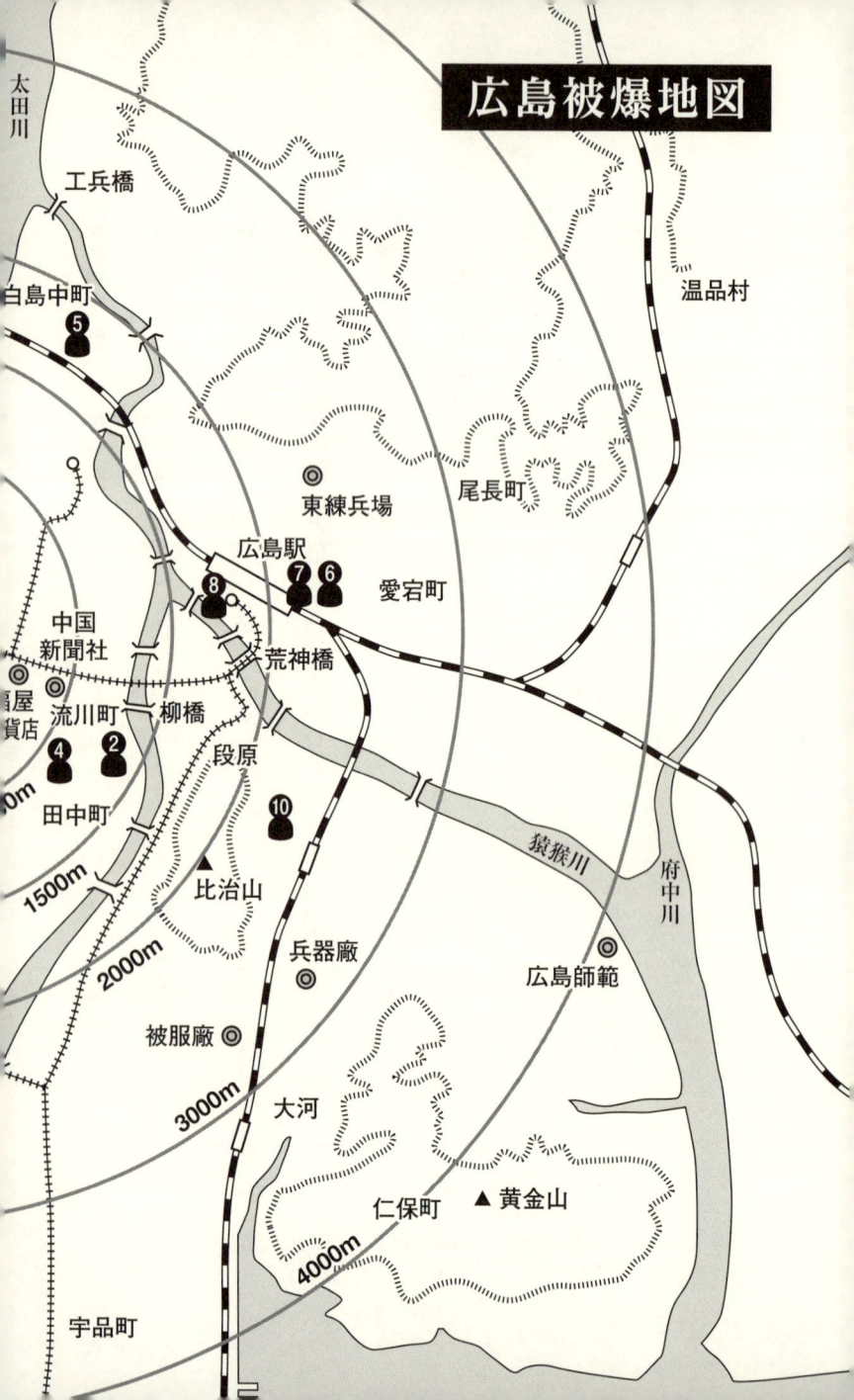

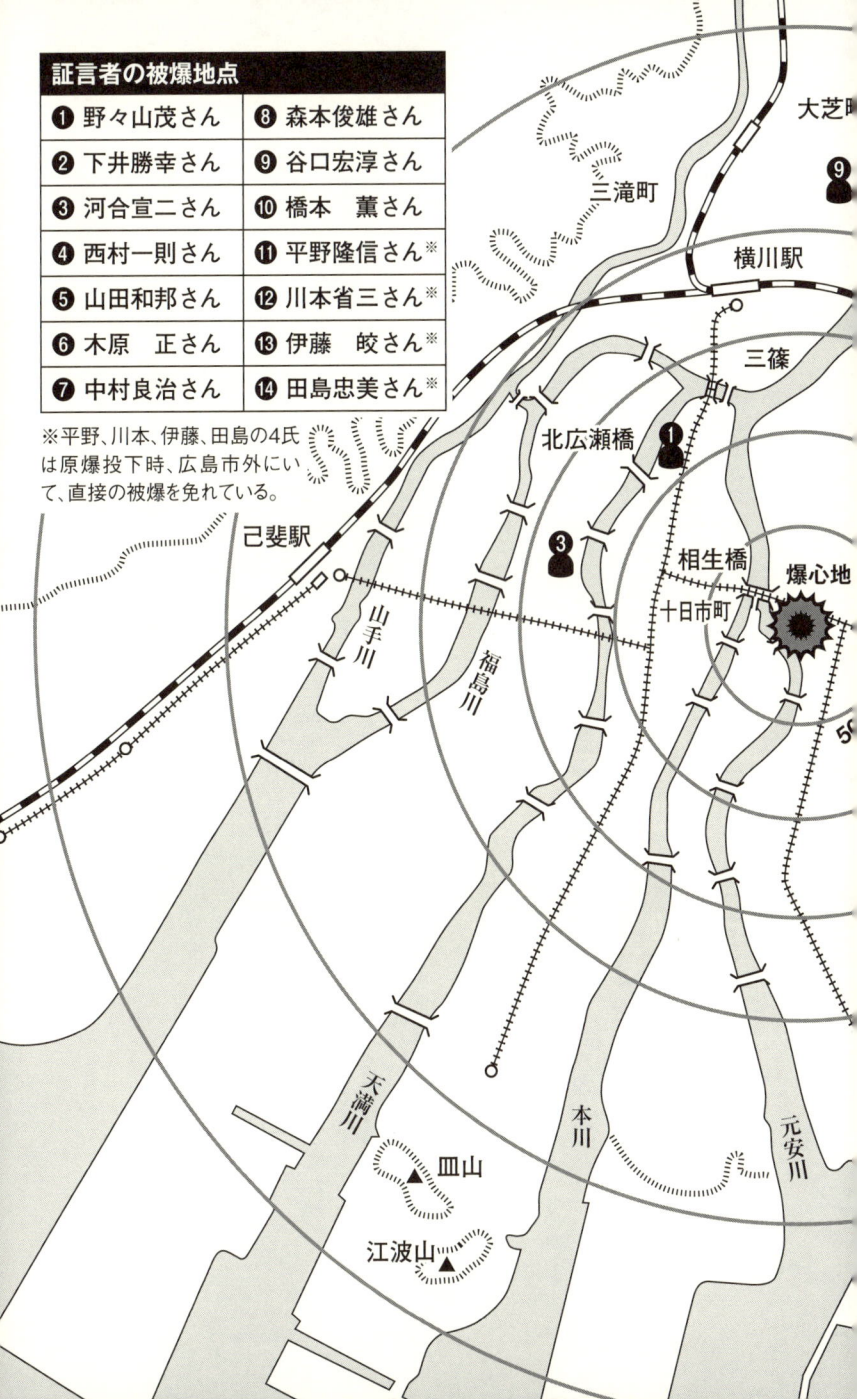

証言1

ローマ、フィレンツェで被爆スピーチ

野々山 茂 さん

ののやま・しげる 一九三〇年（昭和五年）一月生まれ。爆心から一・一キロの広瀬北町（現・中区広瀬北町）の天満川で十五歳のときに被爆。四十歳で結婚。これまで被爆の体験を人に語ったことはなかったが、最近になって、孫たちから聞かれて話し始め、二〇一一年には海外まで被爆証言に出かけた。八十四歳。広島市安佐北区在住。

水泳中に被爆、川面に走る湯玉

愛知県名古屋市で生まれた野々山茂さんは、三人姉弟の末っ子。二人の姉は年齢が離れており、物心ついたころにはすでに広島に嫁いでいた。昭和二十年に入って、東京・大阪をはじめ、各地の都市が次々と空襲を受けたが、広島だけは不思議と爆弾を落とされなかった。そのためか広島に移り住む人が増え始めた。野々山さん一家も、姉たち夫婦を頼って名古屋から広島に引っ越した。長女の恒子さんの家には子どもが六人、次女の姉・春江さんのところには子どもが二人。そこに両親と野々山さんの三人が加わり、三家族十五人が向かい合わせの二軒に住んだ。

10

家は天満川の川土手に立っていました。干潮時にはハゼや川エビ、カニがとれ、満潮のときは、橋の上から飛び込んで遊びました。

当時、私は十五歳。川のない名古屋から引っ越してきた私は川で遊んだことがあります。地元の子どもたちから「ナゴヤ」「ナゴヤ」と泳げないことで馬鹿にされとったことを覚えています。それが悔しくて、私は夜、こっそりと川に入って練習をしました。橋脚の間を順々に泳ぎます。毎夜の練習の甲斐あって、少し泳げるようになりました。

そのころ、私は逓信講習所電信科を卒業して、広島電報局に勤めていました。勤務は三交代制。八月六日、その日は昼二時から夜十時までの勤務だったので、午前中家にいました。たまたまこの日、恒子姉さんの長男の秀明が来ていました。秀明はそのとき、小学六年生。前日まで飯室（現・安佐北区安佐町）に学童疎開していましたが、広島に戻ったところだったのです。

「川へ泳ぎに行こうやー」

ふんどし一丁になったときに、警戒警報が発令。ちょうど天満川は、満ち潮から引き潮に変わる時刻でした。満潮時でないと、橋の上から飛び込めません。いらいらしながら待っていました。しばらくして、やっと警報は解除。私たちはふんどしのまま飛び出して、北広瀬橋の欄干から川に飛び込みました。

そのとき、橋桁には大きな流木が引っかかっていました。秀明と二人で横になっている流木を縦にして、川上に押し戻しながら遊んでいました。川底が深く、秀明は足が立ちません。彼はもたれるように流木につかまり、私が流木を下の方から押し上げていました。

[証言1] 野々山茂

そのとき、どこからともなく、米軍の爆撃機B29の爆音が聞こえてきました。

「撃たれちゃいけんけ、ずんごめ！（水に潜れ）」

とっさに私は叫び、空を見上げました。

その瞬間、「ピカッ」と稲妻のような光が……。

と同時に、川岸に立っていた広瀬国民学校がばらばらになって吹き飛び、人も一緒に飛ばされていくのが目に入りました。そして天満川の水面は、まるで刀鍛冶（かたなかじ）が真っ赤に焼けた刀身を「じゅっ」と水に入れたときのように、野球のボールやピンポン球のような様々な大きさの湯玉が、無数に川面を走り、水面が湯のように熱くなります。

「危ない！」と思ってすぐに水中に潜ると、上から凄（すご）い圧力がかかり、体を動かすことも、泳ぐこともできません。川底から巻き上がった砂混じりの水を何度も飲みました。やっとの思いで、なんとか水面に顔を出します。ついさっきまでぎらぎら輝いていた太陽が見えません。

あたりは真っ暗。

「あの光はなんじゃったんか？」

「この暗闇はどしたんじゃ？」

何が起きたのかさっぱりわからないまま、私は川のなかに突っ立っていました。しばらくして、あたりは少しずつ明るくなりました。

秀明の声が聞こえます。

「兄さん！　その体、どうしたん？」

そういう秀明の髪の毛はちりちりに焼けています。水面から出ている顔も胸も皮膚が剝け、胸のところで昆布のようにぶら下がっています。手の先も皮がずるりと剝け、ゴム手袋のように爪のところで垂れています。お互い、一瞬にして変わり果てた相手の姿を見ました。しかし、自分のことには気がつきません。秀明も私も、まったく同じ姿になっていたのです。急いで土手に上がりました。驚きました。まともに立っている家が一軒もないのです。ふだんは家に隠れて見えなかったはるか東の比治山が、すぐそこにありました。私たちが住んでいた姉たちの家も、押し潰されています。母はそこにいて無事だったのです。

土手の上に建てた家なので傾斜部分が地下室になり、そこが炊事場でした。

恒子姉さんは、胸が裂けて血が吹き出しています。私は、自分が締めていた六尺ふんどしを包帯代わりに巻いて、傷口をふさぎました。

春江姉さんも、ガラスの破片が顔に刺さって血まみれです。春江姉さんの二人の娘は、奇跡的に無傷でした。便所の汲み取りに来ていた荷車を引く牛の腹の下にいて助かったのです。

倒壊した家から抜け出した人たちが、ぞろぞろと逃げていきます。私たちも山手の安全な場所に逃げることにしました。

耳が溶けて垂れ下がり、頬に張りついた人。顎が肩に付いて、首が曲がったままになった人。二の腕が脇腹に張りついて伸びなくなった人。指が五本ともくっついて物がつかめなくなった人。そんな人たちが逃げていきます。百人や二百人ではありません。街全体がそういう状態でした。火災も起きています。

「助けて！　助けて！」

川の洲の下駄屋の奥さんが、倒れてきた柱に足を挟まれています。

[証言1] 野々山茂

必死に叫んでいます。あたりには兵隊も消防団員もいません。後で聞いた話では、下駄屋の主人が、挟まれた奥さんの足を鉈で断ち切って助け出したとか。服も燃え、やけどが酷い。皆、男女の見分けもつきません。防火水槽に人形が浮いている、と思ったらそれは赤ん坊の死体でした。

「あなた、助けて！　助けて！」

と倒れた家の下敷きになった妻の叫び声。泣く泣くそれを見殺しにして逃げるしかなかった夫……。

私たち家族は、母を先頭にして逃げました。

さっきまで遊んでいた北広瀬橋が爆風で崩れています。片側が川のなかに浸かってしまっています。ちょうど引き潮で水量が減っていました。なんとか橋を滑り降りて川を渡りました。一キロぐらい歩いたころでしょうか。山手町（現・西区山手町）の安芸高等女学校の手前あたりで、私はとうとう動けなくなりました。私は芋畑の畝と畝の間に寝かされました。だんだん空が暗くなり、突然真っ黒い大粒の雨が降りはじめました。それはたちまち豪雨になって、私の体は黒い水たまりに浸かりました。かろうじて顔だけが浮いていた状態でした。

野々山さんの父は、三篠（現・西区三篠町）の仕事場に向かう途中で被爆した。背後から熱線を浴び、首筋に重度のやけどを負っていた。それでも懸命に、家族を探しにやってきた。黒い雨を浴びて、白いシャツは真っ黒になっていた。娘たちは、わが子とは思えないほど変わり果てていた。

野々山さん自身も、目が見えないほど顔が腫れ上がり、形相が変わっていた。幸い、父は無傷だっ

た母に気づき、ようやく一家は落ち合うことができた。

　恒子姉さんは面倒見がよく、多くの人たちに慕われていました。そのなかに爆心地から八キロ離れた、安佐郡古市（現・安佐南区古市）の田村さんという農家がありました。ひとまず田村宅にお世話になることになったのです。親戚でも何でもない田村さんに、十四人もの大家族が身を寄せることになったのは、恒子姉さんの人柄によるところが大きかったのだと思います。

　昼間は敵機に狙われ撃たれるかもしれません。私たちは夜になってから移動しました。母が山手町の農家から大八車を借りてきました。胸が裂けて瀕死の状態の恒子姉さん。そしてガラスの破片で顔中血だらけの春江姉さん。上半身大やけどの秀明。まだ二歳だった恒子姉さんの子どもの博巳。この四人を大八車に乗せ、私たちは夜通しガラガラと引きました。明け方ごろに田村宅に着きました。

　私のことを「にいさん、にいさん」と言って付きまとい、実の弟のような存在だった秀明は、田村宅に着いたその日に死亡。夫の実家の飯室に帰っていた恒子姉さんは、一週間後の八月十五日、苦しみ抜いて亡くなったと近所の人が知らせに来てくれました。放心していたのか、母は涙を流すこともなく「ウーン……」と言ったきり。恒子姉さんの三女・昌子は進徳女学校に通っていましたが、いまだに行方はわかりません。原爆投下の八時十五分は、通学の途中だったはずです。春江姉さんの夫・広高さんは名古屋の陸軍兵器廠に勤めていました。久しぶりに妻子に会うために休暇をもらい、広島へ。原爆投下の八月六日に広島に到着し、被爆。八月末、死亡。恒子姉さん、秀明、博巳、広高さん、次々と子どもや孫が死んでいきます。

15　［証言1］野々山茂

家族一人ひとりの死を悲しむ余裕など、母にはなかったのかもしれません。私自身、ほとんど死にかけていた状態だったため、このころの記憶があまりないのです。顔中にガラスが刺さった春江姉さんは、一週間を過ぎたころから顔や体に小豆のような斑点が出はじめました。この斑点が顔から胸にかけて出ると、一週間もたたないうちに髪の毛がずぼずぼっと抜けます。口には出さないものの、皆、春江姉さんが間もなく死ぬだろうと思っていました。

春江姉さんは、こんにゃく玉のような血の塊を「がばっ」「がばっ」と吐き出しました。洗面器がみるみる血の塊でいっぱいです。その血の塊を捨てている間に、もう一つの洗面器が溢れそうになりました。母は毎日、畑に穴を掘って、血の塊を埋めていました。

春江姉さんはその後、奇跡的に持ち直します。「悪い血を全部、吐いたから助かったんかね」と言っていました。九十六歳まで生き続けて昨年（二〇一三年）の二月六日に亡くなりました。

私は八月から十月までの三カ月、生死の間をさまよっていました。化膿した傷口にハエがとまると二、三日で白いウジがわきます。母は一晩中、うちわでハエを追ってくれました。これ以上、息子や娘を殺されてなるものか。本当に必死だったのでしょう。垂れ下がっていた皮膚はやがて乾いて紙のようになりました。母がそれをむしります。そして藁を焼いた灰を食用油で練ったやけどの塗り薬を作り、私のやけどをした頭から顔、胸、指先にまで真っ黒に塗ってくれます。最初はちょっとしみるのですが、すぐにひりひりした痛みが止まります。傷口が乾くとかさぶたになります。乾いたらまたそれをキュウリの絞り汁で浸して取り除きます。そして、また薬で真っ黒に塗ります。乾いたらまた剝（は）がします。母はひたすらそれを繰り返すのでした。

やけどは治っても跡にケロイドが残る。後年、異形の相の人に電車のなかで声を掛けられ、それが昔の知人だった——という光景は、戦後の広島のあちこちで見られた。野々山さん自身、銭湯でかなり長い年月、ケロイドの人たちを見た。

それなのに、私は不思議とケロイドにもならず、傷跡も残っていません。天満川で水泳中に被爆したとき、熱線を浴びた上半身と水中に浸かっていた下半身の境目が、うっすらと残っているだけ。何としても助け出したいという母の執念の賜物だったと思います。

十一月、奇跡的に回復した野々山さんは、電報局に職場復帰する。その際、広島逓信病院で健康診断を受けた。健診にあたった蜂谷道彦院長から「川のなかでピカ（原爆）において、助かったのはあんたぐらいじゃろう。きれいになっとるのお。無理をせんように気をつけんさいよ」と言われた。蜂谷院長は自ら被爆・負傷しながら、破壊された逓信病院のなかで、被爆者を診察・治療にあたった。

袋町（現・中区袋町）の電話局に通う途中、「海軍将兵埋葬の地」と木札がありました。その札のあたりはうっすらと土がかけてあります。土をのけると、腐ってずるずるの死体が出てくるのです。私は、ずっと原爆を「新型の爆弾の一つ」くらいに思っていました。当時は、誰も放射能のことを知りません。行方不明の家族を探しに広島に来て被爆した人たちがたくさんいました。そのうち体はどこも悪くないのに、疲れやすく熱っぽくなります。

17　［証言1］野々山茂

「熱が出たけえ、肺炎かのう」と医者は言います。やがて体に赤い斑点ができ「何だろう」と思っているうちに、髪が抜け、血を吐くのです。自分でも何が起きているのかわからないまま、たくさんの人々が死んでいきました。死んだ人たちを田んぼのあぜ道で毎日焼いていました。棺もありません。死体の脇にまきを積み、野で焼きました。夏なので死体はすぐに腐ります。どの死体にも真っ白にウジがわいていました。死体を焼く臭いが毎日、町に立ち込めていたものです。

野々山さんは四十歳で結婚。相手の公枝さんも被爆者だった。公枝さんは爆心地から二キロの舟入町（現・中区舟入町）で被爆した。もともと公枝さんには結婚を決めていた人がいた。だが、被爆者ということで相手の親族から反対され、破談になった。

被爆者同士で結婚した私たちに
「どうせ、ろくな子は産まりゃせんよ」
と、陰で言う人もいました。幸いなことに、私たちは元気な三人の子どもに恵まれました。孫は五人。そのうちの三人が、あのとき、一緒に川で泳いでいて死んだ秀明と同じくらいの歳になりました。また孫たちが原爆の被害に遭うとしたら、想像しただけでも身震いがします。孫だけではありません。

この地球上の誰の上にもあんな酷いものを落としてはいけません。人類に原爆はいらないのです。
酒を飲むと、やけどをした上半身の肌が赤くなります。次々と最愛の家族を亡くし、悲しみに耐え、私を看病してくれた母の胸中を思うたび、いまでも涙が出ます。

野々山さんはこれまで、原爆についてほとんど誰にも語らずにきた。しかし、平和公園に行った孫たちから、原爆のことを聞かれたのがきっかけで、被爆体験を語るようになったという。そして遂にイタリアでも。

二〇一一年（平成二十三年）のこと。パグウォッシュ会議、核戦争防止国際医師会議（IPPNW）などの平和諸団体から要請を受けて、一月三十日にイタリアのローマ、二月一日にフィレンツェで被爆体験を話しました。慣れないながらも通訳の「次を話してよい」という合図を待って、一生懸命に話します。通訳を通して話すというのは初めての経験でした。皆、目の色を変えて聞いてくれます。このときは、まだ春江姉さんが生きていたので「九十歳を過ぎたいまも健在です」と言うと会場は総立ちになり、拍手と大歓声に包まれました。春江姉さんが被爆しながらも、生き抜いてきたことをわがことのように喜んでくれたイタリアの人たちの、温かい、優しい心に、感動でいっぱいになりました。

来賓のノーベル平和賞受賞者ベティ・ウィリアムズ女史からも、「本当によく来てくださいました」と激励の声をかけてもらいました。終了後も「感動した、グラッチェ」と抱きつかれたり、「蜂谷医師の本を読んだことがある」と握手を求められました。「勇気を出してイタリアまで来て本当によかった」と心から思い、幸せをかみしめました。

これからも子どもや孫たちの笑顔がいっぱいの世界であってほしいと願っています。

人類に原爆はいらない。

証言2

福島原発事故報道を見て放射能の怖さを語る

――下井勝幸 さん

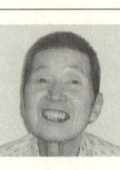

しもい・かつゆき 一九三〇年(昭和五年)一月生まれ。爆心から一・二キロの下柳町の町会長宅で十五歳のときに被爆。十七歳で日本舞踊の花柳流師匠の内弟子になり、二十三歳で、師匠の「幸」の字をもらい、芸名を花柳幸次郎として名取となる。以来六十年のキャリア。八十四歳。広島市中区在住。

電車に乗っていて被爆し、十三歳なのに老人の顔で死んだ弟

私の家は長屋で、前の道路は狭い道でした。道路拡張のために、建物強制疎開が実施されることになっていました。

「九月中に家を明け渡すか、取り壊すように」

私の家は、役所からそう通知を受けていました。当時は空襲警報が頻繁にありました。住宅密集地では、火事の類焼を防ぐため、あるいは避難道路確保のために、強制的に立ち退き要請をされて

いました。

　下井さんは、十五歳。国民学校高等科を卒業して、第二修道中学校に入学したばかりだった。
そのころは、勉強どころか、連日工場への動員。いわゆる「勤労奉仕」である。下井さんは毎朝
七時から、吉島（現・中区吉島）にあった倉敷航空広島工場で飛行機のエンジン部品を作っていた。
仕事は検査係だった。部品を液に漬け、ひびがないかを調べる。そして、合格品には「碇」のマー
クをタガネで刻印する。

　工場では男子生徒のほか、主婦や女子学生も動員されていた。体力がない彼女たちは、タガネで
はなくドリルで検査合格の碇マークを刻んでいた。下井さんが後で聞いた話では、工場は爆風です
べてのガラスが吹き飛んだ。検査係は、いつも明るい窓側で作業をしていた。作業中の主婦や女子
学生は、皆、頭や顔にガラスが突き刺さり血だらけになって死んだという。

　八月六日朝。私はかかりつけの医者による「体調不良」の診断書を工場に出していて、工場を休
んでいました。建物疎開の日が迫っているのに、引っ越し先がまだ見つかっていません。しかたが
ないので、下柳町（現・中区銀山町）の町会長宅で一時的に家財道具を預かってもらうことになり
ました。空襲警報が解除されたのを見計らい、私は作業着に着替えて出かけました。町会長宅は、
私の家から五十メートルくらいのところでした。
　私の家の家財道具は、二階に置いてもらうことになり、まずは二階にある会長宅の家具を下ろす
作業をしていました。私が梯子とロープを使って家具を斜めにして下ろします。そして、それを下

21　［証言2］下井勝幸

で町会長と近所の知り合いの人が受け取ります。そんな作業が始まったときのことです。

突然、カメラのフラッシュの何千倍もの明るさで「ピカッ」と光りました。そして「ドーン」という物凄い音。瞬時に私のいた二階の部屋が地鳴りのような音をさせて崩れちます。私の体は、奈落の底に吸いこまれるように落下していきました。当時、どの家も壁は土壁で、町会長の家もそうでした。構造はもろく、あっという間に家屋は崩れ落ちます。

あたりは真っ暗。柱と壁の間に挟まれていました。必死に体を動かそうとするのですが、身動きできません。左足が崩れた梁に挟まっています。痛い。足首を痛めたようです。

「助けて！　助けて！」と叫ぶと、

「こっちも埋まっとるんじゃ！　行かりゃあせん！」

という怒鳴り声が返ってきます。

その声で、不意に気持ちが落ち着いたのを覚えています。そのまま、しばらくじっと待っていました。がれきが崩れ、少し体を動かせるようになりました。左肩の上の柱の下をくぐって、向こう側に抜ければ助かるかもしれないのです。首の骨が折れるかと思うほどに、力いっぱい首を曲げてみました。やっと抜けました！　ごそごそと這い出します。天井の隙間から見える一筋の光の方向に、必死でがれきをかきわけてみます。そのときまで私は、町会長の家だけが崩れたのだと思っていました。

屋根の上に顔を出し立って見たら、驚きました。爆風のために、町の家屋すべてが同じ方向に将棋倒しになっています。見えるのは屋根ばかり。いたるところにがれきが飛び散っています。後で知ったことですが、一階には町会長の奥さん、娘と先に福屋百貨店や中国新聞社も見えます。

さんなどがおられ、焼死体になって見つかった人も、さっき怒鳴っていた人も見当たりません。ふと、風が出てきました。どこかで火が出たなと思いました。

大阪の空襲で焼け出された叔母から聞いていました。

「火が出て角を回るときなんか、竜巻のような風が吹く！　気をつけなさい！」

私は、風に巻き上げられた埃や壁の土を吸いこんでしまいました。胸がむかつき、思わずその場で大量に吐きます。嘔吐しながらも、何とか屋根から這い出し逃げます。夏だったので、半ズボンと開襟シャツ一枚。それも家の下敷になったので、ぼろぼろに破れています。道路は飛び散った屋根瓦やがれきで、素足で歩けるような状態ではありません。

室内にいたので素足。そのまま道路を歩き、それから屋根伝いに瓦の上を歩いて、倒れた家の下駄箱らしいところから下駄が見えたので、それを履いて、痛む左足を引きずりながら、私は京橋川に向かったのでした。

途中で、共同炊事場のそばを通りました。倒れてきた電柱に挟まれ、動けなくなったおばあさんが叫んでいます。

「助けて！　助けて！」

私は、おばあさんを電柱の下から引っ張り出しました。おばあさんは、そのまま放って置けると思ったのか、いきなり私の腰にしがみついてきます。おばあさんを連れて、私は川土手の広場まで行きました。橋のたもとには、途方にくれている女の人たちが、八人から十人ぐらいかたまりになっていました。

23　［証言2］下井勝幸

あちこちで火が出ています。どこへ行っていいのかわかりません。皆、髪の毛や着物が焼けて全裸同然の格好でした。木片や新聞紙で、前を隠すようにうずくまっていました。そのなかにおばあさんの知り合いがいたらしく、おばあさんはその人たちのなかに入っていきました。膨れ上がって黒焦げになった焼死体が、ごろごろと転がっています。

川土手に上がり、町を見渡しました。
どの家も傾き、潰れています。近くの高い建物は、中国新聞社と福屋百貨店だけ残っていました。そして、そのどちらからも、もくもくと煙があがっています。

「比治山に救護所があるはずじゃー！」
そんな話が広がりました。

川土手に集まっていた人たちは立ち上がり、比治山を目指して歩き出しました。私も一緒に歩き始めました。柳橋まで着いたときです。目の前で橋に火がつきました。たちまち火は大きくなり、橋は燃えています。消す人はいません。ただ、燃えるのを黙って見ているしかありませんでした。

柳橋は、もともと水害によりたびたび落橋しており、このときも柳橋は修理途上で、資材が積まれていた。この資材から発火、橋に燃え移ったのだといわれている。

橋は焼け落ちました。向こう岸に行くには川を渡るしかありません。川は海が近いため、水が引く干潮まで待つしかありません。そのうえ火災で強い風が巻いていて、波も高かったのです。対岸からの川土手の向かいの土手町（現・南区松川町）は、真っ赤な炎が燃え盛っていました。

熱風が吹きつけて熱い。いまにもこちら側に燃え移りそうな勢いです。体が熱いので、川のなかに入って体を冷やしました。私たちは、倒壊した家から畳を持ってきて川に畳を浮かせました。その上に重傷の人から寝かせます。引き潮になるまで、ただひたすら待ちます。土手町の町並みも全焼して、火の勢いは収まったようやっと、立って渡れるまで水が引きました。畳の上に寝かせた重傷人は、真夏なのにぶるぶる震えています。対岸で偶然、父に会いました。奇跡でした。父は正規の兵隊ではありません。建物疎開や工場などに手伝いに行く国民義勇隊で、この日は佐伯郡地御前村（現・廿日市市）の旭兵器製作所へ手伝いに行く途中でした。

広島市内にきのこ雲が見えたので、私たちのことが心配で地御前から船で戻ってきたのだといいます。

比治山は家がないので、火災が起きないだろう。きっとそこに避難しているだろう。そう考えて、歩き通しでやって来たというのです。

父と会えたので、比治山には向かわないことにしました。二人でわが家とは別に借りていた片河（現・東区尾長町）の借家を目指しました。爆風で欄干が崩れ落ちた荒神橋を通って、三十分はかかったでしょうか。真っ黒に焼けて炭のようになった焼死体や、男女の見分けのつかない遺体が転がっていました。

たくさんのかわいそうな人たちを見ました。背中から熱線を浴びた人は衣類が焼け、背中の皮膚が足元まで垂れ下がっています。背中の皮膚をずるずる引きずって歩いています。前面から熱線を浴びた人は顔が赤黒く腫れ上がっています。まるで幽霊のように手を垂らし、その指先から皮膚が

25　［証言2］下井勝幸

ぶら下がっているのです。
母と妹の瑠美子（当時五歳）は、片河の家に疎開していました。その家も爆風で壊れてはいたものの、二人とも無傷で戻った父と私を見て、ひどいやけどを負った人々で溢れかえっていました。
母は無傷で戻った父と私を見て、
「ようけ、たまげたわ！」
と喜んでくれました。
そこへ弟の明夫が戻ってきました。明夫はそのとき、十三歳。東洋製缶へ動員で行っていました。弟の周りにいた人たちは、熱線と爆風でほとんど即死だったとのこと。体の小さい弟と同級生の中村君だけが、大人たちの間に挟まれて助かったというのです。
流川（ながれかわ）で、路面電車のなかで被爆したそうです。弟は被爆したとき弟は帽子をかぶっていたので頭に帽子が焼きつき、黒いやけどになっています。弟は気分が悪そうでした。
まだ町には火が出ていませんでした。何とかその同級生と一緒に二人で帰ってきたらしいのです。
信じられませんでした。広島にこれだけの恐ろしい被害があったのに、うちはこうして家族全員が顔を合わせていることが……。
もうそれだけで思わず笑いがこみ上げてくるようでした。
「よう助かったなあ」と言い合いました。
その日は、大切にとってあった配給米を炒飯（チャーハン）にして皆で食べました。台所も壊れていたので、土間に石油缶で作ったかまを据えました。そして、その上に鍋をかけて母が炒飯を作ります。石油缶

を家族みんなと中村君とで囲んで、母が炒飯を作る様子を見守っていました。いまにして思えば、飯を食用油で炒めて醤油で味付けしただけの炒飯で、何の具も入っていません。あの味はいまでも忘れられません。

翌日、町の火はほとんど収まっていましたが、愛宕町（現・東区愛宕町）だけはまだ燃えていました。茶色に変色した焼けた電車が見えます。

「あれに乗っとったんじゃー」

私たちと一緒に夜を明かした中村君を十日市町（現・中区十日市町）まで送っていきました。

二十日ほどたったころでしょうか。弟は髪の毛が抜け、全身に赤い斑点が出はじめました。ぐったりしている弟に母が、

「大丈夫よ！　いま悪いもんが出とるんじゃけぇ、絶対助かるよ！」

と励ましていました。それは、まるで自分に言い聞かせているようにも見えました。母は弟をさすりながら、何度も何度も元生橋を渡り、十日市町の方に電車道を渡りました。

あんな電車に乗っていて、よく助かったものだと感心しました。そして産業奨励館を見ながら相生橋を渡り、十日市町の方に電車道を渡りました。弟の肩や腕は、割り箸のように細くなっていきました。

八月二十九日、弟は死にました。弟はわんぱくで男気のある性格でした。私とはだいぶ性格は違いましたが、いつも一緒に遊んでいました。路地でのビー玉遊びでも相撲でも、私は弟にかなわなかったことを覚えています。チャンバラ映画を観たあとは、木剣を腰に差して映画のまねをして打ち合いました。そのときも弟が優勢でした。初冬の亥子の祭りでは、いつも弟が赤鬼や青鬼に扮し

27　［証言2］下井勝幸

て町内の子どもたちを追い回します。ときには度が過ぎることもあって、私が止めるとますます暴れました。弟は軍事教練が大好きで「十五歳になったら予科練に入るんだ」と言うのが口癖でした。
母の落胆は、それは深いものでした。とてもかわいそうで見ていられません。弟の頭に塗っていた白い塗り薬の缶を握り締め、母は毎日、声を殺して泣いていました。
弟はまだ十三歳なのに老人のような顔になって死にました。皮膚はボロボロになり、腕も足も細く、体はやせてゴボウみたいな感じでした。あのとき一緒にいた同級生の中村君も、同じ日に死んだと後から聞きました。

私は、爆心地から一・二キロのところにいたのに、やけどもなく急性の原爆症にはなりませんでした。医者も不思議がっていました。「遮蔽があったんじゃろう」と言っていました。屋内にいたことも大きかっただろうと思います。でも、その後、私はずっと病弱でした。いつも体がだるいのです。

よくビタミン剤を打ってもらっていました。学校での体育の時間はいつも見学でした。

戦後すぐに、「変な咳をするね」と言われて病院に行きました。肺結核と診断され、ストレプトマイシンを飲みました。「放射能で白血球が少なくなったら灸が効く」と言われて、灸が流行していました。私も体の具合が悪くなると、灸をすえに行きました。原爆と関係があるのかどうかはわかりませんが、一九六三年（昭和三十八年）、五十八歳の父は肝臓がんで、九〇年（平成二年）、八十歳の母は大腸がんで死にました。妹はその後、結婚しましたが、眼底出血などが重なり失明しました。

一九四六年（昭和二十一年）、友達の姉が事故で亡くなった。友達がその「追善会」で踊るというので、稽古の見学に行った。それが下井さんと踊りとの出あいだった。

稽古場は、福屋百貨店の八階にありました。
「扇子や草履を貸してあげるから浴衣だけあつらえなさい。教えてあげる」
と先生に言われました。
　病弱な体を少しでも丈夫にしよう――。私は日本舞踊花柳流の花柳光幸師匠の内弟子になりました。十七歳のときです。最初のころは体力もなく稽古中に倒れたことも何度かありました。しかし踊りで体を動かすことが良かったのか、私はだんだんと丈夫になっていきました。
　私は、一九五三年(昭和二十八年)六月、名取となりました。それ以降、師匠の「幸」の字をもらい「花柳幸次郎」と名乗ったのです。花柳光幸師匠は後に「花柳梶」と改名、中国地方の邦舞の第一人者となられました。私もまた六十年にわたって、踊りを続けることができたのです。
　一九五六年(昭和三十一年)、最初の原爆手帳をもらいました。爆心地から三キロ圏内で被爆しています。原爆手帳をもらうためには、在住証明者の書いた証明書が必要でした。私の証明書は町会長が書いてくれました。あの日、私たちの家財道具を預かってくれた町会長です。証明書をもらいに行くと、町会長の顔は熱線で焼けただれてケロイドになっていました。
　町会長に「おじさん、ひどい目におうたねぇ」と言うと、
「わしも顔だけが焼けたんじゃ、こがーになったからなあ。こうなったんも運命よ。勝っちゃんも気をつけーよ」
と言ってくれました。
　原爆手帳は、黄色い表紙の手帳です。最初のころは、誰ももらいに行きませんでした。

29　［証言2］下井勝幸

「原爆症は人にうつる！」

そんなことが言われていた時代だったからです。「黄色い手帳」というラジオドラマが放送され、手帳の普及が図られていきます。健康保険証と原爆手帳を見せると医療費がすべて無料だということが周知され、原爆手帳をもらう人はだんだんと増えていきました。証明者を見つけられない人が、ラジオで「〇〇町の〇〇さんを知っている方は連絡ください」と尋ね人をするようになりました。

結婚は三十一歳のとき。日本舞踊の先輩から、いつも脅かされていました。

「三十歳までに結婚しないと大変よ。一生独身だよ。いい人がおったらすぐしんさい！」

妻は徳島出身で被爆はしていません。

「被爆者には障害を持った子どもが生まれる」という話が広がっていました。妻が妊娠したときは心配で心配で、居ても立ってもいられませんでした。幸い、娘二人は今日まで健康で過ごしています。そのころ「被爆二世」に原爆手帳を発行するという話が出ていました。

「娘さんに原爆手帳を申請しますか？」

と聞かれたのです。断りました。原爆は私一人でたくさんです。子どもたちにまで引きずらせたくなかったのです。

原爆慰霊碑の近くに住んでいるので、毎朝五時に起きてお祈りに行きます。

私自身が原爆に遭ったことは、これまでほとんど詳しくは話しませんでした。

しかし、東日本大震災（二〇一一年三月十一日）の福島第一原発事故で、それが変わった。福島第一原発事故の国際原子力事象評価尺度は最悪のレベル七。旧ソ連のチェルノブイリ事故（一九八

30

六年〉と同じだった。核廃絶運動のリーダーだった森滝市郎さんは「核と人類は共存できない」と訴えていた。何かがあってからでは遅い。いまは、機会があれば、自分の被爆体験を語るようにしている。

「一人は微々たる力でも、まず一人ひとりが声をあげることから始まる」と下井さんは言う。

テレビのニュースで、福島第一原子力発電所の建屋で作業をしていた人の姿を見ました。作業員の腕に、赤い湿疹が出ているように見えました。――あのとき、弟の体に見たものと同じだ。ぞっとしました。まだ原子炉のなかを確認することさえできないのに、国は早々に事故の収束を宣言してしまったのです。放射能はそんな簡単なもんじゃない。国は曖昧なことを言うべきではない。原爆によってひどい目に遭って、放射能の怖さを一番よく知っているのは私たち被爆者です。いまこそ私たちは声をあげないといけないと思います。

31　［証言2］下井勝幸

証言3

誰が被爆を伝えるん？ 妻の一言で告白

河合宣二さん

かわい・せんじ 一九三〇年（昭和五年）二月生まれ。爆心から一・二キロの上天満町（現在の西区上天満町）の自宅で十五歳のときに被爆。背中のケロイド、前立腺がん、心臓病などの後遺症も続き、医者通いの毎日。十年前まで、建築関係の仕事に携わってきた。八十四歳。広島市西区在住。

いまなお続く後遺症
原爆は絶対に「悪」だ

「母は芸者あがりで、とにかく派手で気っぷがよかった」と河合さんは言う。父は真面目で仕事一途。地下足袋(たび)の改良を研究し、製品化した人だった。好対照な夫婦だった。河合さんは、そんな夫婦の次男として生まれた。

屋敷の一角にミシンを置いた作業場があり、若い衆が二人雇われていました。家にはお手伝いさ

んが二人いて、母はいつもあれこれと指示をしていました。商売が軌道に乗っていて、羽振りもよかったのです。屋敷は上天満町（現・西区上天満町）にありました。間口が五間、奥行が十六間の広い二階建てで、私は「坊っちゃん、坊っちゃん」とちやほやされて育ちました。正月などは、来る人来る人に酒と雑煮が振る舞われます。噂を聞いて見知らぬ人もやって来ます。

誰かれ構わず母は、

「上がりんさい！　上がりんさい！」

と座敷に上げて、飲み食いさせていました。

母に連れられて、よくお茶屋にも行きました。母が芸者衆にご祝儀をあげるのを見ました。市立の第一商業学校（現・広島商業高校）に入ってからは、家に学校の友達が大勢遊びにきていました。男女共学ではないから男ばかりです。酒を覚えるのも早かったと思います。隣が酒屋だから、ツケでいくらでも買える。友達が来るといつも酒を飲みました。

一九四五年（昭和二十年）、私は三年生。卒業まであと一年。旧制中学は五年制でしたが、非常時下の当時は修業年数が四年に短縮されていました。

学校の友達が予科練（海軍飛行予科練習生）に合格したのを祝って、仲間五人が外の店で飲めや歌えの大騒ぎ。飲み疲れの翌日。あのときも、疎開作業のため学校を休んでいた私のところへ、昨日の飲み友達四人が登校途中に来て「あんたが学校へ行かんのんなら、わしらもたいぎゅう（＝おっくう）になった」と言って、ずる休み。わが家の二階で、雑談したりごろ寝したりしていました。

「弾丸が切れたんじゃろ！」

空襲警報が解除になり、高射砲の音が消えました。

33　　［証言3］河合宣二

などと話していたそのときです。

「ピカッ」と光りました。

と思ったら、どどーんという凄い音がして家が崩れました。まるで鋳型にはめられたかのように、体がぎゅっと締めつけられました。崩れた家から無我夢中で屋根の上に這い出しました。周りの家はすべて倒れています。普段はまったく見えないのに、産業奨励館がよく見えました。天満川では、窓枠や家具、馬と一緒にたくさんの人々が悲鳴をあげて流されていきます。まだ朝なのに、あたりは夜のように真っ暗。自分が三途の川にいるのではないかと思いました。そう思ったほど、いま見ている光景が現実のものとは思えなかったのです。

突然、親父の声がします。

「宣二！ 母さんが下敷きになっとるけえ！ 来い！」

家が倒壊していて、どこがどこなのかわかりません。とにかく屋根からもう一度潜って、一階のあたりに行ってみました。仰向けに倒れた母の左腕は、家の鴨居に挟まれています。腕が裂け、骨が出ていました。母の顔は蒼白で死人のようです。呻き声さえも出ていません。「こりゃ助からん！」。直感的にそう思いました。父と一緒に必死に、母を鴨居の下から引っ張り出しました。裏の天満川の川土手に寝かせます。

「若い衆を呼びに行ってくるけえ！ おまえはともかく友達を連れて逃げえ！」

父はそう言って工場の方へ走っていきます。ふと気づくと、そのすぐそばに弟が倒れていました。私の顔を見て、よろよろと立ち上がりました。

「あんちゃ〜ん」

34

河合さんの弟は学校で水泳の選手だった。この日、建物疎開に行く予定だったが休んだ。そして川で泳ごうと、雁木（川の船着場の階段）にいたところで直接、原爆の閃光を浴びた。当時十三歳だった。

前に差し出した両手の皮膚が垂れ下がっていました。

弟を連れて、友達四人と三滝（現・西区三滝町）まで逃げました。

弟は体が熱いのか、

「水が飲みたい！」

と川の方に行きます。とたんに、遠くの消防団の人が怒鳴りました。

「水は飲ませるな！　死ぬぞ！」

水を飲ませるわけにはいきませんでした。

近くの山すそでは、救護の兵隊が負傷者の治療をしていました。そこに弟を預けて、友人たちとさらに山の上の方に向かいました。皆、ガラスや、土壁の竹が体に刺さっていて血だらけでした。

やがて、黒い雨が降ってきました。雨はどんどん激しくなり、土砂降りになりました。このとき、自分の背中から血が流れていることに初めて気づきました。背中に無数のガラスの破片が刺さっています。雨にぬれ、血が流れています。寒い。村の氏神の社がありました。四人で社に入って横幕を剝いで体に巻きつけて休みました。雨がやみました。変な話ですが急に大便がしたくなりました。我慢できません。

「先に行っとってくれ」

35　［証言3］河合宣二

友達にそう言って、畑のそばで用を足しました。これが凄かったのです。真っ黒い便が大量に出ました。
「これが全部、わしの腹から出たんか……」
信じられないほどの量でした。
後日、医者から言われました。
「それがよかったんじゃろ。悪いものを全部出したんじゃから」
ひと休みした後、みんなで近くの友達の家に行こうとしたら、一人が三滝の自宅へ帰るというので、仕方なく残った三人で行き先を変えて、祇園町（現・安佐南区祇園町）へ向かいました。しかし、そこもまた死体の山でした。私たちの治療どころではありません。
「祇園町で治療している」という噂を聞いたからです。古市（現・安佐南区古市）まで、また歩きました。嚶鳴国民学校（現・古市小学校）が避難所になっていました。校舎の壁に一人の兵隊が頭をつけてかがんだまま、死にかけていました。背中は焼けただれ、白いウジが一面うごめいています。
「死んどるんかのう？」
と言ったら、その兵隊がじろりと振り向きました。
「人間はなかなか死なんもんだな」と思いました。背中一面、焼けているのに生きているのです。
しかし、そういう私も、背中にウジがわき、その兵隊とほとんど同じありさまでした。やけどの人たちは順番に並びます。湯飲みに入れた赤チンに脱脂綿を浸し、やけどの傷口に塗ってもらいます。するとすぐに「はい、次！」と廊下に出されるのでした。あのとき受けた「治療」はせいぜいそんなものだったのです。後日、背中か

36

らいくつものガラスの破片が出たし、取り出せなかったガラス片は、そのまま埋まって小さなこぶになりました。

学校の廊下には椅子が並べられ、被爆した人たちが寝ていました。ほとんど死にかけている人も、すでに死んでいる人も多くいました。その枕元に乾パンが置いてありました。「あれは無駄じゃろ」と、乾パンを盗んでわけて食べました。初めて他人のものを盗んだのです。

どこの救護所も被爆者で満員でした。軍は民間人を決して診ようとしませんでした。

「医者のいる可部（現・安佐北区可部）まで行くけぇ、重病人を乗せぇ！」

という声が聞こえました。

トラックが重病人を乗せていました。軍隊ではなく民間のトラックでした。誰かがトラックを調達して、重病人を可部へ運ぼうとしたのでしょう。私たちも、死にかけた人たちと一緒にトラックに乗り込みました。トラックの荷台には二十人以上の人がいました。ほとんどの人が真っ黒に焦げて男か女かさえもわかりません。ただ、河岸のマグロのように寝転がされ、かすかな声で「水。水……」と呟いていました。皆、力なく寝ていました。救護の消防団員と私たち四人だけが、寝ている人たちの体と体の隙間に足を入れ、座っていました。

可部に着く前に、トラックのなかで娘さんが二人死にました。皮膚が剥げて赤黒く人相もわかりません。あれはかわいそうでした。夏だから薄着だったのでしょう。爆風と熱線で焼かれ、裸同然でした。

「こりゃあ死んどるけぇ！　下ろせ！」

消防団員がトラックを止めて遺体を下ろします。

37　［証言3］河合宣二

せめてもと、乳房や陰部にヤツデの葉をかぶせ、手を合わせました。埋める道具も時間もなかったのです。

一人を下ろせば、一人のけが人を乗せてもしょうがないのです。死んでいる者を乗せて、トラックのなかで突然、発作を起こした者がいました。友達の杉田忠治でした。白目を剝（む）き「うー！ うー！」と唸（うな）っています。いまにも死にそうな顔をしていました。私はその杉田に馬乗りになりました。

「おじ（杉田のあだ名＝素振りが大人びて落ち着いていたので）！ 死ぬなよ！ おまえの家へ行くんじゃけぇ」

と殴りつけました。そのビンタで杉田がはっと正気に返りました。

可部の警察も被爆者でいっぱいでした。被爆者に包帯を巻き、赤チンを塗っていました。警察署の裏の空き地に、消防団員がやってきました。死んだ人間を手錠（てじょう）で引っかけ、ずるずると死体置場まで引いていきました。死者は地面に山積みにされていました。ここも私たちを診るどころではありませんでした。赤ん坊や小さい子どもを連れた母親はほったらかしにされ惨（みじ）めでした。途方にくれたように座りこんでいるだけでした。

私たちは、もう一人の友達の実家の大朝（おおあさ）（現・北広島町大朝）に行くことにしました。再び、死にかけている人たちと一緒にトラックに乗り込みました。大朝のその家を訪ねると、そこのお母さんが私たちの姿を見てびっくりしていました。

「女物しかないんじゃが……」

そう言って三人に浴衣（ゆかた）を着せてくれました。そして古畳を敷いたトラックを用意してくれました。

私たちはそのまま、杉田の実家の壬生（現・北広島町壬生）まで行きました。訪ねていった壬生の帽子屋には杉田のお母さんが疎開していました。お母さんはすぐに、近所のおじさんに大八車を頼んでくれました。私たち三人はそれに乗せてもらって、やっと医者に診てもらうことができました。医者は、赤チンを塗り背中のガラスや竹片を抜いてくれました。大朝で着せてもらった女物の浴衣は、背中のところが血と膿で真っ赤になっていました。杉田のお母さんから新しいシャツを着せてもらい、そこに一週間滞在し、毎日、大八車で病院に通いました。赤チンを塗った傷口が乾いて、かさぶたになりました。

　上天満町の河合さんの家の近所に、笠坊医院という大きな病院があった。その病院の院長夫妻が「可部にウチの実家がある。戦争がひどくなったら、来んさい」と常日ごろ言ってくれていた。河合さんの親も「何かあったら、可部の笠坊さんに疎開させてもらおう」と言っていた。河合さんはそれを思い出し、可部の院長の実家を訪ねていった。

　門から庭を通って奥に入っていく。すると、縁側にちょこんと座っている人がいます。「母ちゃんだ！」。母は昔から背筋をしゃんと伸ばした粋な人でした。母はその格好のままで座っていました。
「まさか！　こりゃー、夢じゃなかろうか」。目の前に居るのは間違いなく、母ちゃんじゃ。無我夢中で走り抜けて抱きつきました。
「母ちゃーん」
　もう言葉にはなりません。大声をあげて泣きました。

39　［証言3］河合宣二

「怖かった」「寂しかった」「辛かった」「痛かった」
これまで、こらえてきたたくさんの気持ちが、いっぺんに溢れ出して泣き続けました。
母も泣きました。
「よう生きとった！　よう生きとった、宣二」
母はぐっと強く私を抱きかかえて離しませんでした。

被爆して十日——。
母は無事でした。親切な朝鮮の青年に助けられたのでした。その青年は、川土手の橋の下に焼けたトタンで雨除けを作ってくれたそうです。そして「ここで休んでいなさいね」と母を運んでくれたといいます。しかし、若い衆を呼びにいった親父も、三篠橋で治療を頼んだ弟も行方がわかりませんでした。あのとき、父は元気だったはず。それなのに、なぜ可部に訪ねて来ないのか——。いらいらしながら、一カ月が過ぎました。当時、占いの「コックリさん」が流行っていました。五円玉と割り箸で占いました。「二人とも死んでいる——」と出ました。
弟は、直接被爆したから助からなかっただろう。それならあれほど水を欲しがっていたのだから、水を飲ませてやりたかった。いまでも悔いています。親父はあの後、火や煙に巻かれたのだろうか。

河合さんはその後一年あまり、可部の笠坊宅に世話になっていた。そこへ、四歳上の河合さんの兄も除隊して岐阜から戻ってきた。母と兄と河合さんの三人の生活が始まった。

私は白血病になりました。輸血が必要になり、兄の血液を太腿に筋肉注射で何度も輸血しても

いました。そうこうするうちに、今度は兄が高熱と下痢が続くようになりました。腸チフスでした。兄は隔離され、私の輸血もそこで断念することに。とにかく、体がだるくてだるくて仕方がありません。湯飲み茶碗を持ち上げることさえ、できなくなりました。九月に大きな台風（＝枕崎台風）が来て床下まで浸水しましたが、逃げようにも体が動かずそのまま寝ていました。

広島の家には、母の誂えた高価な着物がたくさんありました。戦争中、それらの着物を可部の笠坊宅に預かってもらっていました。母は預けていた着物を売り食いする生活を始めました。人徳もあったかもしれません。除隊して戻ったのに、坊っちゃん育ちの兄はまったく働こうとしません。母はあまりそういう風でした。芋や野菜を持って集まってきた農家の人たちを前に、母はまるで呉服屋のように、着物を並べて見せました。母はいつも毅然としていました。

このときも「着物を持って芋と交換」という感じではありませんでした。母は、なぜかいつもそういう風でした。芋や野菜を持って集まってきた農家の人たちを前に、母はまるで呉服屋のように、着物を並べて見せました。母はいつも毅然としていました。

笠坊宅に来て一カ月ぐらいしたころでしょうか。私の髪の毛が抜け始めました。髪に手を入れるとぼごっと抜けます。眉も陰毛も体毛はすべて抜け落ちました。そして歯茎が紫色になり、腐っていきました。出血し膿が出ます。歯ブラシで歯を磨くと、ぶよぶよの歯茎の肉が歯ブラシについてきます。

不思議なことに一年たったら、出血も膿も止まりました。髪の毛もまた生えてきました。背中はかさぶただらけ。痒くて痒くて気が狂いそうになりました。まるでトカゲのように、かさぶたでデコボコしていました。それを乾いたタオルで、乾布摩擦をするみたいにごしごしやります。すると、かさぶたが剝がれて痛痒いものの、気持ちよかったのです。その後、膿が出て熱を持って、またか

さぶたになります。その繰り返しでした。
背中一面はケロイド状に引きつっています。体を動かすのも不自由でした。軍国少年だった私は、負けん気だけは強かったと思います。背中のケロイドをものともせずにこられたのは、この気の強さのおかげだったのでしょう。

河合さん一家は、そのまま二年間を可部で暮らした。家や工場のことが気になって、一人で広島に出た。驚いたことに、従姉弟が工場を再開させてくれていた。「よう生きとったのう！」。ほんとうに喜んでくれた。芋粥をふるまってくれたことが忘れられない。そんなころのことだった。当時診てもらっていた可部の町医者と母が話している。偶然、河合さんはそれを聞いてしまった。
「この分だと、宣二さんは三十歳までしか生きられんよ」

前から気の強い性格でしたが、これを聞いてからは、もう怖いものがなくなりました。どうせ、あと十年と生きられん。命なんて惜しくない。荒れ始めました。十九歳ころの私は、赤線（当時売春が行われていた地域）に入り浸っていました。目玉をグリグリ動かすので「グリちゃん」という仇名がついていました。赤線は町の東西にありました。「西のグリちゃん」といったらちょっとした顔でした。

あのころ自暴自棄になった原因は、もう一つありました。仕事をしようと就職試験を受けると合格です。しかし身体検査になると、必ず不合格になってしまいます。原因は背中一面のケロイドでした。体調が悪く病院に行きます。医者は背中のケロイドを見て「写真を撮らせてくれ」と言いま

す。どの医者も、治療法はわからないというのです。皆が気味悪がります。だから銭湯へは行きませんでした。情けない思いでいっぱいでした。さりとて、冬でも家で行水でした。旅行も行ったことがありません。極道にもなりきれなかったのです。宇品港（現・広島港）で小麦を運ぶ仕事があるというので行ってみました。しかし、体力がないのでそのまま帰されてしまいました。

　その後、友人の紹介で左官屋に弟子入りし、河合さんは左官になった。一九七四年（昭和四十九年）に結婚。四十四歳のときだった。河合さんの妻は呉市の出身で原爆には遭っていなかった。河合さんの放射能の後遺症は、いまなお続いている。

　被爆から七十年近くがたちます。いまでも、雨が降ると背中のケロイドが痒くなります。太腿や腕の裏側に紫の斑点が浮き出ます。前立腺がんや心臓病なども患いました。毎日、かかりつけの病院に通います。それが日課です。

　「核を持つ国は悪魔だ」と言った人がいます。その言葉に尽きると強く思います。アメリカも一回原爆を落とされてみないとわからんだろう。それがどれほどに辛いことか。アメリカだけじゃない。ロシアも中国もフランスもイギリスも、核を持っている国は皆、悪だ。自分たちは核を持っておきながら、他の国には核を持たせない。

　「自分たちも持たないから、他の国も持ったらいかん」と言うならわかります。おかしな話です。自分をこんなにした戦争が、いまでも憎い。当たり前だろう。人生をめちゃくちゃにされ、苦し

43　［証言3］河合宣二

み続けて生きてきた者の感情はきれい事では済まされない。
「直接、原爆に遭うた人が年々少なくなる。あなたが黙っとって誰が伝えるんね」。夫人のこの強い勧めが、これまで語ることを避けてきた河合さんの重い口を開かせ、このたびの証言となった。
しかし、河合さんの思いは複雑だ。「何をいくら言うても、原爆に遭うてない者にはこの気持ちはわからん。腹へったもんの気持ちは腹へったもんにしかわからん。それと同じよ。言葉じゃないけえ」

証言4

命の恩人のためにも語らねばならぬ

西村一則 さん

にしむら・かずのり　一九三三年(昭和七年)十一月生まれ。爆心から一・五キロの比治山橋のたもとで、十二歳のときに被爆。地元の町内会長、防犯組合長を十年。公民館等で被爆体験を通し、子どもたちに命の大切さ、どう守るのかを考えてもらう活動に取り組んでいる。八十一歳。安芸郡府中町在住。

担任から「二人は死んだ」
友達は逝ってしまった

　西村さんは被爆当時、十二歳。私立松本工業学校(現・瀬戸内高校)の一年生だった。豊田郡小谷村(だにむら)(現・東広島市高屋町)の農家に生まれ育った。小谷村は広島市内まで汽車で一時間ほどのところにある鄙(ひな)びた村だった。小学生のころの思い出を聞くと、西村さんは記憶のなかの唱歌をいくつも口ずさんだ。

♪肩をならべて兄さんと／今日も学校に行けるのは／兵隊さんのおかげです

♪お国のために戦った／お国のために戦った／兵隊さんのおかげです
戦争の正義を信じて疑わない世代だった。

 私は六人姉弟の三番目。上に二人の姉がおり長男でした。私はとくに一番上の姉にかわいがられていました。何かあればすぐに「大っきい姉ちゃん、大っきい姉ちゃん」と姉を頼りにしていました。
 その日の建物疎開は、中学一年生ばかり二十人が集められていました。私たちは、広島駅まで七つの駅から順次汽車に乗って、広島駅に向かっていました。白市駅を出発し、西条駅のあたりで空襲警報が鳴りました。広島駅に到着する前には、車掌が警報の解除を知らせていました。
 建物疎開は田中町（現・中区田中町）の予定でした。
 広島駅に到着した私たちは、弥生町（現・中区弥生町）に向かって隊列を組みました。当時の学生は、皆、戦闘帽にカーキ色の学生服、足にはゲートルを巻いていました。物資不足ゆえ、制服の色も大きさも揃ってはいません。色違いや帽子もばらばらでした。私たちは、京橋川沿いを行進していました。柳橋のところでB29の爆音を聞きました。B29は大型爆撃機なので、他の爆撃機より爆音も太く大きいのです。当時、広島はほとんど空襲がありませんでした。私たちは防空壕に避難した経験もなく、そのまま行進していました。
 テレビの画面がプツンと消える。あのとき、私に起きたことはそれでした。私自身は、「ピカ」も「ドン」も見ていませんし、聞いてもいません。突然、視界が真っ暗になり、意識を失いました。気がつくと、体の上に木材やがれきが覆い被さっていました。どれくらいの間、気絶していたのかはわかりません。当時の建物はほとんどが木造家屋だったので、それらが飛んできたのだと思います。

がれきの隙間から大勢の人たちが逃げていくのが見えます。上半身は身を乗り出せたのですが、私の左足は大きな材木に挟まれて動けません。

五十メートルほど先の家から火の手があがりました。

「大っきい姉ちゃん！　お父さん！　助けて、助けて！」

われ知らず、そんな叫び声をあげていました。

「もう一度、家に帰りたい」。たくさんの思いが去来し、瞬時にそれまでの人生が走馬灯のように浮かびあがりました。人間は死が近づくと、ほんとうにそれまでの人生の瞬間が次々と蘇ります。

「助けて、助けて！」

必死に大声で叫ぶのですが、誰も他人のことを気にかける余裕などありません。助けて！　もう足なんていらない！　火がすぐそこ一メートルほどのところまで。やっぱりだめじゃ、終わりじゃ、死んだらどうなるんか──。死を覚悟したときのことをいまも鮮明に覚えています。

そのときでした。

「いま助けちゃるぞ！」

比治山の憲兵さんか、兵隊さんだったと思います。がれきをのけながら木材をテコに、材木を斜めに押し上げてくれました。全身に力を入れて抜け出せました。

「抜けた！　抜けた！　ありがとう！　助かった！」

その人のおかげで、かろうじて焼け死ぬのは免れました。そして、がれきから出て気づいたと──。私は右半身に大やけどを負っていました。気絶して、飛んできたがれきの下敷きになるほんの一瞬。その瞬間に私は右半身にピカを浴びたようです。顔から肩、腕、腰、足のゲートルまで

47　　［証言4］西村一則

右半身がすべて焼けていました。

見渡す限りがれきが広がっており、どこに道路があるのかさえわかりません。そして、私は、木材の下敷きになった私の左足の関節は砕けていました。

そのまま仰向けに倒れこみました。

──父さんが助けに来てくれたときにわかるように！　仰向けに倒れたのは、かすかにそんな意識があったからだと思います。「西村！」と呼ぶ声がしました。目眩がするほどに、太陽がまぶしくて苦しい。どれくらいの時間がたったでしょうか。煤けて真っ黒な顔が見えました。焼けただれた顔の皮膚はところどころめくれています。知り合い……だろうか？

「誰？」

「柳田じゃ！」

一緒に隊列を組んで歩いていた同級生の柳田でした。彼は、いつも白市駅の次の西高屋駅から汽車に乗ってきます。座る席も決まっていたので、いつも一緒に待ち合わせて通学していました。

「また今度来たら皆殺しにされるで！　早う逃げようや！」

「……わしは動けん。足がダメじゃ」

「なら、わしが負うて逃げちゃる！」

気がやさしくて体が大きい柳田は、面倒見のよい親分肌の男でした。私を背負い、尾長（現・東区尾長）の学校に向かって歩き出しました。しかし、すぐに柳田の息が切れ始めます。

「柳田！　下ろしてくれ。わしも、ちーたー（＝少しは）歩ける！」

そう言って下ろしてもらい、何とか片足で跳び、ものにつかまって這いました。ほとんど歩けな

い私を見て、柳田はまた私を背負ってくれました。
「柳田、やっぱり無理じゃ」
「おまえだけ先に帰ってくれ。うちのもんに知らせてくれ」
何度そう叫んだことでしょう。
また「西村！」と呼ぶ声がしました。西久保でした。色白で可愛い顔をした金持ちの坊ちゃんで す。よし、三人で逃げよう！　西久保と柳田の肩を借り、私はほとんど担がれるようにして学校ま で行きました。学校へ行けば、薬もあるし手当してもらえる——。そんな期待はあえなく砕かれま した。学校は焼失し、何の跡形もありませんでした。
「ここからだと船越の家が近い。行こう！」
西久保がそう言い、私は再び二人の肩を借りて歩き出しました。当時、難所といわれた大内越 峠まで来たときでした。そこまで逃げてきて、ほとんどの人が力尽きて倒れまし た。新たな死人が死体の上に倒れ、山となって幾重にも重なり合っていました。一度倒れると、もう 起き上がれません。おびただしい数の人々が死んでいました。——この人たちにも家族がいたろう に！　そうして今度は、逃げてくる人が押し寄せる。後から後から死体を踏み越えていく……。 まだ息のある人もいました。踏まれながらその足にしがみついて「助けて！」と叫んでいる人さえ いました。

大内越峠をどうやって越えたか、よく覚えていません。峠を越えて、温品（現・東区温品）に着いたら、 そこに小川がありました。体が熱いので川に手を入れたとたん、腕から肩まで水ぶくれができました。 柳田も顔を洗おうとすると、顔の皮膚がほとんどめくれて口のところまで垂れ下がりました。体中

がヤケド状態だったのです。片目は塞がり、もういっぽうの目も細くしか開きません。西久保だけは、体の損傷が少ないように見えました。近くの畑にトマトがなっていました。三人でちぎってかぶりつきました。柳田が吠えるような大声で泣き出しました。
「わしはトマトが食えん！」
顔の皮膚が剝がれて口のなかに入っています。もはや食べることができません。かわいそうでした。

——こんな体で、柳田はわしのことを思い出します。焼けて水ぶくれになった腕が、直射日光に当たって痛かったのを覚えています。少しでも手を下に垂らすと、血が下がって激しく痛みます。ようやく、船越（現・安芸区船越）の西久保の家に着きました。

西久保のお母さんが、息子の姿を見るなり飛び出してきました。泣きながらすごい勢いで、西久保を家に引っ張りこみました。そのまま玄関の前で立っていたら、隣の家のお婆ちゃんが「うちに来んさい——」と柳田と私を招き入れ、一晩泊めてくれました。ご飯を出してくれましたが、柳田は食べられません。「食べにゃいけん！」とお婆さんはお粥を作ってくれました。そして、柳田の唇のところをつまんで口のなかにひと匙ひと匙、お粥を流しこみます。「やけどには油がいちばんだから」と、私には食用油を右半身に塗ってくれました。

翌日そのお婆さんは、一緒に汽車に乗ってくれて、私の実家のある小谷村まで送ってくれました。私は右半身がやけど、足もけがをし自宅に戻ると、母の驚きと喜びは尋常ではありませんでした。

ていて異様な格好だったはずです。

「一則、よう戻ってきてくれた！」

母はその場にしゃがみこんで泣きました。

「広島に爆弾が落ちて大変なことになっとると聞いて皆、心配しとった」。父は、前の日もその日も、私を探しに広島に行っていました。夜、広島から戻った父は私を見てとても喜んでくれました。自宅に戻っても「助かった！」という安堵の思いしかありません。生き延びるだけで精いっぱいでした。感覚そのものが麻痺していたのだと思います。

被爆から一週間たって初めて、痛みや痒さを感じ始めました。小谷村には病院がありません。病院は西条に行くしかありませんでした。やけどの体ではとても通えないうえに、病院にも満足な薬はありません。原爆が落ちてなくても、あのころは日本中、薬のない時代でした。

「このまんまにゃしとけん。何としても治しちゃる！」

母はあちこちにやけどに効く治療法を聞いて回っていました。いろいろ試しました。まず入道草（ドクダミ）を蒸して練ったものを塗りましたが、効き目はありませんでした。次に「ジャガイモは熱を取る」と聞いてきて、母は彼岸花の根とジャガイモを擦って食用油を混ぜたものを塗ってくれました。患部に塗られたジャガイモは、熱を吸ってだんだん乾きます。すると古いジャガイモを取り除いて、また新しいジャガイモと彼岸花の根を塗ります。これを繰り返すうちに、ゆっくりとやけどはかさぶたになっていきました。体の右半分が重度のやけどで風呂にも入れません。井戸水で手拭いを冷やして、患部に当てるだけ。あとはただ自然に治るのを待つしかありません。仰向けもうつ伏せもできない。右半身は何かに触れると痛みます。布団を折ってそれに左半身を寄りかか

51 ［証言4］西村一則

るようにして生活していました。

家で牛を飼っていたので、ハエがたくさんいました。そのハエが傷口にたかります。姉たちが団扇（うちわ）で追い払ってくれますが、いくら追ってもハエがいます。ほんとうにハエには苦しめられました。そのうちに、白いウジ虫がちょろちょろとうごめき出しました。自分の体ながら、もはや人間の体ではありません。姉たちが箸（はし）やつまようじでつまんで取ってくれました。

こうした家族の献身的な治療のおかげで、西村さんは翌年の二月に学校に戻ることができた。自分は治療に長くかかったが、ほかの皆は、もうとっくに学校に戻っているはず。西村さんは喜び勇んで学校に向かった。しかし……。

教室に入っても、柳田も西久保もいません。不思議に思って先生に聞きました。

「柳田と西久保が来とらん。何で休んどるん？」

先生は言いました。

「二人とも死んどるぞ」

信じられませんでした。目の前が真っ白になりました。先生が嘘（うそ）をついているのだと思いました。気をとりなおして周りを見ると、組の半分ぐらいが来ていないのです。皆、死んだと聞きました。本当なら私が死んでいるはずでした。

二人の肩に背負ってもらって私は助かった。被爆したとき、私たちは京橋川を弥生町に向かって行進していました。だから爆心地は右手にあたります。川を挟んでいるので、遮蔽（しゃへい）物がありません。皆、熱線をまともに浴びたのです。おそら

柳田は、あの瞬間に原爆の方を向いてしまったのでしょう。だから顔が焼け焦げました。私は頭から右耳、首、肩、右腕、腰、太腿、足首と全身の右半分にやけどを負いました。腰と太腿は最後まで治りにくかったのです。
　被爆から二年後の一九四七年（昭和二十二年）、父が死にました。ずっと寝こんでいて髪の毛が抜け出し、やがて血を吐くようになり弱っていきました。医者も原因がわからず、結局「肺病（肺結核）」という診断になりました。肺病は栄養をつけなければ、ということで、私はよく西条まで牛乳を買いに行きました。いま、思えば父は急性白血病だったのでしょう。私を探しに直後の広島市内に入ったための「入市被爆」にほかなりません。

　西村さんは学校を卒業して、佐竹製作所に入社。塗装を覚えた。被爆して左足が不自由であった西村さんは人一倍努力した。入社の一年後に早くも独立。精米機の塗装を一手に引き受けた。その後、六一年（昭和三十六年）に東洋工業（現・マツダ）に入社。塗装工、生産管理部、人事部教育センターを経て、六十歳で定年を迎えた。
　定年退職後は、身障者訓練センターでふすま張りや掛け軸の表装などを勉強した。マツダの社宅のふすま張りを一手に引き受けるなど、仕事をたくさんもらった。忙しくもあり、ありがたくもあった。ただ、仕上げたふすまをエレベーターのない社宅に運ぶときは困った。不自由な左足をかばいながら、重い板戸やふすまを一生懸命運んだ。

　結婚をしたのは二十八歳のとき。マツダに入社して二年目のころです。妻は呉市出身ですから、

原爆には遭っていません。村の知人の紹介で見合いをしました。私が被爆していることがわかり、妻の父親から「考えさせてください」と言われました。妻と義母が義父を説得し、なんとか結婚することができました。

妻が最初の子どもを身ごもったときは、特に心配しました。当時「結婚しても、まともな子はできん」などという噂が流れていました。いまでも結婚の話が出ると気を使います。娘や息子たちの結婚のころはいまから三十年前。結婚相手のご両親が気にされるのは明らかで、被爆のことはとても口にできませんでした。そしていままた、孫たちの結婚の時期に来ています。妻もできれば話さないでほしいと思っているようです。

日本の敗色が濃厚になった一九四五年（昭和二十年）夏、中国・四国地方にも空襲が繰り返された。六月二十九日に岡山、七月四日には高知、高松、徳島の四国三県の県庁所在地、同二十六日には残る愛媛の松山が空襲の被害を受けた。多くの地方都市が空襲の被害を受けるなか、八月五日まで、広島市だけは被害がなかった。これは米軍が原子爆弾を投下したときの被害を調べるために、意識的に空襲を行わなかったといわれている。

「アメリカは、広島の人たちを人体実験に使ったのだ」と西村さんは憤る。原爆投下時も爆撃機はたった三機のみ。空襲警報が解除されたところに、「エノラゲイ」が原爆を投下した。いわばアメリカは「実験」のために、原爆の効果を最大にする環境を作りあげたのだ、と。

私は八十歳過ぎまで生き延び、私を助けてくれた二人の同級生は十四歳で逝ってしまったのでし

た。

この二人が声をかけてくれんかったら、私は死んでいた。命の恩人の二人の友達のためにも、私は原爆のことを話さなければいけんと思っています。

二〇一〇年（平成二十二年）秋、府中小学校で子どもたちに話しました。子どもたちが私ら被爆者の話を聞いて作詞した歌「あの夏を忘れない」の発表会にも参加。「わかってくれるかのう」と思っていましたが、子どもたちはしっかり受け止めてくれていました。うれしかった。

いま福島の人々のことを考えますと、辛いだろうなと思います。私たちのときは「放射能」というものの恐ろしさを理解していませんでした。放射能だらけの土地の上にバラックでも何でも建てました。がむしゃらに明日に向かって生活を始めました。そして鼻血が止まらなくなり、髪の毛が抜けて「これはなんだろう？　なんだろう？」と、わけもわからず人々は死んでいきました。

いまの時代は、放射能の怖さがわかっているだけに、福島の人たちにはいまもって故郷に戻ることさえできない人が大勢おられる。前に向かって一歩踏み出すことさえできません。これほど、大変なことはありません。ただただ、どんなことがあろうと、気持ちの上でくじけないでほしい。自分に決して負けないでほしい、そのことだけを強く願っています。どう立ち上がり、どう現実に挑むか。挑戦する限り、必ず希望はあると思います。

55　［証言４］西村一則

証言5

平和利用の核ならよい、というのは嘘だ

山田和邦 さん

やまだ・かずくに　一九三〇年（昭和五年）三月生まれ。爆心から一・七キロの白島中町の自宅で十五歳のときに被爆。中学校教員を務め、その後教育委員会、大学教員に。町内会長や社会福祉協議会会長を歴任し地域に貢献。八十三歳。広島市中区在住。

教え子たちに訴えた
わしより先に死んだら承知せんぞ！

被爆当時、私は広島師範学校の生徒でした。父の勧めで教師になるために進学したのです。学校とはいいながら、授業はとうに停止されており、毎日学徒動員で働いていました。最初の動員は、撥水テント工場で縫ったテントをたたんで運ぶ仕事でした。その後、宇品の暁部隊（陸軍船舶司令部）の弾薬庫で爆弾を積み込む作業になりました。あの日も、暁部隊に行くはずでした。

あの日、私は母と白島中町（現・中区白島中町）の自宅にいました。父は軍需工場の重役で、吉田（現・

安芸高田市吉田町）の工場に泊まり勤務のため留守でした。ちょうど空襲警報が解除になり、動員に出かける用意をしているところでした。家の仕切り壁にもたれてゲートルを巻いていると、どこからともなく「ブーン」という爆撃機の音が聞こえてきました。

次の瞬間「ピカッ」と視界が真っ白になりました。

何も考える間もなく凄まじい轟音とともに、私の体は壁ごと数メートルふっ飛ばされました。天井は崩れ、畳ごと床が抜け落ちていました。私の体は血だらけでした。母も台所のガラス戸にぶつかり、肩から胸が裂け、血が吹き出ていました。私は、母を背負って外に出ました。

そのときの光景はむごいものでした。電柱は倒れ、道路に電線がうねっていて、見渡す限り、看板や板切れ、トタン板が散乱していました。家はほとんどが倒れ、潰れ、屋根瓦が狭い道路を覆い尽くしていました。そして、そこかしこに転がる無数のけが人や死体——。どの死体も真っ黒で、男女の区別もつきません。

兵隊は皮のベルトと革靴を履いているので、それだけが燃えずに残っていました。蒸したジャガイモは、薄茶色の皮が剝ける。あれとまったく同じです。皆、手からも顔からもジャガイモの皮のような皮膚が垂れ下がっていました。

私たち母子は近くの永山病院に向かいました。しかし病院は崩れていて、とても手当ができるような状態ではありません。ふたたび母を背負って、もう少し先の逓信病院を目指しました。屋外にいた人々は、顔も手足も焼けただれています。頭髪も衣服も焼けて皆、半裸です。がれきの下から「助けて！ 助けて！」と叫ぶ声が聞こえてきましたが、どうすること

57　［証言5］山田和邦

ともできませんでした。

山陽本線のガード（高架）は崩れて、渡れなくなっていました。私たちは逃げてくる人々の流れに逆らって進みました。しかし、母を背負ったまま、何度も何度も押し戻されてしまいます。もう病院は諦めるしかありませんでした。兵隊たちが口々に「北に逃げろ！」と言っていました。

潰れた家の間を縫って、私たちも北に向かいました。白島北町と牛田町をつなぐ工兵橋の土手に着くと、そこも地獄絵図でした。逃げてきた人々が、次々と土手の草の上に倒れこむのです。草の匂い、生物の匂いに気が抜けるのか、たくさんの人が倒れ、そのまま死にました。

原爆の爆風で多くの橋が崩れたが、工兵橋は吊り橋だったために奇跡的に無事だった。この橋は近くの駐屯地と演習場を結ぶために作られたもので、橋の下は工兵隊の演習場になっていた。普段は吊り橋の前と後ろに衛兵が立っており、地元住民が近づくことも禁じられていた。背後から迫る火から逃れるために、この日多くの被爆者がこの工兵橋を渡った。工兵橋はたくさんの被爆者たちを救った「命の橋」であった。後年、老朽化により橋の撤去が検討されたが、住民の反対により残されることとなった。

橋の向こう側には、兵隊たちがひとかたまりになって座っていました。彼らは皆、一様に眼をやられていたのです。何も見えないので互いの肩につかまって、何か見えるものはないかと、しきりに顔を動かしていました。そして、彼らのその顔は熱線で焼けただれ、赤黒く腫れ上がっているのです。

「何を見たんや⁉」と聞く声がありました。
「火の玉じゃ！」「大きな火の玉が光っとった！」と応える声がありました。
原爆の光をまともに見た人たちは、皆、眼にやけどを負い、次々に死にました。体を焼かれ「水！」「水！」と呻きながら、這って雁木(川の船着場の階段)を下りていった人々は、水に入りそのまま流されていきました。流されながら「助けてくれ！」「起こしてくれ！」と手を差し出すのです。
しかし、その手を引っ張ると、ずるずると腕の皮ごと剝ける。倒れた者を助け起こすこともままならない、まさに地獄でした。

原爆の熱線で焼かれると、一瞬にして衣服は燃え落ちます。全裸にわずかなぼろ布がまとわりついているだけの状態になってしまいます。しかしもはや皆、「恥ずかしい」などと感じることさえできないのです。逃げる者は逃げ、動けない者はその場で命を落としました。もし逃げる途中に転べば、その上を無数の人々がわれ先にと駆けていきます。踏まれて亡くなった人も多かったはずです。逃げ惑うなか、誰も他人のことを思いやる余裕などなかったのです。

何が起きたのかさえわからないまま、時間が過ぎていきました。私たち母子も、もはや何も考えられず、ただ人の流れに押し流されて、工兵橋を渡りました。
全裸同様の見知らぬ女性に頼まれ、崩れた家から衣類をひっぱり出してきて渡したこともありました。工兵橋のたもとには、そんな女性がたくさんいました。
橋を渡って、私たちはさらに北へと逃げました。土手から先は、あまりやけどやケガのむごい人は見なくなりました。「何かあったら、白島中町の人たちは長束町(現・安佐南区長束)へ逃げよう──」。
当時は、非常時に備えてあらかじめ町ごとに避難場所が決められていました。私たちは昼まで土手

59 ［証言5］山田和邦

にとどまり、そこから長束に向かおうとしたときだったと思います。
夏の昼間だというのに、急に空が真っ暗になりました。後で聞いた話ですが、そのほんのすぐそばで「黒い雨」が降っていたそうです。幸い、私たちは「黒い雨」に遭遇することはありませんでした。

夜半、ようやく私たちは、長束の鎮守の森にたどり着きました。ふと、広島の方を見ると町が燃えていました。牛田あたりの山も燃え出しました。新聞が読めるほどに明るくなりました。私たちは、そのままそこで野宿しました。

「痛いよう――」
「水くれ！ 水！」
呻き声、泣き声で一睡もできません。
その翌日。私たちは付近の農家の人たちに仮住まいを提供していただきました。畳の上にあがったときの感激は、いまも忘れられません。ようやく、私たちは落ち着いて傷の手当てをすることができました。体に刺さったガラスの破片を抜き、傷口を拭き……。初めて人心地がつきました。そのときにいただいたトマトの美味しかったこと。母はそのまま農家に一泊お世話になり、翌朝、親類の家へ向かいました。可部（現 安佐北区可部）には父の姉と三人の従姉弟がいて、従姉弟たちが、学徒動員でよく父の広島工場へ来ていたので、お互い知っていました。
母は、首から肩にかけて傷が化膿していました。
「痛い！」「痛い！」
母が泣くものの、私にはどうすることもできません。可部の陸軍病院は、学校の教室を代用した

60

もので、満足な設備などあろうはずもありますことさえできません。唯一の医薬品ともいえるヨードチンキで消毒するのがせいぜいでした。

そして、それから一週間もしないうちに、私の体に異変が現れました。何もやる気が起きません。歯茎から血が出て止まらない、蚊に刺されてもいつまでも赤く腫れて治らない……。調べてもらうと、通常七千～八千の白血球が十万以上もありました。急性白血病だったと思います。

そして母も急性白血病でした。白血病のために傷口がいつまでたっても塞がりません。かわいそうだった。いま思えば死ななかったのが不思議なくらいです。早くに広島を離れたのがよかったのでしょう。

当時は、いったい自分たちの体に何が起きているのかさえわかりませんでした。まさか、あれが原因で白血病になるとは……。ただの「新型爆弾」だとしか理解していませんでした。そのことだけが唯一の救いです。あの爆弾はただの「新型爆弾」だとしか理解していませんでした。そのことだけが唯一の救いです。情報がなかったから、余計な不安を引き起こしませんでした。

その年、母子は秋ごろまで可部にとどまった。十月になってようやく、山田さんは師範学校に戻ることができた。後年、学校制度が変わったため、師範学校は広島大学となり、そのまま入学。二十一歳で大学を卒業し、山田さんは幟町(のぼりちょう)中学校の社会科の教師になった。しかし、そこでもまた、原爆の爪痕(つめあと)と対峙(たいじ)する運命が待ち構えていた。

最初の年、一九五一年（昭和二十六年）、私は一年生の担任になりました。そして、その最初の教

え子が被爆の影響で亡くなりました。色白でおかっぱ頭のおとなしい子でした。その年の年末ころから体調を崩して、学校に来なくなりました。翌年四月にクラス替えがありますが、しかし彼女は登校できません。籍だけは残し、二年にそのまま進級ということになりました。

私は、当時の鉄道病院へお見舞いに行きました。病室の前に立ったときでした。なかから彼女の呻き声が聞こえてきました。私はドアを開けることもできず、その声が収まるまで病室に入ることができませんでした。

白血病は、しばしば全身に激痛をもたらします。しばらくして病室へ入っていきますと、彼女が嬉（うれ）しそうに笑みを浮かべてくれましたので、ほっとしました。

枕元には真新しい二年生の教科書が置いてあります。社会科の教科書を開いて、

「いま、ここまでやりよるよ」

と言いますと、彼女は「うん、うん」とうなずいていました。

それから間もなく、彼女は亡くなりました。授業があって私は葬式には行けません。クラスの同級生たちは、湯本さんは被爆が原因で入院し、登校できないのだと皆、知っていました。そしてその彼女と同じように、幼いころ被爆している子どもたちが何人もいました。その子たちを不安に陥（おとしい）れてしまうことがわかっていながら、彼女の死を伝えました。どれほど辛（つら）かったことか。私は直接にはかかわっていませんが、「原爆の子の像」で有名な佐々木禎子さんも幟町中学校に在籍していた生徒です。

私は四十年近い奉職で、五回学校を替わりました。どの学校でも、幼児被爆や胎内被爆の生徒が

62

必ず何人かいました。引地馨君のことも忘れられません。三年生の担任のときの生徒で、ほんとうに優秀な子でした。クラス対抗のバレーボールの試合でも活躍していました。ところが、勉強にもスポーツにも優れた子で、親御さんもずいぶん期待されていたと思います。幼児被爆による白血病——。そのときは、声も出せんでした。

「こんなことが続くと、教師というのは本当に辛い職業です」。そう山田さんはつぶやく。彼は、その後も何人もの教え子を原爆症で亡くした。「私自身も被爆していますが、教え子を亡くすのはもっと辛いです」

「○○くんが白血病で去年亡くなりました——」。久しぶりに同窓会に顔を出しても、教え子の死を伝え聞くことになります。六十歳を過ぎても、なお原爆症は発症します。やり切れません。東京で結婚して、いまはいいお婆ちゃんになっているかつての教え子が、「最近、頭髪が抜け、体調も悪いです」と話していました。その女性も先日亡くなりました。

私は同窓会のたびに「わしより先に死んだら承知せんぞ！」と言います。卒業した後に死んだ者を含めれば、二十四、五人の教え子を原爆症で亡くしています。若くして亡くなった子どもたちのためにも、残った私が真相を語っていかなければいけないと思います。私は、教師時代から機会があれば被爆体験を語るようにしていました。妻とも「せめて記憶が残っている間だけでも語っておこう」と話しています。

63　［証言5］山田和邦

山田さんは、一九五六年（昭和三十一年）に結婚。山田さんは、「直接被爆対象地域」といわれる爆心地から約二キロ以内で被爆したが、妻も同じく二・三キロ地点で被爆していた。被爆者同士の結婚、ということになる。

原爆症の後遺症のことはもちろん考えましたが、「被爆者同士で助け合っていけたらいい──」と思い結婚しました。片方が被爆していなかったら家族の反対ということもあったかもしれませんが、私たちに反対者はいませんでした。子どもは三人。最初の子を妊娠したときは、不安になりました。

「風聞に惑わされるな。現実にはそんなことはない」と、医者である妻の兄が力づけてくれました。あのときは、本当に励まされました。

山田さんは、原爆には三つの被害があると言う。まず、熱線によるやけど。そして爆風によるけが。山田さんの母がそうであったように、多くの人が無数のガラスが体に刺さり、あるいは倒壊した家の下敷きになった。そして放射能──。

放射能は得体が知れません。とくに入市被爆や胎内被爆は、どこで被爆したのかも判然としないのに発症してしまいます。私も放射能が危険だと知っていれば、白島中町には戻らず、田舎に避難していたに違いありません。ちょうどいま福島の人たちが原発から避難しているように。

終戦直後、「ABCC(原爆傷害調査委員会)」という米国の調査研究機関が比治山に開設されました。そこは治療をするのではなく、原爆のデータ収集のため検診を行う施設でした。食糧難の時代でしたので、検診を受けるとカレーライスを食べさせてくれたり、チョコレートをくれたりします。私も何度か行きました。当日は、車で迎えが来るほどの待遇だったと記憶しています。

放射能は「死の科学」とも言われます。当時、放射能のことを何も知らなかった私たちは、焼け跡にバラックを建てて住み、あるいは畑を耕して野菜を植えていました。

そしてたくさんの人たちが、すさまじい倦怠感で働けなくなりました。当時は、「ぶらぶら病」とか「横着病」と呼ばれていました。そして、十年くらいして、それらの人たちは次々に亡くなりました。一九五七年(昭和三十二年)、国が初めてその原因が放射能であることを発表しました。このとき初めて「原爆症」が認定されたのです。この認定の前の十年間は「空白の十年」と言われています。広島にはあちこちに慰霊碑がありますが、早い時期に建てた慰霊碑には「原爆」という文字は入っていません。占領下におけるプレスコード(言論統制)の影響もあって、アメリカに気兼ねして「原爆」の文字を使えなかったからでしょう。

山田さんは、市内の公立中学校の教師を定年近くまで務めた。その後、教育委員会に移り、さらには広島文教女子大学で、七十歳まで教壇に立った。町内会長や社会福祉協議会会長を務め、また二十年以上保護司をやっていた功績が認められ、叙勲を受けることになった。山田さんの父も叙勲を受けていたので、父子二代にわたって叙勲されたことになる。そう話す山田さんの表情は、初めてほころんだ。しかし、原爆の話に戻るとまた表情は硬くなった。

65　［証言5］山田和邦

十五歳で被爆して、八十三歳のいままで──。私の人生は、あらゆる原爆症の連続だったような思いがします。ちょうど被爆から十年目、二十五歳で肝臓病を発症。四十代後半になりますと、ちょっと油っぽいものを食べると、ひどい腹痛がするようになりました。「胆囊炎」と診断され、胆囊を切除。いまは、甲状腺機能障害と前立腺がんの疑いで薬を飲み続けています。
 だから、福島の原発事故のことは他人事ではありません。東電も政府もすべてをつまびらかにしていないと思います。「平和利用の核ならよい」などというのは嘘です。人類と核は絶対に共存できません。

証言6

あの原爆を忘れさせてなるものか

木原 正さん

きはら・ただし 一九二七年(昭和二年)二月、和菓子屋の家に生まれた。爆心から一・九キロの広島駅に停車中の汽車内で十八歳のときに被爆。広島鉄道局に勤務。被爆後、家業を継いだが、その後に就職した会社で、得意の毛筆書きが認められる。現在は独立し、毛筆専門に筆耕を手掛ける。八十七歳。広島市東区在住。

命ある限り語り継ごう

私は、男五人女三人の八人兄弟の四番目で三男。実家は岡山県津山市で、小さな和菓子屋をやっていました。店は一家総出で働きました。尋常高等小学校の低学年のころから、兄や姉たちと一緒に工場であんこ作りを手伝いました。父は、昔気質の職人でした。だから、いい加減な仕事をしていると叱られました。まきで叩かれたこともあります。

私は最中が得意でした。濡れ布巾の上に、最中の皮を伏せて並べます。皮の縁がほどよく湿ってから片方の皮にあんこを詰めると、面白いようにピタッとくっつきます。小豆を煮ながら、そっと

スプーンですくっては舐めていました。これが楽しみでした。

一九四一年(昭和十六年)四月、木原さんは広島鉄道局の施設部電修場信号室での仕事についた。当時十四歳。そのころ、国鉄(現・JR)には全国で八つの鉄道局があり、その一つが広島鉄道局である。施設部電修場は、鉄道局のなかでもかなり特殊だった。主な仕事は、鉄道信号の切替器である継電器の定期検査と修理。ほかに時計、配電盤メーターなどの点検修理なども行っていた。

「鉄道」という印象よりも「工場」でした。私の職務は技工で、メッキやコイル、木工、鋳物、旋盤などを扱いました。ときどき上司の目を盗んではベルトのバックルや指輪、登山用のピッケルなどを作ったこともありました。当時、国鉄は軍用物資や兵隊の輸送を行っていました。人手が足りず、軍隊の応援もありました。白い軍服を着た兵隊が、貨物列車で石炭を窯にくべているのを見たことがあります。軍も国鉄を別格扱いしていたのでしょうか。国鉄職員の徴兵は、遅いように思われました。それでも、同期の仲間五人に「赤紙」が来ました。

休日にはよく職場の仲間と、道後山へハイキングやキャンプに行きました。道後山は、広島・鳥取・岡山の三県にまたがる山です。国鉄職員なので、汽車賃は当時無料。みんなで芸備線に乗りました。夜九時過ぎに、カーバイトランプを点け、山小屋に行ったものです。そのころの仲間も、原爆で一人は行方不明になり、一人は死にました。

四五年(昭和二十年)になると、食糧不足はいよいよ深刻さを増した。そのため木原さんたちは、

呉線小屋浦駅の線路脇の空き地を整備して、塩田を作ることになった。当時、小屋浦駅の線路そばの道路を降りると、すぐに海があった。砂を撒き、バケツリレーで海水を汲み入れる。天日で自然に干すと、食塩ができあがる。

八月六日は、塩田整備作業の初日でした。学徒動員で仁保国民学校の六年生が来ていました。さすがに、子どもたちに難しい仕事はさせられません。せいぜい「これをメッキ場に持っていきなさい」などといった小間使いの雑用がほとんど。その朝、私は、同僚や後輩の四人と、十人の子どもたちを引率して、塩田に行くことになっていました。集合場所は、広島駅の呉線ホームでした。

そのとき、呉線の汽車は十分ほど遅れて到着しました。運命のいたずらだった。もし時間通りに発車していれば、原爆投下の時間に汽車は向洋駅か、またはその次の海田市駅に着いていたことになる。そこまで行っていれば、木原さんたちは被爆することはなかっただろう。

汽車に乗る直前、上空に米軍Ｂ29爆撃機が見えましたが、空襲警報もなかったので、気にもとめず、先に子どもたちを乗車させました。続いて私も車両の入り口近くに乗り、立って子どもたちと話をしていました。

当時は、汽車の窓に木製の鎧戸が付いていました。発車の前には、いつも車掌が「鎧戸を降ろしてください」と案内します。しかし、子どもたちは遠足気分でワイワイとはしゃいでいました。夏なので車内は暑く、子どもたちは皆、窓を開けていました。

69 ［証言6］木原 正

発車の予定時刻は八時十五分。

突然、写真を撮るときのマグネシウムのフラッシュ——その何百倍もの閃光が走りました。瞬時に、目の玉がえぐられるように感じました。ほとんど同時にドーンと汽車が大きく揺れました。駅舎の屋根のスレートが全部、崩落してきました。落下したスレートと埃で、視界が暗くなりました。

それまで広島に空襲はありませんでしたが、他の都市に焼夷弾が雨のように落とされていたことは知っていました。爆弾が一発ということはないはず。「次の爆弾を落とされる前に手で目と耳を塞ば！」と思いました。子どもたちは大声で泣きながらも、訓練で教えられた通りに手で目と耳を塞ぎ床に伏せています。どの子にも割れた窓ガラスが刺さり、けがをしていました。子どもたち一人ひとりを抱き線路に下ろしました。

線路づたいに、それぞれが前の子のベルトをつかみ、数珠つなぎに進んでいきました。向かったのは、二百メートル先にある大須賀町（現・南区大須賀町）の踏切です。私は、栄橋のたもとの鉄道病院に連れて行こうと思っていました。しかし、大勢の人が街中から栄橋を渡って洪水のように向かってきました。皆、やけどで顔や腕の皮膚がただれています。

私たちは人々の渦に巻き込まれ、東練兵場に入ってしまいました。仕方なく、東練兵場の隅に子どもたちを集めました。顔や腕から血を流して、泣きわめいています。「すぐに薬を持ってくる。ここを動くな！」そう言って、私は南蟹屋（現・南区南蟹屋）にあった仕事場に向かいました。足の踏み場もありません。それでも、何とか仕事場も爆風で柱が折れ壁や窓も壊れていました。ところが、子どもたちの姿が見えません。何か救急箱を探し出して、急いで練兵場に戻りました。そのとき、私は初めて自があって移動したのでしょうか。しばらく、そこで待つことにしました。

分がけがをしていることに気づきました。東練兵場に戻るときに、線路の枕木やレールにつまずいて転んだときの傷だったのでしょう。白い半袖シャツは、胸から袖や腰の辺りまで血で真っ赤に染まり、右足からも出血していました。足の傷は骨まで達しています。救急箱から薬を取り出して止血しました。

一時間ほど待っていましたが、誰も戻ってきません。仕方なく、仕事場に戻りました。数日後に知ったことですが、子どもたちは互いに「市内は危ないから」と、東練兵場近くの山の側を通り、仁保（現・南区仁保）まで帰ったそうです。

母親の乳首をくわえて死んだ赤ん坊

私は汽車のなかにいたので、直接の熱線を浴びませんでした。だからけがだけで助かりました。職場の電修場は、負傷者の手当に追われていました。私は当直員として助役の他四人と寝泊まりするように命じられ、前庭に板とむしろを敷き、蚊帳を吊って寝ました。その夜、電気コードの先に豆球をつないだ特製電灯を作りました。信号機を動かす試験のときの特大乾電池を使ったのです。この特製電灯で、付近の路地や崩れた建物の陰にけが人がいないか探し回りました。仕事場では百人以上いた職員が、このとき、二十人ぐらいに減っていました。

見回りをしていると、電灯の明かりを見た負傷者が「水、水を！」と懇願します。その暗闇のなかに、やけどで上半身裸の一人の婦人がいました。乳飲み児を抱いて「兵隊さん、お水をください！」と声を掛けてきます。近づく人は、皆、兵隊に見えたのでしょう。その声はか細く、必死に

[証言6] 木原 正

訴えてきます。抱いている乳児は、母の乳首をくわえたまま、すでに死んで体の色が変わっていました。それでもわが子を抱こうとするのは、母親の本能だったのでしょうか。その婦人は顔から肩にかけ、とくにひどく焼けただれていました。私は何もしてやれませんでした。手を合わせて詫び、その場を去りましたが、いまも心が痛みます。

原爆投下直後、多くの被爆者が水を飲んだ直後に死んでいった。そのため、水を懇願されても、水を飲ませないことが多かったとされる。実際には、それらの人々はほとんど水を飲まなくても死んだという。

私たちがいた東練兵場は広大な敷地でした。日ごろは兵隊が銃剣の稽古や隊列を組んで行進しているところですが、そこは避難してきた被爆者がぎっしりと詰めかけていました。けがをして横になっている人々。かたまっている家族の群れ。一体どれぐらいの人数がいるのか、わからないほどでした。

しかし、日を追うごとに、人々の数がみるみる減っていきます。身内のところに避難する人もいましたが、死んでいく人のほうがたくさんいたのです。そうした遺体を貨物車両に積み込み、何両も繋いで運んでいました。あるとき、空の貨物車両を覗き込んだら、何とも言えない異様な臭いが鼻を突き、思わず吐きそうになりました。

周囲の木造の屋根は波のように歪んで見えました。原爆は上空で炸裂し、凄まじい力で押さえつけるように襲ったのでしょう。

東練兵場に近い愛宕町は、夜中まで激しく燃えました。消防団員が号令をかけ、それに従って市民が手押しポンプで水をかけていました。その二、三日後。熱線を浴びて死んだ多くの軍馬を一列に並べ、重油をかけて焼いているのを目撃しました。被爆して死んだ馬は、両足をぴんと伸ばして腹が膨れていました。ビニール風船を膨らませたようにも見えました。とりわけ、その悪臭はすごいものでした。

被爆して十日。私は下痢（げり）が続きました。続いて頭髪が抜け出しました。いま思えば、それは原爆症の症状でした。被爆後、長い間、広島ではスカーフをかぶっている女性を多く見かけましたが、おそらく私のように頭髪の抜けた女性たちだったのでしょう。

木原さんは、そのまま翌年の四月まで鉄道局の施設部電修場信号室に勤めた。その後、家業を継ぐため、神戸市の和菓子屋に住み込みで修業を始めた。そして、郷里の津山市に戻り、父を手伝うようになる。

昔の和菓子作りしか知らない父は、新しい技法を知ってとても喜んでくれました。新しい和菓子が評判になりました。「この和菓子を販売させてください」という人も現れました。小売りをやめ、和菓子の製造に専念することにしました。二十七、八歳のころのことです。原爆に遭った人には原爆手帳が交付される、と聞きました。そして、その手帳があれば医療費が免除されるといいます。私は、爆心から二キロ以内で直接被爆したので、すぐに原爆手帳が交付されました。けれど、原爆手帳など本当はもらいたくない。手帳をもらったら結婚に影響すると考えていました。できれば

[証言6] 木原 正

「普通の人間」でいたかったのです。

私の体調は悪化する一方でした。結果として、原爆手帳には大いに助けられることになりました。三十二歳のときに膀胱の手術。四十五歳のときに腸閉塞ました。三回も同じところを開腹しましたので、ヘソがなくなってしまいました。五十五歳で胆石症を発症し、手術を受け大病続きも、原爆手帳のおかげで助かったのです。

一九六七年（昭和四十二年）には、木原さんは新聞広告で見かけた山陽事務光機という会社に入社。やがて、得意だった毛筆書きが認められ、表彰状や宛名書きを専門に頼まれるようになる。山陽事務光機に定年まで勤めたが、その後も取引先などから毛筆の賞状書きなどを頼まれるようになった。九五年（平成七年）には「きはら企画」として独立し、現在も毛筆書きの仕事を続けている。

若いころは被爆したことを隠し通していました。還暦を過ぎ、六十五歳ころになって「やっぱり生きている間に語り継ごう」と心に決めました。まず趣味の仲間や仕事で知り合った友人に話し、それから語り伝え始めました。一番衝撃を受けたのは、若い人たちが原爆に無関心だったことです。私は、地獄のような出来事を二度と起こさせないために、いまこそ語ろうと強く思っています。

証言7

人間の宿命を感じつつ、平和のために尽くしたい

中村良治 さん

なかむら・よしはる　一九二七年（昭和二年）五月生まれ。広島商業学校卒業後、国鉄に勤務。車掌を目指す勉強中に爆心から一・九キロの広島駅車掌区の建物で被爆した。避難先は落合村を経て、母の故郷の九州・佐賀県へも行く。八十六歳。広島市佐伯区在住。

かえらぬ親友五郎君からの返信はなかった

上に姉が二人と兄が一人。私は四人兄弟の末っ子でした。近所に男の子兄弟三人がいる家があって、皆でよく日が暮れるまで空き地でサッカーをして遊びました。思い出すのは、父が元気だったころの正月です。父が餅をつき、母が合いの手で餅を返します。その餅を姉たちが丸めていました。父は相撲が好きで、いつもラジオに耳をつけるようにして、相撲の実況放送を聞いていました。

中村さんが国民学校に通うころ、戦争は激しさを増した。学校で勉強したのは二年生の一学期まで。その後は学徒動員に駆り出された。三菱重工広島造船所で、溶接やパイプを曲げる作業の日々が続く。勉強は一週間に一回。土曜日に学校の先生が来て、造船所の食堂で三時間ほど話を聞くだけだった。

もともと父は、職人を集めて海軍省に窓枠などの建具を納入する仕事をしていました。しかし、もうそのころには、体を壊して寝たきりになっていました。食料難の時代でしたから、とにかく食べ物が手に入りません。新鮮な魚など、とっくに庶民の口に入らなくなっていたので、私は造船所の食堂で出た鯖(さば)の煮付けをよく持って帰りました。いつも父は喜んでくれました。気管支炎の父は、激しく咳(せ)き込んでは、母が背中をさすります。それ以外は、ただ寝ているだけ。それが精いっぱいの「治療」でした。父はだんだんと衰弱していき、一九四四年(昭和十九年)、五十六歳で亡くなりました。

中区江波)で、米ヌカで作った「江波団子」が売り出されると聞くと、あわてて出かけます。江波(え ば)(現・よければ、手に入る。運が悪ければ、空(から)で帰る。そんな時代です。当時は食べ物だけでなく、薬もありません。

父の死の翌年の三月。十八歳の中村さんは、県立広島商業学校を卒業して、国鉄に就職した。

当時は、軍需産業しか働くところがありませんでした。同級生のほとんどが、動員先の造船所に残ります。他には、国鉄に入って軍用物資を運ぶ貨物車両の車掌ぐらい。とても自由に職業を選べ

るような時代ではありませんでした。

　父の死後、母は自分の故郷である九州の佐賀県に帰りたがっていました。私が国鉄に入ったのも「佐賀に行けることがあるかもしれない」と思ってのことでした。でも働いてみてわかったのは、広島に入る貨物列車は、上りは姫路、下りは下関まで。そこから先は管区が違っていたので、佐賀へは行けませんでした。

　中村さんの主な仕事は、貨物車両の連結の入れ替えだった。連結の入れ替えと一口にいうのは簡単だが、なかなか大変な仕事だった。機関車の馬力を考慮して、繋ぐ貨物車両の車両数を考える。そして、駅ごとに貨物を切り離す順番を考えなければならない。最初にとまる駅の貨物を最後尾にする。そして、次の駅の貨物は順にその前に連結した。

　当時の機関車は、蒸気機関車でD51やC31が主流です。D51は四個の動輪を持つ馬力のある機関車で、三十車両の貨物を引いて走ることができました。D51の「D」はアルファベットの四番目。動輪が四つあることを表しています。C31の「C」は三番目だから動輪が三つ。従って、C31は三個の動輪で走る機関車のことです。「51」や「31」などの数字は型式を示します。貨物車両の車掌になるには試験があります。私たちは、勤務のない日は、車掌試験の勉強をしていました。広島駅の隣にある木造建ての車掌区建物の二階でした。

　あの日も、私は朝から十二人の仲間とともに勉強をしていました。朝の八時十五分、私は窓際にいました。その瞬間、まるで電車のスパークのような「ピカッ」と

77　［証言7］中村良治

いう光とともに、私の体は吹き飛ばされました。音は何も聞こえませんでした。その日はカラリと晴れた日だったのに、周囲はまっ暗になりました。手探りで階段の手すりにつかまり、なんとかそれを頼りに一階に降り、外に出ました。

そのとき、異様な光景を見ました。真っ暗だった周囲が、下の方から少しずつ明るくなります。そして、黒い埃のようなものが、スーッと空に昇っていきます。気がつくと、私は、肩から腕にかけて血が、あれが空に昇って「黒い雨」になったのでしょうか。雨は降りませんでしたで真っ赤になっていました。詰め襟の紺色の鉄道員服の上から、無数のガラスの破片が刺さっていました。車掌になったばかりのため、襟章は白い模様のバッジでした。その襟章は血で赤く染まっていました。

広島駅前は大混乱で、すごい人だかりになっていました。駅の増築部分は、すべて崩落していました。上司に「家のことが心配なので見に行ってもいいですか！」と叫ぶと、

「行きなさい！」

と許可してくれました。

私は駅を飛び出し、力の限り走りました。自宅は、いつもなら歩いて二十分ほどの距離にあります。私の家の向かいにあった段原国民学校が、出火し激しく燃えていました。私の家がめちゃくちゃに壊れていました。そして、爆風に吹き飛ばされて血だらけになった母と下の姉が、家の前にぼーっと立っていました。二人とも潰れた家から這い出して、大けがを負っています。足の踏み場もないくらいの壊れた家から、よくも出てくることができたものだ、と思いました。髪はくしゃくしゃで、二人の顔は煤けていました。

家の裏側で、三人の衛生兵がテントの救護所を建てはじめました。やけどに油を塗り、傷口に包帯を巻いて応急処置をしています。私もそこで処置をしてもらいました。そこへ、女子挺身隊として陸軍兵器廠に勤めていた上の姉が戻ってきました。爆風で兵器廠もめちゃくちゃになったそうですが、けがはありませんでした。電話局に勤めていた兄は、召集されて山口県の小月部隊の通信隊に配属になっていました。おそらく無事のはずです。私たち家族は、本当に運がよかったのです。

 中村さんたち家族四人は落合村（現・安佐北区落合）に向かった。以前から町内で決められていた避難先が、落合村だったのだ。途中、被爆して皮膚が焼けただれた大勢の人の群れとすれ違った。

 恐ろしいともかわいそうとも思う心の余裕はありませんでした。感覚が麻痺していたのでしょう。電柱は倒れ、周囲に電線が散乱し、あちこちに焼死体が転がっていました。たくさんの死体を跨ぎ、避けながら逃げました。川には無数の死体が浮いていました。二人の兵隊が乾パンを配っていましたので、私たちは乾パンをもらい、他の逃げる人たちと先になったり後になったりしながら、東大橋を通って逃げました。
 夕方に着いた落合村は原爆の被害はなく、随分のんびりしていました。がっくり力が抜けたのを覚えています。落合村では、あらかじめ受け入れ先の農家が決まっていました。その晩、避難先で蚊帳を吊ってくれたのです。「本当に嬉しい」と実感しました――。

 しかし、中村さんたち一家には、もう帰るべき家がなかった。たとえ薄い縁でも、頼って行くし

かない。翌日、一家は可部(現・安佐北区可部)へ向かった。可部には、亡くなった父の兄嫁が住んでいたからである。

あの日、広島の方角に大きなキノコ雲が可部から見える、と思うた」と可部の人は口々に言っていたそうです。「何かわからんが、えらいことが起こっとる、と思うた」と可部の人は口々に言っていたそうです。可部に着いて四、五日目のこと。私は原因不明の高熱に襲われました。立っていられないほど体がだるいのです。しゃがんだまま、ずっと必死に耐えるしかありません。それが原爆の症状だとわかったのは、半年くらい後のことでした。
八月十五日、玉音放送がありました。つい一週間前までは「天皇陛下」という言葉だけで全員が直立不動でしたが、そのときは皆、立ったまま、ぼーっと聞いていました。

当時、市民は天皇陛下の声を聞くのは初めてであった。「本当に戦争が終わったのか」「意味がよくわからなかった」。そんな人も多かったという。

終戦の日、私たち家族は母の故郷・佐賀へ出発することになりました。少しだけ体調がよくなっていた私は、抱えられるようにして汽車に乗り込みました。私たちは被爆当日に「罹災証明書」をもらっていましたので、汽車賃は無料でした。「罹災証明書」は、兵隊たちが乾パンと一緒に配っていたものです。同じ町内で一塊になって逃げていたし、同じ避難場所に行きますので、一人ひとりを確認はしていなかったのでしょう。「証明書」とはいいながら、名前も生年月日も記入されてはいません。ただ「罹災証明書」と書かれた紙切れ一枚でした。そしてそれが後に、原爆手帳と差

し替えられました。
　私たちは広島駅を出発して大竹駅まで行きました。そこからは空襲で線路が寸断されていましたので、小瀬川の鉄橋を歩いて岩国へ。そして岩国から再び汽車に乗って佐賀まで行きました。母の実家は、佐賀県の鹿島(現・鹿島市)にありました。佐賀で読んだ西日本新聞は、新型爆弾で広島が全滅したと報道していました。母の親戚は、私たち家族が「全員死んだ」と思っていたところへ、母と二人の姉と私が戻ってきたので、びっくりしていました。
　終戦と同時に兄は除隊となって、母の実家を訪ねてきました。
　上の姉は、実家の向かいにあったうどん工場に働き口を見つけましたが、他の者は食べていく手段がありませんでした。そこで下の姉と兄は元の職場である広島の電話局に戻りました。私も姉と兄を頼って、広島の電話局に勤めることになりました。戦争と原爆の投下でとにかく人手が足りないころでしたので喜んで採用してくれました。愛宕町の父の実家に間借りして、兄姉と私の三人は広島で働きました。母と上の姉は、母の実家の佐賀で暮らしています。そんな、家族ばらばらの生活が続きました。
　被爆した翌年春には、首のリンパ腺が腫れました。しかし広島には診てくれる医者も病院もほとんどありません。佐賀の母のところで医者を探すことにしました。佐賀の病院では「すぐに手術」ということになり、そのまま電話局に休暇願を出して手術しました。やがて回復し、その後も二カ月に一回は佐賀の母の実家に行きました。広島では食べるものがありませんが、田舎の鹿島には米や芋が豊富にある、という事情がありました。
　母はいつも「ちゃんと食べとるか」と、心配して米や野菜を持たせてくれました。母からもらっ

81　[証言7] 中村良治

た米や野菜はリュックサックの底に隠しました。当時は、警察による闇米の摘発がよくありました。門司駅で、乗客は駅地下道に四列に並ばされて検査を受けました。私は米の上に野菜を載せていましたので、見つかりませんでした。

そんなころ、広島商業学校時代の友達と会いました。彼の家は、かつては大きなお屋敷で豊かな生活でした。原爆ですべてが焼けてしまい、流川町の焼け跡地にバラックを建てて住んでいました。

「ワシも隣にバラックを建てて住んでもええかのう」と言うと、「来んさいや」と喜んでくれました。

私は早速、彼の家の隣に、十二坪のバラックを建てて住みました。壁は板を打ちつけただけ。屋根は木の皮が付いたままの削ぎ葺きでした。六畳二間に台所と便所のついたバラック。そこに兄姉と三人で三年近く住みました。

やがて、母と同居していた上の姉が結婚。私たちの生活も落ち着いたので、佐賀から母を呼ぶことができました。五日市町（現・佐伯区五日市町）の楽々園に移り、四人で生活しました。その後、私は結婚して家を出ました。私は三十四歳、妻は二十六歳。妻は広島の出身ですが、当時は学童疎開で広島市にいなかったため、被爆を免れました。私が被爆者だからといって妻の家族から何か言われたことはありませんでした。

この後、中村さんの姉が「交易営団」という三菱系列の貿易会社に転職。その会社の待遇がたいへんよかったので、中村さんもその会社に転職した。「交易営団」は、呉市に住んでいた進駐軍の家族のために、家具や冷蔵庫などを納入する会社だった。会社は進駐軍の引き揚げと同時に役目が

終了、閉鎖された。そのため、中村さんは兄の紹介で証券会社に勤務することとなった。やがて、その証券会社が出資する「広島砂糖」へ引き抜かれ、そこで定年まで勤めた。

　いまだに忘れられないのは、広島商業学校で親友だった光田五郎君のことです。彼はスポーツマンでした。鉄棒の蹴上（けあ）がりがうまく、同級生のヒーローでした。五郎君の家は「光田ヒヨコ店」といって雛（ひな）を売っていました。私が佐賀の母の実家に移ったばかりのときでした。とにかく仕事がないので、何か仕事をしようと思い「雛を育て鶏にして卵を産ませたい」。そう五郎君に手紙を書いたのです。彼からの返事はありませんでした。代わりに、彼の死を告げるお兄さんからの手紙を受け取りました。短い手紙でしたが、私は本当に悔しくてたまりませんでした。

　あの日、広島商工会議所で特別幹部候補生の身体検査があり、五郎君は朝八時に、爆心から二百六十メートルのところにある会場に向かったそうです。五郎君は優れた体格がありながらすぐに亡くなってしまい、体が細く病弱な自分が、この年齢まで生きている。つくづく人間には、宿命や運命というものがあると感じずにはいられません。だからこそ、平和のためにいまここで、自分のできる精いっぱいを尽くしたいと固く心に誓うのです。

証言8

毎年、八月六日に韓国人原爆犠牲者慰霊碑へ

森本俊雄 さん

もりもと・としお　韓国名：金寿甲（キム・スガプ）。一九二九年（昭和四年）、韓国釜山市生まれ。四歳で来日。爆心から一・七キロの松原町（現・南区松原町）のトラックの下で十六歳のときに被爆。戦後、音楽喫茶「ムシカ」の支配人など喫茶店の仕事を六十年間続けた。八十四歳。広島市西区在住。

韓国から来日し被爆
広島で必死になって家族と生き抜く

　森本さんは、韓国生まれで、四歳のときに両親に連れられて来日し、広島に住んでいた。先に日本に来ていた父親の弟がクリーニング店を経営していた。近所に韓国出身者も多かったという。中学生になり、一九三九年（昭和十四年）の創氏改名で、それまでの「金」から「森本」となる。森本さんは、十六歳で軍関係の物資を輸送する運送トラックの助手として働いていた。

あの日、私は六十俵の米をトラックで運んでいました。トラックとはいえ木炭車です。もともと、電気系統やエンジンはトラブル続きでした。いつものことながら、この日もエンジンの調子がよくありません。広島駅あたりまで来たとき、どうにも馬力が出なくなってしまいました。運転手が「オイルが漏れているかもしれん。見てくれ」と言うので、トラックの下に潜り込みました。オイルの状態を点検するために。

私がトラックの下に体を入れた瞬間。そのときです。

「ピカッ」

と目を開けていられないほどの強い光が、あたり一面を覆いました。

「ドッカーン」

という、これまで聞いたこともない凄まじい爆発音。そして、強い風が巻き起こりました。爆風で木片などが飛びかっています。空には大きな雲がむくむくと立ちのぼっています。塵やゴミのようなものが降るように落ちてきました。幸いなことに私はトラックの下にいたために助かりました。運転手も車内にいたためか、体に傷ひとつありませんでした。

とりあえず、二人で宇品の支店に戻ることにしました。宇品に向かう比治山線の電車通りは、惨状を呈していました。道路いっぱいに、崩れた家屋の木片や瓦が飛び散っています。もちろん、電車は止まったまま。付近を歩いている人は、皆、頭の毛はちりちりに焼けています。服も破れている人ばかり。歩くのがやっとというようすです。なかには歩けなくなった人もいます。

宇品支店の建物は無事だったのですが、社員は自宅が心配だろうから、すぐに家に帰るようにとの指示が出されました。歩くといっても歩いて帰るしかありません。御幸橋を渡り、日赤病院の前か

85　［証言8］森本俊雄

ら鷹野橋商店街にさしかかりました。そこでは、大勢の人が裸同然の姿で逃げ惑っていました。明治橋や住吉橋を渡るとき、川を見下ろしました。すると、たくさんの人が流されていました。誰もそれを助ける余裕などありません。すでに死んでいる人もいたのかもしれません。私はただただ無事を祈って見るだけでした。

森本さんは、必死の思いで河原町（現・中区河原町）の自宅付近にたどり着く。しかし、自宅は完全に崩壊。家族で決めてあった避難場所に向かう。そこでは母と妹、末弟に落ち合えたが、家の外に遊びに行っていた弟は行方不明だった。

以前から、わが家では、緊急避難場所を佐伯郡河内村（現・佐伯区五日市町）の知人宅と決めていました。そこは、荷物疎開で、たんすなどの家財道具を運んでおいたところです。母と妹、一番下の弟の三人は、すでにそこに避難していました。宇品にあった陸軍糧秣廠の缶詰工場で働いていた父も、そこにやってきました。父の頭にはガラスで切った傷がありました。
しかし、自宅の近所で遊んでいたはずの二番目の弟だけが行方不明。ずいぶん探したのですが、なかなか見つかりません。私は避難所となっていた学校を中心に見て回りました。負傷者の顔を一人ひとり確認することが続きました。草津国民学校に弟と思われる子どもがいるということで駆けつけました。原爆投下から三日目のことです。負傷者が教室にあふれていました。そのなかに大やけどの子どもが倒れていました。大声で弟の名前を呼んでも返事はありません。頭から顔にかけて大やけどをしていて、人相もまるでわかりません。体も焼けただれて裸同然。

86

しかし、その子どものズボンについているベルトのバックルに見覚えがありました。それはたしかに私の手造りのバックルでした。弟があまりにほしがるので、私があげたものに間違いありませんでした。

右足首に傷があったことも思い出しました。見ると同じような傷があります。体をゆすり弟の名を呼びかけてみました。かすかにうなずいたので、ようやく弟と確認できたのです。家族全員が、とにもかくにも日本語だけは助かったことが確認できたのです。しかし、その後の弟は悲惨でした。寝ている体を起こすと背中に白いウジがわいていることもありました。「人間の骨が効く」といって人骨の粉末を飲ませることまでしました。

その年の大晦日(おおみそか)、三家族で韓国への帰国問題をめぐって話し合いました。その結果、まず私の家族が韓国に帰ることになりました。私はすでに働いていましたし、韓国語が話せません。四歳のときから日本語の環境のなかで育ってきました。韓国に帰っても、韓国語での会話や読み書きがまったくできないことが何より気になりました。言葉の面が不安で、帰国することはためらわれました。最終的に私も広島に留まる決意をしました。

広島に残った私は、駅前にある食堂を手伝うようになりました。在日韓国人で広島駅前で喫茶・食堂をはじめた親戚がいたのです。店主の奥さんが父方の叔母にあたることもあり、その店で働くようになったのでした。当時、駅前の猿猴橋町(えんこうばしちょう)（現・南区猿猴橋町）は、戦後いち早く復興した闇市の町でした。縄張り争いが激しく、テキ屋とやくざの闘争は、東映の『仁義なき戦い』でも有名になりました。

その喫茶・食堂はやがて音楽喫茶「ムシカ」として生まれ変わり順調に営業を続けました。店主

87　［証言8］森本俊雄

は、闇市でクラシック音楽のレコードを入手。「音楽で広島の人たちを元気づけたい」という動機で音楽喫茶をはじめたのです。「ムシカ」とはスペイン語で「音楽堂」という意味です。

音楽喫茶を開店した一九四六年(昭和二十一年)の大晦日には、ベートーベンの『交響曲第九番』のコンサートを開催しました。このレコードは店主が苦労して大阪の闇市で入手してきたものでした。その日のことはいまでもよく覚えています。雪が降っていました。会場は三十人も入ると満員というスペースしかありません。

店の外から窓越しにたくさんの人が耳を澄ませて『交響曲第九番』に聴き入っていました。音楽に国境はありません。食べるものにも事欠く時代に、多くの人がベートーベンの音楽に心を癒やされた感動的な光景でした。以後、この「第九コンサート」は長く続き、多くの広島市民に親しまれたのです。

十年続いた闇市のなかの「ムシカ」はその後、中心街の中区胡町に移転。木造三階建ての広島唯一の音楽喫茶店となっていました。五五年(昭和三十年)一月、中区胡町への移転を機に、私は正式に「ムシカ」の支配人となり、喫茶店運営の一切を任されるようになりました。喫茶店「ムシカ」は非常に繁盛していて、ウェートレスは二十人近くいました。ウェートレスの一人で一歳年下の女性と結婚。現在の妻、万里子です。

しかし、妻の親族が私たちの結婚に大反対。私が在日韓国人であり、爆心地近くで被爆していたためだろうと思います。さらに、妻の実家では、すでに嫁入り先を決めていたこともあって、親族一同が、私たちの結婚に猛反対しました。

「ぼんくらしやがって!」

と、妻は責め立てられました。
「私は恋愛はしたけれども、ぼんくらはしとらん！」
と、妻が反論したことは、後々までの語り草となりました。
妻の実家付近では、
「あそこの娘は朝鮮人と駆け落ちしたらしい」
という噂もささやかれたそうです。妻の親族の反対を押し切っての結婚でした。しばらく妻の実家からは勘当同然の状態に置かれました。それが、いまでは妻も親族から、「あんたが一番優しい人と一緒になれて、幸せじゃね」と言われるほどになりました。

森本さんは、この「ムシカ」で十年間支配人を務める。「ムシカ」はますます盛況となり、恒例の年末「第九コンサート」には、二百人もの聴衆が集うようになる。常連客のなかには、市長や広島在住の作家、芸術家、詩人、学生など多くの音楽ファンがいて、クラシック音楽を楽しんできた。
その後、森本さんは独立して、自分の喫茶店をオープン。以来、閉店までの四十年間にわたって喫茶店の経営一筋に生きてきた。このように、被爆を乗り越えて必死で生き抜いてきた森本さん。だが、自身と家族に原爆の影響は強く残っている。

私は爆心地から一・七キロの松原町（現・南区松原町）で被爆しました。その後長年にわたって体調が悪く、とくに下痢がとまらなかったりします。ビタミン剤を打ってもらうためにたびたび病院に通っていました。胃潰瘍、腎臓病など内臓も患っています。心筋梗塞で倒れて救急車で運ばれ

たことが七回もありました。妻も被爆者です。あの日、妻は下宿屋の地下室でずっと寝ていました。妻にも被爆の影響があるのかもしれません。

長女は子宮がん。次女は舌がんで三回手術、いまは甲状腺がんで治療中です。「被爆二世」は、原爆の影響はないと言われ、原爆手帳もありません。しかし、現に娘二人ががんを患って苦しんでいます。孫たちにもいつ症状が出るかと思うと不安でたまりません。

広島を離れ韓国に帰った私の家族も悲惨です。父は、帰国後十年を経ずに亡くなりました。次男は、動脈りゅう破裂。妹は、急性白血病。三男は、肝臓がん。それぞれ母を残して若くして亡くなりました。明らかに被爆の影響があったのだろうと思います。

猿猴橋町での「ムシカ」から始まって、通算六十年間の喫茶店での仕事。四歳で韓国から日本にやって来て、もう八十年になります。周りの人たちに支えられ、異国の地に生きているという不自由さも感じることなく生きてこられました。私自身は日本人から差別的なことを言われたことはありません。在日韓国人であるからと不当な扱いも受けませんでした。たまたま広島に住んでいたために、人間としてめったに経験することはない原爆に遭遇してしまいました。

もし、今度また戦争が起きたなら人類はおしまいだと思います。いま、軍備の増強だとか、国防軍の必要性というようなことを主張する人もいるようですが、これはとんでもないことです。戦争となれば、殺し合いなのです。必ず、問答無用で人が人を攻撃し合うでしょう。そして、私たちのように戦争が終わっても苦しむ人が出てしまいます。それも、二代、三代にわたって長く苦しむことになってしまいます。

戦争などないのが一番いいのです。平和が一番いい。私は、本当にいい人生でした。日本は美し

90

い、すばらしい国です。私が生まれた韓国と、人生の大半を過ごした日本が、私たち夫婦と同じよ
うに、互いに信じ合い仲良く助け合って、永遠の平和の道を築いていってほしいと願っています。
　広島の平和記念公園のなかに「韓国人原爆犠牲者慰霊碑」があります。毎年、八月六日には、早朝
四時半から五時にお参りに行っています。

証言9

いつか中国語で被爆体験を話したい

谷口宏淳 さん

たにぐち・ひろあつ　一九三八年(昭和十三年)十月生まれ。爆心から二・三キロの大芝町の大芝国民学校グラウンドで六歳のときに被爆。七十歳近くまで運送会社で働いた。チャンスがある限り被爆体験を世界中の人に訴えていきたいと、いま、中国語に挑戦中。七十五歳。広島市東区在住。

自ら被爆しながらも必死で看病してくれた母

　谷口さんの母は子連れの再婚だった。兄は母が最初に結婚したときの連れ子。そのころ、谷口さんの父は中国・大連に航空技士として出征していた。父が不在の家では、母は肩身が狭かったのだろう。母は三人の子どもを連れて、嫁ぎ先から大芝町の実家に戻り、祖母の食堂を手伝っていた。

　あの日は朝、空襲警報がありました。家族五人で防空壕に避難していましたが、七時三十分ころには警報が解除。私は、歩いて十分ほどの大芝国民学校(現・大芝小学校)に登校しました。そのころ、

学校には兵隊が駐屯していて教室は使えませんでした。私たち児童は、校舎の手前に建てられたバラック小屋で勉強していました。上級生たちは工場へ動員されています。兵隊たちも出払っており、学校には私たち下級生しかいません。授業にはまだ少し時間があります。一年生の私は、グラウンドの朝礼台のところで遊んでいました。

どこからともなく微かに爆撃機の音が聞こえてきました。夏の朝の太陽は眩しくて、目を細めていたときです。突然「ピカッ」という鋭い光で目が眩みました。思わずしゃがみこんだのと爆風で吹き飛ばされたのが、ほぼ同時です。あたりは異常な静寂に包まれています。薄目を開けてみると、もうもうたる砂煙がたちこめ、一緒にグラウンドで遊んでいた十人ぐらいの子どもたちが倒れ、あるいは尻餅をついて泣き崩れています。バラック小屋の教室は跡形もなく潰れてしまっています。

次の瞬間、「ドドーン」という轟音が耳を貫きます。思わず自分の紺の半ズボンを見ました。半ズボンは焼けてぼろぼろ。あとで見ると自分の半ズボンは右の後ろが焦げ茶色に焼けていたのでした。後ろ側だったので、まったく気がつきませんでした。

立って大声で泣いている男の子。何ともないので、自分は大丈夫だと思いました。しかし、頭と服から出ていた右手と両足にやけどを負いました。

そのとき私は半袖の白い開襟シャツを着ていました。頭をかざしていた右手は、大やけどを負ってしまいました。坊主頭でしたが、頭がいちばんひどい状態でした。その代わりに、かざしていた右手の陰になっていたからでしょう、顔は手の陰になっていたからでしょう、顔に幸い顔にやけどはありませんでした。爆撃機を探すのに眩しくて右手をかざしていたため、顔ルタールをかぶったようになっていました。頭はがさがさになって、手でさわるとずるっと皮ごと

剝けてしまいます。

私は、泣きながら自宅の方に歩きだしました。靴は爆風で飛ばされたときになくなり、裸足です。わが家は傾いており、母は外に出て私を待っていました。あのとき、母は黒い水玉模様のブラウスを着て庭で水を撒いていたそうです。黒い水玉模様がそのままやけどと化して黒い斑点ができていました。母も埃まみれになって私を待っていたのでした。泣きながら帰った私は母を見るなり抱きつきました。母も「ようもどった！ ようもどった！」と泣くばかり。私は怖くて母の着物の裾を摑んだまま。どこへ行くにも母の後をついていました。

祖母は二階の仏間にいて無事でした。三歳上の兄は学校の教室にいたため助かり、すでに帰宅していました。

近所の人たちが逃げはじめていました。市内で火が出たらしい。皆、まだ火が出ていない三滝の山に逃げようとしていたのです。三滝の竹林のなかでは、家族や知人同士がかたまりになって座っていました。やけどを負った人。むごいけがをした人。死んでいるのか生きているのか──ぐったりと頭を後ろに垂れた赤ん坊を背負った母親が夢遊病者のようにうろうろしています。着衣ごと焼かれて煤けたような全裸の人。座りこんで意味不明なことを口走っている人。幽霊のようにただ立ちつくしている人……。

ほどなく黒い雨が降ってきました。やけどの痛みに雨の冷たさが気持ちよく感じられます。皆、雨に当たり、上を向いて口を開けて黒い雨を飲んでいました。私も口を開けて雨を受けました。母が飛んできて、

「勝手に動いたらいけん！」と皆のところに連れ戻されました。

焼けたトタンを拾ってきて、雨を防いでいる家族がいました。母は必要なものだけでも取ってこようと家にもどりました。しかし、家は完全に倒れています。食堂にあった蒸したジャガイモを持ってくるのがやっとでした。

谷口さんの一家は、再び父の実家の西原（現・安佐南区西原）に行くことになった。祖母と母、兄弟三人の家族五人で約四キロの道を歩いた。谷口さんは、やけどで肌が引きつって、屈んだ姿勢しかとれなかった。よたよた、のろのろと進んだ。

道端はどこも死体が転がっています。私たちは死体をよけながら歩きました。水を求めて防火用水槽に顔をつっこんで息絶えた死体を数多く見かけました。新庄橋のたもとでも、川に入った人が死んで水に浮いています。私も水が飲みたくて何度も川に行こうとしました。そのたびに、母が私の手を握って引きもどしました。
「いけん！　飲んだら死ぬ！」
母は、父の実家に着くまで私の手を離しませんでした。父の実家に着いたとたん、祖母は動けなくなり、三カ月間、寝たきりのまま他界しました。

私のやけどは重度でした。とくに半ズボンから出ていた両膝の裏側からふくらはぎの損傷がひどいのです。足が「く」の字に曲がったまま、伸ばすことさえできません。夜は膝を立てて眠ります。剥がすと凄まじい痛みが襲います。母が着物を裂いて膝裏がくっついてしまうこともありました。天花粉のような粉薬を患部につけてくれたすき状にした布が包帯がわりにして巻いてくれました。

95　［証言9］谷口宏淳

ました。しかし、翌朝になると血と膿で布は固まっています。それを剝がすのがまた痛いのです。毎朝毎朝、私は脂汗をかきながら唸っていました。母は「ちょっとずつ剝がす方が痛いけえ」と一気にバリッと剝がします。そのたびに私は大声を上げます。病院に行っても治療薬などありません。これ以外の治療方法はなかったのでした。

そのうち殺虫剤工場の油紙が手に入るようになり、布が油紙に代わりました。やけどのただれからくる臭いが凄まじいので、兄弟は近寄りません。母だけが「絶対、ようなるけえ」と毎日、解毒剤として効き目があるとされるドクダミ草を煎じて飲ませてくれました。もう皆に採り尽くされて、家の周りにはドクダミ草がなくなりました。

そこで母はドクダミ草を探しに行くために、自転車に乗る練習をはじめ、乗り方を覚えたらすぐに片道一時間以上かかって、山奥までドクダミを採りに行ってくれました。

それから二年半、ひたすらやけどのただれとかさぶたの繰り返しでした。私はずっと、家のなかで座ったまま手と尻だけを使って移動していました。ただれているので冬も布団がかけられません。夏はハエがとまるとすぐにウジがわいてきます。いつも母が箸でつまんでとってくれました。髪の毛もすべて抜け落ちていました。

谷口さんの父が復員してきたのは、そのころだった。父は絵に描いたような軍人気質で、いつもしかめっ面をしていた。谷口さんは被爆以来、ほとんど学校へ行っていない。勉強ができないので、父に怒られてばかりいた。食事前にはいつも父にかけ算九九を暗唱させられていた。学校に行きはじめたのは四年生からだった。小学三年の終わりに、ようやくかさぶたがとれた。

父の実家のまわりは、ほとんどの家が爆風で少しずつ傾いていました。服と足のやけどの跡がケロイドになっていた私は、皆から「くさい！　やけど！」と言われ、いじめられました。当時「原爆は伝染する」と考えられていました。「谷口の息子は原爆じゃ！」と陰口を言われるのが辛くてたまりませんでした。とりわけ運動会は嫌でたまりません。半袖、半ズボンなので他人にケロイドを見られてしまいます。やけどの跡は皮膚が突っ張り、いつもぎこちない動きになります。私はどんないじめにあっても、母にはそのことを話しませんでした。母を悲しませたくなかったからです。

それでも、これみよがしな陰口が聞こえたことがありました。母は厳しい顔をして黙ったまま、聞こえないふりをしていました。

被爆したとき、かざしていた右手はげんこつのまま固まってしまいました。小指や薬指、中指で握った形で、かろうじて親指と人差し指だけが動く程度。無理に動かそうとすると、小指と薬指の間が裂けて血が吹き出してきます。曲がってくっついている指の皮を切り裂いてしまいます。血と膿で固まったところをまた剥がす……。その繰り返しでした。

「尻や腿の皮膚を移植して顔のケロイドをきれいに治した」というニュースを聞いて、医者に相談したこともありましたが、「指はしょっちゅう動かすところだから手術はできない」と言われました。

六年生になって、ようやく髪の毛が生えてきました。母がうれしそうに言いました。

「ひろちゃん、髪が生えてきとるよ」

頭に手をやると、じゃりっという髪の感触があります。うれしくてたまりませんでした。やけど

97　［証言9］谷口宏淳

の治りかけはとても痒いのです。かさぶたの周囲を掻くと、膿がたまりかさぶたになります。それでも中学校に入ったころには、何とか右手は動くようになっていました。
　右手と両足の後ろ側はケロイドなので、皮膚呼吸ができません。夏でも、この部分の皮膚は冷たいのです。いまでも右足を胡座の姿勢にするとケロイドが突っ張ります。胡座をかくことができません。
　体はいつもだるい状態です。とにかく疲れやすく、立っていられません。すぐに横になってしまいます。晴れた日は、日射病のように気分が悪くなります。これはいままでずっと続いています。
　不整脈もありますが、これだけは原爆と関係があるのかどうかわかりません。
　被爆している私と母に、父の実家は辛くあたってきました。母が嫌味を言われ続ける姿を見るのは耐えられませんでした。父の実家には、除隊して早くに帰った父の弟や親族もいました。私の家族五人が一度に押しかけたのですから、厄介者扱いされたのも仕方ないとは思います。叔母にいじめられて、かまどの火を見ながら涙を流す母を何度か見ました。一度、叔母が「この家から出ていってくれ！」と言ったことがありました。
　さすがに私も我慢できずに言い返しました。
「母が被爆したんは、ここにおられんようになって、大芝に行ったけえじゃ！　追い出されんかったらこんなことにゃ、ならんかった！」
　谷口さんは高校を卒業し、運送会社に勤めた。二年ほどして、大阪への転勤願いを出した。無事、それが受理され、谷口さんは一人で大阪に行った。

母は体調が悪くなり、寝たり起きたりの日々が続きました。ついには肝臓がんで入院し、その後の二年を病院で過ごしました。母の入院もあって、私は大阪での仕事を辞めて広島に帰りました。

当時、私は二十一歳。病院に見舞いに行ったとき、母は言いました。

「宏淳、あんたは原爆に遭うとるんじゃけえ、体だきゃ気をつけて長生きしんさいよ」

「兄弟のなかでおまえが一番親孝行じゃった」。それが母との最期の会話でした。享年四十九歳。母は被爆してからの十五年間、苦労の連続でした。自らも被爆しながら、息子の私のケロイドを必死になって治そうとしてくれたのです。母の死後、母をいじめた叔母も亡くなりました。叔母は最期に「宏淳さん。お前の母さんに悪いことしたなあ。許してね」と謝ってくれました。

谷口さんは一九五六年（昭和三十一年）に、原爆手帳を申請した。それ以来、月に一回は健康診断を受けに行く。

私は一度体に放射能を浴びています。いつ白血病を発症するのか。いまだに「原爆症が発症するのでは」という恐怖は拭（ぬぐ）えません。思えば、私は夏物の半袖シャツを持っていません。どんなに暑くても必ず長袖を着ています。運送会社やタクシー会社に勤めていたときも、社員旅行には何かしらの理由をつけて行きませんでした。風呂のことを考えると気持ちが重くなるのです。原爆に遭ったことを自分からは言い出しません。人と歩くときも、無意識にその人の右側に立っています。いつも右手のケロイドを気づかれまいとしてきました。一度だけ、大阪の勤務先で親しくなった人に原爆に遭ったことを告げたことがあります。

99 　［証言9］谷口宏淳

「原爆症！　伝染らんか？」と言われました。手足のケロイドを見て気づいた人はいただろうと思います。それでも、自分からは言いませんでした。

当時の結婚は、見合い結婚がほとんどであった。「身元調査」のことを、そのころは「問い聞き」といった。谷口さんの縁談は、「問い聞き」で、被爆していることがわかったとたんに破談になった。「見合いでは結婚は無理だ」。谷口さんはそう思った。一九六六年（昭和四十一年）、谷口さんは結婚。

妻も生後一歳三カ月のとき、宇品で被爆しています。私も、それ以上のことは何も聞きません。聞くのが怖いのです。私が妻に聞いたからといって、どうしてやることもできません。そして、妻も私の被爆について何も聞いてはきません。いままで私は、妻にさえ原爆に遭ったことを話していません。妻が私に何も聞かないのはすべて妻の優しさだと思っています。

三十歳のときに妻が妊娠しました。不安でした。「障害をもつ子が生まれる」という噂も聞いていました。夜も眠れません。長男が五体満足で生まれたときはうれしくて一人泣きました。次男が二歳のときに、神経性皮膚炎（ヘルペス）にかかりました。首から顔にかけてケロイドのようになった顔を包帯でぐるぐるに巻いていました。思わずぞっとしました。自分のことを思い出したからです。

広島にいながら、七十一歳になるまで原爆資料館（広島平和記念資料館）に入ったこともありませんでした。思い出したくない。他人に知られたくない。原爆の話題は、極力避けてきました。毎年、八月六日が近づくとテレビのニュースは見ないようにしていました。

ある平和展示を見たのがきっかけで、原爆・平和について、ちょっと考えてみようと思いはじめました。初めて原爆資料館に行ってみてわかりました。アメリカによる原子爆弾投下を、日本は察知することができなかったのです。
大本営発表では国民に嘘ばかりついていました。原爆投下の一週間前、家の近くで大人たちが防空壕掘りをしていました。母がその人たちにお茶を出しに行ったので、私も一緒について行きました。大人たちは笑いながら口々に言っていました。
「勝った！　勝った！　また勝った！」
「広島は空襲もない。ほんまにええところじゃ――」。
あの日も、先に来た偵察機には空襲警報を出していたのに、原爆を投下した爆撃機に対しては警報を出していません。もしあのとき、空襲警報が出ていれば、私はグラウンドにいなかったでしょう。原爆の被害に遭うこともなかったかもしれません。それが悔しいのです。
「戦争の早期終結」などというのはただの言い訳です。明らかにアメリカは広島と長崎を原爆実験の場にしたのです。それも、威力の差異を調べるために、広島にはウラン爆弾、長崎にはプルトニウム爆弾と使い分けて――。

GHQが比治山に作った「ABCC（原爆傷害調査委員会）」は、治療が目的ではなく被爆者のデータ収集が目的でした。治療してもらえると思って行った被爆者たちは、裸にさせられ、ケロイドの写真を撮られ、血液検査と体調の変化を質問されて帰されるのです。アメリカは徹底して被爆者をモルモットとして扱っていたのではないでしょうか。

一昨年、広島駅前で東京から来たという人に呉行きの列車を尋ねられました。福島第一原発の事

101　[証言9]谷口宏淳

故で、風向きによって放射能の数値が高くなったので、呉市にいる子どもたちのところに一時避難するとのことでした。放射能は風に乗って流れます。あのとき、私たちは三滝の山の方に逃げましたが、考えてみれば、それは黒い雨、放射能の流れと同じ方向だったのではないでしょうか。

「広島ピースボランティア」をやっている方にすすめられ、私は初めて、知らない人たちを前にして、被爆体験を話しました。妻もその場にいました。私が話している間、ずっとうつむいていました。私はあと何年生きられるかわかりません。しかし話せるチャンスがある限り、話していきます。そのことを私は決めたのです。

世界中の人たちがいま、関心を持って広島に来ています。なかでも中国の人たちが多いことを知りました。以前、福岡市に住んでいる長男が、

「これからは中国の時代がくるでぇー。中国語を勉強しとったほうがええかもしれんよ」

と言っていました。友人の誘いもあって、毎日のように広島大学にある社会人向け放送大学の中国語講座に通っています。いつか中国の人に中国語で被爆体験を語りたいと思っています。

102

証言10

世界平和への使命と信じて真実を語りたい

橋本 薫 さん

はしもと・かおる　一九二九年（昭和四年）十月生まれ。爆心から二・八キロの段原町の路上で十五歳のときに被爆。八十四歳。東広島市在住。

ピストル一丁と現金千円
遺体を焼き続けた二十日間

　橋本さんの家は七人家族。父は床屋を営んでいた。兄は、海田（現・安芸郡海田町）にあった陸軍兵器廠に軍属として勤めていた。その下に姉が二人いて、二人とも広島貯金支局に勤めていた。橋本さんは次男で四番目。下にもう一人妹がいた。橋本さんは、中野（現・安芸区中野）にある国民学校に進学した。

高等科の二年生のとき、先生からこんなことを聞きました。
「軍属はお国のためになるし親孝行だ」
「配給物もいい、他の者が食べられんようなものを食べられるぞ」
 同級生五十八人のうち、六、七人が満蒙開拓青少年義勇軍に、残りのほとんどは国鉄に行きました。一九四四年（昭和十九年）三月、私は国民学校高等科を卒業。四月一日付で陸軍兵器補給廠兵器科の修理班に配属になりました。待遇は、先生から聞いた通り、恵まれていました。いつも冷凍みかんや馬の干し肉などを家に持って帰っては、家族を喜ばせたものです。
 八月六日。私はあと二カ月で十六歳になるところでした。あの日は夜から明け方まで任務でした。友人の林君と歩いて帰る途中、段原（現・南区段原）あたりまで仕事から開放されたのが午前八時。比治山が私たちを守ってくれたのです。
「バシッ」と轟音がし、瞬時に爆風で吹き飛ばされました。周囲は真っ暗。気がつくと周りに人がいません。爆心地は比治山の西側にあたり、私が被爆した段原は、山のかげになっていました。いわば比治山が私たちを守ってくれたのです。しかし、上空からの爆風はすさまじいものがありました。
 段原国民学校がすごい勢いで燃え盛っています。崩れた建物の下敷きになって、「助けて！ 助けて！」と児童たちの叫び声。炎のなか、私たちはなす術もなく見ているだけ。まだ生きている子どもたちを救うこともできません。いまも悔やまれてなりません。生きたまま焼かれた子らが地獄なら、ただ見ていることしかできない私たちも地獄でした。
 道端に備え付けてある用水に飛び込んだまま死んだ人も見ました。路傍に横たわって動かない人、

立ったまま死んでいる馬も。爆風で飛んできたガラスの破片が戦闘帽を突きぬけて私の頭に刺さっていました。腕も血だらけでしたが、そのときは痛いとも感じませんでした。

 原爆投下の夜、橋本さんは軍のトラックで仁保町（現・南区北大河町）の洞窟へ連れて行かれた。そこには、白いドロドロした薬のようなものを塗られた被爆者が何百人もいた。応急処置も施されないまま、被爆者たちは次々とトラックに乗せられ運び込まれてきた。皆、やけどを負い、顔や体から血を流している。
 しかし、軍のトラックに女性や子ども、そして瀕死の重傷者はいなかった。いや、トラックに乗ることができなかったのだ。橋本さんは、この洞窟のなかで流れ作業に従事することになった。

 次から次へと、けが人に水銀軟膏とチンク油（外皮用薬）を溶いてつくった白いペンキ状の薬を塗ります。薬を塗られた人々は、皆、「これで助かる」と喜んでいました。洞窟のなかは涼しくて、比較的過ごしやすい場所でした。それでも夏でしたから、傷口の化膿からくる悪臭が洞窟内にこもっていました。皆、体が腫れあがり、身動きができません。寝たまま糞尿を垂れ流しています。
 そのとき一人の若い上官が、興奮して精神がおかしくなってしまい、突然「アメリカ兵を皆殺しにしてやる！」と叫んで、洞窟のなかでピストルを撃ちはじめるという場面も見ました。
 少しでも歩ける者は、広島湾に浮かぶ似島（現・南区似島）に運ばれました。しかし、動けない者は洞窟に残され、三、四日で髪が抜け、皆、死んでいきました。
 それでも洞窟には、焼けただれて髪が抜け皮膚の垂れ下がった人たちが続々と運ばれてきます。

105 ［証言10］橋本薫

「水くれぇ！　水を」
　しかし、私たちは上官から止められていました。
「水をやったら死ぬ。飲ませるな！」。私たちは、そばで見守るだけで何もしてやれません。
「死んでもいいから水をくれ！」とうめいて死んでいく人も大勢いました。哀れに思って水をやり、上官に殴られた者もいました。

　八月十日ごろから、橋本さんは現在の西区古江辺りでの遺体処理の仕事につかされることになった。

　遺体処理作業は食事付きでした。あちこちの川から、遺体が引き揚げられ、トラックで運ばれてきます。広島には七本の川がありますが、被爆者たちは熱さと乾きで水を求め、川に飛び込み、川のなかで死んでいったのです。数えきれない遺体が川に浮いていました。干潮と満潮の寄せ返しで沖まで流されず、河口から広島湾まで遺体だらけの地獄の光景です。
　一週間も十日も水に浸かった遺体は、どれも腹が膨れ、腐ってずるずると抜けてしまいます。臭いとか気持ちが悪いなどと思う余裕はありませんでした。いま思うとぞっとするのですが、手袋もさせてもらえず、作業は素手でした。腕を持つとすぽっ
　古江のあたりは田んぼが広がっており、麦を刈った後に「掘り上げ田んぼ」を作り五十センチほど畝を高くしてありました。この田んぼの畝に枕木を渡すと、一度に六、七人の遺体が並べられます。畝の間に空間ができて風が通り、よく燃えるのです。古い枕木は、兵器廠のトラックで国鉄か

らもらいました。わらは近くの農家に行ってもらいました。
効率よく多くの遺体を焼くために、はじめは頭と足を交互にして並べます。そして重油をかけます。水に浸かり腐った遺体を焼くとはじめは膨れ上がります。そのうち陶器のように固くなります。そして、「ボーン」と頭部が破裂します。破裂した頭部が飛ばないように、わらを大量にかぶせておきます。そして、次々に頭部がはじける音がして、やがて燃え尽きて骨に……。古参の軍属が、たまった骨を熊手のようなもので掻き出して集めます。そして、頭蓋骨とともにどこかへ運んでいきました。

こうして毎日毎日、遺体を火葬し続けたのです。一日に三～四百体も……。二十日間の作業で、八千体ちかく焼いたことになります。

遺体を焼いていると、身寄りを亡くした人たちが大勢集まってきました。母がいないという人。「その骨を分けてくれ」と身元不明の遺骨を持って行く人もいます。せめて自分の肉親の身代わりに供養しようというのでした。徐々に広島市内の各所に遺体を焼く場所が増え、町単位で焼く煙が立ち昇るようになりました。遺体はどんどん腐敗していきます。もし遺体のまま埋めるには広い土地が必要ですが、焼いて骨にすると十分の一以下の大きさですから、焼くしかなかったのです。

子どもが行方不明のままだという人……。

秋風たなびくころ、軍属だった橋本さんたちには、弾抜きのピストル一丁と現金千円が配られた。十月末、橋本さんは、ようやく家に戻る。

当時の千円は、現在の貨幣価値でいえば八十万円ほどにもなるだろうか。

107 ［証言10］橋本薫

看護師をやっていた母が、私の頭や腕に埋まっていた小さなガラス片を探し出しては、一つ一つピンセットで抜いてくれました。破片は三十個近くもありました。被爆から三カ月ほどたっていました。ガラス片は半年以上体内に放っておくと取り出せなくなってしまうのだそうです。

千田町（現・中区千田町）の広島貯金支局に勤めていた二人の姉は、無事でした。原爆投下の日、上の姉は朝、安芸中野駅に着いたところで、上着のボタンが取れ、家に戻ってボタンを付け直し、汽車に乗り遅れたので助かったと言います。姉の職場の人たちはほとんど死亡したそうです。てっきり死んだと思っていたら、ぼろぼろの格好で帰ってきました。はいていたモンペが焼けてパンツのように短くなっていました。そんな状態で二日間も市内にいたのに、幸いその後も原爆症になりませんでした。

下の姉はあの日から二日間、行方がわかりませんでした。

橋本さんは軍の仕事が終わり、そのまま仕事を失った。そこで友達と進駐軍相手の闇物資のブローカーをはじめる。たばこの「ラッキーストライク（LUCKY STRIKE）」、人工甘味料のサッカリンなどを進駐軍が分けてくれていた。しかし、闇物資を扱う仕事を姉が心配し、姉から新たな仕事を紹介される。住み込みで働く医療器具の営業だった。

営業回りでは、いつも仕事帰りに的場町（現・南区的場町）にあった「丸松」という、うどん屋に寄りました。一杯が十五円。そこで働いていた笑子と親しくなって結婚しました。私が二十三歳、笑子は十八歳。終戦から七年がたっていました。その後、生命保険のセールスに転身しましたが、結婚して十一年目に長女をさずかりました。なかなか子どもができませんでしたが、

東京オリンピックが開かれるなど当時は日本の高度成長期のはじまりでもありました。オリンピックの翌年、私は「これからは腕一本で稼げる仕事に就こう」とタクシーの乗務員になりました。まだ自動車も少なく、道路は空いて走りやすく、一日の売り上げの半分が乗務員の取り分で、骨身を惜しまず働き、いい収入になりました。私は営業成績がよく、会社からも信用され、推されて組合の委員長も務めました。

あるタクシー会社に勤めていたころ、四十すぎの独身女性がいましたが、結婚には縁がなかったようです。

「あれはピカをうけとる」

そう言われていたのです。ケロイドがあるわけでもでも、体が弱いわけでもないのに……。原爆に遭ったというだけで、差別され結婚できなかった人たちが当時は大勢いました。だから私の姉も、原爆手帳をもらうことをためらったのでした。私は手の甲をやけどしましたが、腫れやケロイドにはなりませんでした。打ち身のように皮膚が青黒くなっています。いまだにそこが切れて血が出ます。原爆と関係あるのかどうかわかりませんが、前立腺を患い、薬を飲み続けています。

原爆はどこまで人間を苦しめ、地獄に落とそうというのでしょうか。そのすべてが戦争の真実です。だから、どんなに顔をそむけられようとも、真正面から原爆を語りたいと思っています。いま、それが私にできる最大限の世界平和への使命と信じて……。

109　[証言10] 橋本薫

証言11

八十歳を前に「ヒロシマの心」の継承を決意

平野隆信 さん

ひらの・たかのぶ　一九三五年(昭和十年)十一月生まれ。爆心から三百メートルの材木町に実家があり、一週間後に入市被爆。当時九歳。父親は被爆死、母親は戦時中病死で、祖母に育てられた。理髪店、建設業を経て現在、地域活動に活躍中。七十八歳。安芸高田市在住。

「入市被爆」した私

私の家は爆心地のど真中にあった

平野さんの家は材木町(現・中区中島町)の二十五番地にあった。現在の広島平和記念公園の原爆慰霊碑の近くだ。当時は、商店が立ち並ぶ賑やかな繁華街だった。平野さんは一九四五年(昭和二十年)三月まで、この材木町に住んでいた。家は「平野靴下商」という靴下の製造業。毎日、数人の従業員が、六、七台のミシンを使って糸から靴下を編んでいた。

110

私の家の隣にはたばこ屋がありました。よく父に頼まれて、たばこを買いに行くと、釣り銭がもらえるので、このお使いが楽しみでした。たばこ屋の隣が下駄屋で、周囲の人々から、私の顔を見ますと、姉は「お嬢ちゃん」、私は「ぼくちゃん」と大事にされていたのを覚えています。

私には二歳上の姉と二歳下の妹、そして四歳下の弟がいました。

一方の隣には、二井谷呉服店本宅のお屋敷がありました。近所には「五色劇場」という映画館がありました。その二階から眺める庭園の景色は素晴らしいものでした。本川のたもとには、本川橋があります。夏は橋から川に飛び込みました。水がきれいで、砂地にはカニやエビがいます。この橋のあたりは少し登り坂になっているので、重い荷を引いた馬車がよく立ち往生します。私たちはそんな馬車を見かけると、押してあげたりしました。

この本川を挟んで、本川小学校がありました。私のいた中島小学校とは、いつも仲が悪いのです。川を挟んで「本川学校〜。ぼろ学校〜。なかに入ってもぼろ学校〜」とはやし立てると「中島学校〜。ぼろ学校〜」と言い返してきます。こんなことも懐かしい思い出です。

平野さんの母は産後の肥立ちが悪く、弟の出産以来、ずっと寝たきりだった。平野さんの家は工場と住居が一緒になっていたが、母だけは向かいに建てた部屋で療養していた。一九四三年（昭和十八年）、平野さんが七歳のとき母が亡くなった。

111　［証言11］平野隆信

その日、学校の先生から「すぐに家に帰りんさい」と言われました。家に戻ると、母が布団のなかから手を出して黙って握ってくれました。それが母との最期の別れでした。

葬式のこともあまりよく覚えていません。

四歳のときでしょうか。父は出張で留守でした。私が二階の階段から転げ落ちて、唇の右下を切ったことがあります。母はあわてて私を抱きかかえて、近くの病院に走って行きました。そのときの母の温もりだけは、はっきりと覚えています。後年、辛いことがあると、よく口元の傷あとを鏡で見ました。そうすると、母の温もりを思い出します。

母の死後、父は工場で働いていた親類の女性と再婚することが決まっていました。「おまえたちの新しいお母さんになる人なんよ」と女性を紹介されました。いちばん下の弟は、その人が面倒を見てくれました。

戦時中のこと、茶の間の下には防空壕が掘ってありました。空襲警報が鳴りますと、子どもたち四人は防空ずきんをかぶり、床を開けて地下へ降りて行きます。警報が解除されるまで、息を殺してじっと静かにしていました。空襲警報は慌ただしく何度も鳴りましたが、解除のサイレンはのんびりした音でした。子ども心にもほっとしたものです。田舎の八千代町（現・安芸高田市八千代町）に帰るバスをもう少し大きくなってからのことです。

突然、空襲警報が鳴りました。バス停にいた人たちは、皆、近くの西練兵場の防空壕に逃げこみ、私も一緒に飛び込みました。上から毛布のようなものをかけられ、私たちはじっとしていました。そして、それも毛布の端をめくって、防空壕の隙間から空を見ます。B29の編隊が飛んでいました。

に向かって次々と高射砲が放たれていました。高射砲の弾丸は、どれ一つとしてB29に当たりません。当たるどころか、弾丸がまったく届いていませんでした。B29が悠々と飛んでいきました。「これでほんまに日本は勝てるんじゃろうか」。子ども心にそんなことを思いました。

 戦火が激しくなった一九四五年（昭和二十年）三月。平野家の子どもたち四人は、八千代町の父方の祖母のところに疎開することになった。

 それまでおばあちゃんとは、さほど親しくありませんでしたから、私たちははなはだ心細かったのです。いつも四人一緒に固まっていました。戦争で世間が不安な空気のなかで、母親がいない心細さは言葉にできないほどでした。
 おばあちゃんの家には、電気が引かれていませんでした。夜、便所に行くときはカンテラを持っていきます。お風呂に入るのもカンテラ。不便だし不安でした。八千代町のあたりは、戦争中も比較的のんびりした雰囲気でした。隣の家に、同じくらいの年格好の男の子が三人いて、夏になると川に泳ぎに行ったりして、一緒に遊んだものです。おばあちゃんのところには、父の弟のお嫁さんも従弟と一緒に身を寄せていました。この人が、私たちのお母さん代わりとしてよく面倒を見てくれました。

 いっぽう、新しい母になる女性は、広島の工場兼自宅で父と同居していた。各地で続く空襲の悲報に、平野さんの父は工場を疎開させることを決意した。八千代町に工場用地を確保し、引っ越し

が始まった。平野さんの叔父が、八月六日早朝、馬車で荷物を取りに行く。いつもはあっさりと工場に引っ込む父が、その日に限って、街角を曲がって姿が見えなくなるまで、別れを惜しむように叔父を見送っていた。虫の知らせだったのだろうか。

原爆投下の前日、父は材木町に戻りました。「もう少し整理することがある」。父はそう言っていたそうです。

翌八月六日の朝。八千代町の家の前の空き地で、隣の家の男の子たちと遊んでいました。
「バーン」「ドーン」。凄まじい地響きがしました。南の方を見ると、巨大なきのこ雲が立ちのぼるのが見えました。電気が来ていないので、おばあちゃんのところにはラジオもありませんでした。
「可部の方で何か大ごとになっとるらしいで」。そんな噂が流れた程度でした。そして、その日はそのまま寝ました。

翌日になって、近所の人から聞きました。
「広島市内がやられたらしいで！」。夕方、いちばん下の弟をおばあちゃんのもとに残して、姉と妹と私は国道五四号線まで父を迎えにいきました。姉が妹の手を引きます。市内から三十キロも離れているので、トラックもほとんど通りません。姉と妹はくたびれて、道路にしゃがみこみます。妹と私は立ち上がってのぞき込みました。トラックは、たくさん遠くからトラックがやってくると、私たちのけが人を乗せて走ってきました。荷台には包帯を巻いた人や焼けて煤けた人々がたくさんいました。そのトラックが止まり、いまにも父が降りてくるのではないか――。トラックが通るたび、三人で目を凝らして見ていました。

114

日が暮れるまで父を待ちました。その夜、父は帰って来ません。おばあちゃんは気丈にふるまっていました。

「大丈夫！ すぐ戻ってくるけえ！」

翌日も翌々日も、私たちは国道に迎えに行きました。父は帰ってきません。いよいよ四日目。おばあちゃんと継母になる人の姉が、材木町へ行くことになりました。父は帰ってきたといいます。焼けたミシンや機械類の残骸（ざんがい）があったからです。「平野靴下商」の跡地はすぐにわかったといいます。そして、階段の踊り場に父の遺体があったそうです。

祖母は、救護の兵隊に、父の遺体の処置を頼んだ。継母になるはずだった人は、八月六日の早朝、妹と外出し、そのまま行方がわからなくなった。そして、祖母たちは八千代町に戻った。

一週間後の八月十四日。おばあちゃんと姉と私は、市内に向かうトラックに乗せてもらって、材木町のわが家に帰りました。トラックから降りたときの驚きはいまも忘れません。あたり一面、焼け野原。隣のたばこ屋も下駄屋もなくなっていました。見たこともない光景に、膝（ひざ）ががくがくと震え、止まりません。

川には死んだ馬が浮かんでいました。焼けたミシンを目印になにか川に入って行くと、焼けたトタンの上に人骨が盛られていました。「兵隊さんがやってくれたんじゃね」と、おばあちゃんがぽつんと言いました。あたりを見回すと焼け残ったやかんがありました。そのなかに父の骨を入れ、私が持って三人で帰りました。そのときのやかんはいまでも大切に持つ

ています。これだけは私が死ぬまで守りたいと思います。
父の葬儀を終えた八月十九日には、おばあちゃんと私たち姉弟は材木町で父の追善回向をしました。

それから二カ月後。
「夫が兵隊に行ったまま消息がわからないから」。父の弟のお嫁さんが、従弟を連れて再婚しました。八千代町のおばあちゃんの家で、私たちの母代わりになってくれていた人です。ショックでした。「この人までいなくなるんか」。何もかも突き放されてなくなってしまうような気がしました。
おばあちゃんは、あまりに年をとりすぎていました。おばあちゃんのほかには、この世に私たち姉弟四人だけ。誰にも頼れない心細さで胸がいっぱいになりました。
あのとき、おばあちゃんがいなかったら、私たち四人は原爆孤児として生きるほかありませんでした。おばあちゃんにはいまでも感謝しています。私たち姉弟は、そのままおばあちゃんの家で暮らしました。いま思えば、おばあちゃんはわずかに米や野菜は作っていましたが、ほかには何も収入がありませんでした。
あのころは皆、いつもお腹を空かしていました。わずかなお米に、大根をきざんで入れて量を増やします。来る日も来る日も、大根めしやさつまいもを入れたご飯ばかりでした。靴がないので、草履をはいて学校に行きます。雨が降ると草履が泥をはね上げるので雨の日はいつも裸足でした。
これはずっと後で聞いた話です。小学校の先生が、家に訪ねてきて「（妹を）養子としてもらい受けたい」と、言ったそうです。
「どんなことになっても姉弟が離れるのはいやじゃ」と姉は最後まで頑張ったそうです。おばあちゃ

んも「孫は皆、わしが育てますけえ」と言い、妹は残ることができたのです。

その後、平野さんは新制中学を卒業し、十五歳で理髪店に弟子入りした。なぜ理髪店だったのか？

国道沿いに一軒の理髪店がありました。その近くを通ると、いつも電気がこうこうと点いていて華やいでいました。そのころはランプやカンテラで生活していましたから、電気の灯を見ると心が躍りました。それで「散髪屋になりたい」と思ったのです。

四年の徒弟生活を経て、一年間の御礼奉公。平野さんは二十歳で八千代町に戻り、理髪店を開業した。理髪店の稼ぎで、平野さんは姉と妹を嫁がせた。

理髪店をはじめてすぐのころです。仲のよかった近所の材木屋に、見かけない少年がいました。材木屋は「戦災孤児なんじゃ。うちで雇っちゃろう思う」と言います。その子は年のころ、十五、六歳。どことなく寂しそうな表情が抜けませんでした。おばあちゃんがいなければ、自分たちもその子と同じような運命をたどっていたでしょう。

その後、平野さんは友人の紹介で見合い結婚をした。二十六歳のときだった。妻は平野さんの二歳年下。彼女は美容師をやっていた。結婚を機に、国道沿いに理容兼美容院を建て、夫婦で働いた。三年目に長男が生まれた。

「これから」という結婚四年目、一九六五年(昭和四十年)のことでした。突然、背中が痛くなり微熱が続きました。いつもの医者に行っても「何の病気かわからない」と言われ、大学病院を紹介されました。大学病院で「結核」と診断されました。結局入院はせず、ストレプトマイシンを飲み、通院しながら治しました。子どもがいるので、どうしようか悩みました。ベッドが空き次第、入院と言われました。

元気にはなったものの、近所に結核であることが知れ渡っていた。もう理髪の仕事は続けられなかった。妻の美容院は継続させて、平野さんは、妻の弟がやっていたアルミサッシ業を手伝いはじめた。その後、独立。二十年間、平野さんはずっとアルミサッシ業を続けてきた。「被爆者の感情は複雑だ」と平野さんは言う。被爆からまもなく七十年。原爆はずっと平野さんを苦しめ続けてきた。

「そっとしておいてもらいたい」という気持ち。そして「この苦しみを伝えにゃいけん」という気持ち。相反する感情にずっと苛（さいな）まれ続けてきました。じつは結婚するときも、妻には被爆者であることを隠していました。口に出すのも怖かったのです。生涯、誰にも言うまいと思っていました。「七十五年間は、広島には草木も生えない」と言われていた時代です。原爆投下時、私は八千代町にいました。八千代町ならば、直接は被爆とは関係のない場所です。父の骨を拾いに行って入市被爆した——。その事実さえ言わなければ、誰にもわかりません。

しかし、結婚から三年後、妻が長男を身ごもりました。前置胎盤で吉田町の病院では手に負えないといいます。なんとか紹介された広島県立病院で出産することはできましたが、八カ月の早産。千八百グラムの未熟児で生まれました。

私の被爆が原因なのか——。不安な日々が続きました。

そして長男が一歳半になったとき、今度は脱腸になりました。次々と起こる長男の体のトラブルに耐えられなくなり、私はとうとう妻に、原爆投下直後の八月十四日、爆心地近くの材木町に行ったことを告白しました。妻はただ一言、「大丈夫よ」と言ってくれました。長男は、その後は何ごともなく健康に成長しました。

私たちの継母になるはずだった人のお姉さんを探しました。頼みこんで何とか「入市被爆」の保証人になっていただきました。

ずいぶん遅れましたが、私も原爆手帳をもらうことにしました。爆心地に二週間以内に入った者は「入市被爆」と認定されます。原爆手帳があれば、健康診断も無料で受けられるそうでした。「入市」を証明するには保証人が必要でした。しかし、おばあちゃんはすでに亡くなっています。

私は、若いころから耳鳴りに悩まされていました。よく目眩（めまい）もします。脳外科に行っても「原因はわからないし、処方する薬もない」と言われます。「これは入市被爆の影響だろうか」と、つい考えてしまいます。体調が悪いときは、不安になって眠れません。

子どもが熱を出します。のぼせて鼻血を出します。普段なら何ということのないことでも「放射能のせいでは」と怯（おび）えてしまいます。何かあるたびに不安を抱きます。他の人ならどうということのないことにも凍りつきます。

119　［証言11］平野隆信

私の姉も「入市被爆」を隠して結婚しました。「口に出したら結婚できんかもしれん」と姉は言っていました。それ以来、姉とも材木町の話はしていません。隠せるものなら隠し通したい――。姉が誰にも相談できず、どんなに苦しんだか。かわいそうでした。

姉や私と同じ苦しみを、きっといま福島の人々が味わっている。将来もまた見知らぬ誰かが、同じ苦しみを繰り返すのだろうか――。だから福島の人たちの苦しみは決して他人事ではありません。

八十歳を目前に「ヒロシマの心」を継承していかなくてはならないと思うようになりました。昨年、広島市が被爆体験の継承者を養成する事業を始めたことを新聞で知り、応募しました。DVD「ヒロシマの証言 被爆者は語る」に私の証言を収めていただきました。また、地域では、地域振興会の役員を十年（うち会長四年）、八千代開発公社理事、八千代体育協会理事として活動しています。

地域から希望を広げ、平和のために生涯尽くしていきたいと思っています。

証言12

原爆孤児を二度と出さないために

川本省三さん

かわもと・しょうそう　一九三四年（昭和九年）三月生まれ。双三郡神杉村の疎開から原爆投下三日後に塩屋町の実家に帰り入市被爆。当時十一歳。家族五人が死亡や行方不明で原爆孤児に。七十九歳。広島市西区在。

忘れ去られた原爆孤児
浮浪児として生きるしかなかった

　川本さんは爆心から六百メートルの塩屋町（現・中区大手町）で七人家族の長男として生まれた。一九四五年（昭和二十年）四月、袋町国民学校の六年生は田幸村、川西村、和田村、そして川本さんが疎開した双三郡神杉村（現・三次市）に別れて学童疎開。神杉村には男子四十五人、女子三十二人。宿舎は善徳寺というお寺だった。

疎開先での食事は、茶碗一杯のご飯と味噌汁と漬物だけでした。皆、育ち盛りの年ごろでとても足りません。いつもおなかを空かせていました。昼食の時間、疎開先の地元の同級生が開いた弁当箱は輝いていました。白い米粒がぎっしり詰まっているのがうらやましくてうらやましくて……。
「おい、わけてくれよ。鉛筆やるから、消しゴムも」と、物々交換で弁当をわけてもらったりしたものです。とにかく口に入るものがほしかった。農家の子どもたちに、食べられる野草を教えてもらいました。イタドリ、ノビル、セリ、スギナ……。麦の穂をしごいて、手で揉んで生のまま食べたこともあります。田んぼのあぜ道に植えてある枝豆もむしって口に入れたりもしました。おいしいかどうかではありません。とにかく口にものを入れるだけで、気を紛らすことができました。おいしかったのは、トノサマガエル。両脚を引っ張って、つるりと皮を剥いで、炊事担当の人が天ぷらにしてくれました。鶏肉のササミに似た味で、貴重なたんぱく源でした。あのトノサマガエルを食べたから、いまの体があるとさえ思っています。あとは、イナゴやバッタも食べました。なんでもありです。

疎開先ではほとんど勉強はしませんでした。松の幹に傷をつけて松ヤニを竹筒で受け、松根油とともに集めることがいわば勉強に代わる作業でした。松根油は航空エンジンの燃料にするのが目的だったようです。私たちは荒れ地の開墾もやりました。そこにサツマイモやジャガイモを植えました。

八月六日も朝から畑づくりをしていました。ふと気づくと、空が異様です。広島市の方角に入道雲のような白い雲がむくむくと湧いてきます。あまり見たことのない光景でしたので、気になってしかたがありません。「この雲の湧き方は普通じゃないぞ」と思ったものです。神杉村は広島から

距離にして五十キロ以上も離れています。原爆の光も音もまったく感じることはできませんでした。ただ、雲の湧き方で何かが起きたのではと非常に気になっていました。夕方までに先生方には村役場から何らかの連絡が入ったようすでした。しかし、私たちには広島の出来事は何も教えてくれませんでした。

その後、疎開している子どもを迎えに来た家族の口を通じて、いろいろな話が伝わってきました。「特殊爆弾により広島は全滅した」と聞いても、私はあまり実感がありませんでした。次々と家族が訪れ、友達の多くが疎開先から去っていきます。疎開先にはもう何人も残っていません。ようやく、八月九日になって、広島から五歳年上の姉が私を迎えに来てくれました。私の顔を見るなり姉は「ワー」と泣き出しました。聞くと、姉は原爆投下の翌日、塩屋町の自宅に行ったと言うのです。見ると、居間のあたりに母と妹と弟の三人が抱き合って焼け死んでいた。顔は真っ黒で見分けがつかなかったけれども、場所からいって、母と弟妹の三人だろうというのです。父と中二の次姉は建物疎開で外出していて行方不明でした。

川本さんは、姉とともに焼け跡となった広島に戻る。自宅は焼け落ち、行き場もなく母と弟妹の遺骨を持って親戚を転々とする。どこも二人を引き取ってくれるような余裕はなかった。結局、十六歳になったばかりの姉が部屋を借りて姉弟二人の生活が始まった。

広島駅のホームに立ち、驚きました。駅から瀬戸内海の島が見わたせるのです。あたりはシーンとして、物音一つしませんもありません。目の前には何もありません。そこからの光景は信じられないものでした。

123　［証言12］川本省三

ん。私は気持ちが悪くなってしまいました。とりあえずは、姉の勤め先のビルの一室を借りて、そこで寝起きしました。姉は、国鉄管理局に勤める日々ですが、私は何もすることがないので町中をうろつくようになりました。そこには両親を亡くした身寄りのない孤児が多くいました。袋町小学校の同級生も何人かいました。姉は、炊き出しの後ろに並んでいる孤児に順番を譲ってやったり、一緒に鉄くずを拾ってやったりしました。私は孤児たちから受け入れられるようになりました。孤児かどうかは服装を見ただけでわかります。親のいる子や施設にいた子とは、明らかに服装が違ったからです。

週に二回炊き出しもありました。彼らと一緒に焼け跡で鉄くず拾いやモク拾いをしました。友達がほしくてたまりませんでした。私は、炊き出しの後ろに並んでいる孤児に順番を譲ってやったり、一緒に鉄くずを拾ってやったりしました。私は孤児たちから受け入れられるようになりました。孤児かどうかは服装を見ただけでわかります。親のいる子や施設にいた子とは、明らかに服装が違ったからです。

夜になると帰るところのない彼らは、橋の下やビルの焼け跡の隅、防空壕などしかありません。寝るときぐらいは固まっていた方がいいだろうという程度の集団でした。朝になると、それぞれ勝手に自分の食べ物を探しに出かけるのでした。

それは、五、六人ずつ着の身着のまま固まって眠りました。

そこで、一つの「グループ」とか「仲間」ではありません。寝るときぐらいは固まっていた方がいいだろうという程度の集団でした。朝になると、それぞれ勝手に自分の食べ物を探しに出かけるのでした。

浮浪児たちは、食べ物を入手するため、食べ物の露天商を狙いました。まず店頭の餅を摑んで逃げる。それを店主が追いかける一瞬の隙に、ほかの子どもが次々に餅を盗むといった具合です。盗む方も必死。いつまでも手に持っているとは危険です。次の瞬間にほかの孤児たちに狙われます。ですから餅を盗むのと口に入れるのは同時です。小さい子は大きい子に横取りされます。飲み込む前に口をこじ開けられ、取り出されて食べられてしまう。まさに餓鬼そのものでした。

四カ月後、突然姉が体調を崩した。足のまめがつぶれて出血し、血がとまらない。髪の毛も抜け出し、一週間ほどで姉は亡くなってしまった。川本さんは翌年二月に沼田（現・安佐南区沼田町）の村長に引き取られる。当時、疎開した広島の小学生は、八千六百人。そのうち二千七百人が孤児となったが、孤児院に収容されたのはわずか七百人。正確な数字は不明だが、残った二千人は町に放置され浮浪児となったことになる。

　六人いた私の家族は、私一人だけになってしまいました。周囲の人たちが、孤児収容施設に私を入れようと尽力してくれたのですが、そうした施設は孤児たちであふれかえって満員。施設に入ることもできませんでした。
　原爆投下の翌月には、枕崎台風が広島を襲いました。橋の下をねぐらにしていた多くの浮浪児が流されました。あふれた浮浪児の面倒をみたのは暴力団のお兄さんたちでした。バラックを建て、二階に自分たちが住んで、階下は家畜小屋のような状態で浮浪児が雑魚寝していました。寝場所と食料を提供する見返りに、浮浪児を働かせて、その稼ぎをピンハネするのです。漫画『はだしのゲン』のように集団を作りリーダーがいるのは、中学生以上の孤児のこと。かっぱらいぐらいしかできない小学生は一人では生きていけません。
　仕事は暴力団のお兄さんが持ってきます。浮浪児を五人一組にして靴磨きの道具一式を貸してくれます。二人は靴の汚れ落としと磨き係。あとの三人は客引き。夜、仕事が終わると、暴力団のお兄さんに稼ぎを渡します。ところが、稼ぎの少ないチームは交代させられ、食事も抜きになったり

125　［証言12］川本省三

しました。だから皆、必死で仕事をしました。浮浪児仲間同士のけんかもしょっちゅうでした。ほかに仕事はいくらでもありました。メチルアルコールを十倍の水で薄めて一杯十円で売る。ヒロポン（覚せい剤）の販売。再生たばこ。これは、進駐軍が捨てたたばこの吸い殻を拾い集めてほぐし、紙に巻き直してたばこを再生して売るのです。こうした仕事も暴力団のお兄さんが教えてくれます。ただ、売上金はすべて巻き上げられてしまいます。それでも浮浪児たちが逃げ出さなかったのは、食べて寝られたからです。こうして孤児たちは何とか生き延びることができたのです。

この事実は、ほとんど知られていません。町中に放置された孤児たちの実像がまったく伝えられていないのです。「孤児」という場合、「両親をなくしてしまった子」と理解され、孤児院などの施設に収容された子どもたちをイメージされることが多いようですが、実際には、施設の孤児を大きく上回る数の孤児が浮浪児となっていたのです。

町中にあふれた孤児たちは、小さい子からどんどん死んでいきました。食べ物を持っているのを見つかると大きい子に取り上げられてしまいます。口をもぐもぐ動かしているので、押さえ付けて口をこじ開けてみたら小石だったという話さえあったものです。病気になりぐったりしていても誰も気にしません。死んだらいち早くその子の衣服を剥いでしまいます。だから、路上で死んだ子はたいてい裸でした。暴力団のお兄さんに拾われた孤児は助かったのです。

やがて、川本さんの父方の叔父が現れる。施設はどこも満員だった。川本さんは、この叔父のところにだけは行きたくなかった。結局、翌年の二月、父親の実家がある沼田の村長で、川中醤油店主に引き取られる。

川中醤油店では「中学に通わせるわけにはいかないが、手伝いをしたら食べさせてやる。ゆくゆくは家も持たせる」という条件でした。どこにも行くところはありません。叔父のところにだけは行きたくなかったので、必死に働きました。朝から牛の世話、草刈り、田んぼの株切り、畑仕事……。なんでもやりました。醤油の仕込みも覚えました。無休で働き十年。私は二十三歳になっていました。約束通り、家も建ててもらい、村の青年団長も引き受けました。

そして、村の娘を好きになって求婚しました。しかし、相手の親が大反対です。
「あんた、あのとき、広島におったの。広島におった者は放射能に汚染されとる。あんたと結婚させたら障害児が生まれる。あんただって長生きできん。そんなもんと一緒にさせるわけにはいかん」

悔しくて、悔しくてたまりません。「結婚もできんのに、家なんかもらってもしょうがない。これからは、自分の好きなように生きるんだ」。そう思いました。

この出来事で川本さんは、村を飛び出し、広島に舞い戻る。十二年ぶりの広島は、すっかり変わっていた。偶然、小学校の一年下の孤児仲間と再会。彼はいっぱしの暴力団員になっていた。暴力団のもとでしか生きられなかった浮浪児のことやその生きざまは世間ではほとんど知られていない。

疎開先で一緒だった友達は若い者を引き連れて、自分の縄張りを肩で風を切って歩いていました。運転免許証を持っていた私は彼の口利きで運送会社に就職。夜になると町中をのし歩き、博打場に出入りするような生活でした。暴力団にあこがれて「仲間に入れてくれ」と頼んだことも。しかし「お

127 　［証言12］川本省三

まえは、やくざには向かん。優しすぎるわ。暴力団に入れるわけねえわ」と断られてしまいました。
　その友達はしばらくしてけんかで命を落としました。
　そんな荒れた生活が十年ほど続き、三十歳を過ぎたころのことです。交通違反で、反則金二千円が科（か）されました。ところが、その二千円がどうしても工面できないのです。つくづく自分が情けなくなりました。人に金を借りてまで反則金を払って生きていこうという気力がなくなってしまいました。もう生きている価値はない。「死のう！」と決意しました。でも、広島では死にたくありません。「とにかく、だれも自分のことを知らないところに行こう。そこで死にたい」。広島を出ることにしました。
　ポケットのなかには六百四十円。岡山までしかたどりつけません。岡山駅を出て、どっちに行こうかと歩き出したときのことです。目の前のうどん屋に「住み込み店員募集」の張り紙があります。「この岡山には、自分のことを知っている人はだれもいない。ひょっとしたら、もう一度人生をやり直せるかな」と考えたのです。うどん屋の店主に頼んだところ「本当にやる気があるんなら、やってみんさい」とすぐに雇ってくれました。そこで頑張りました。結局、三十年間、岡山で必死に働きました。小さな食品会社を経営できるまでになりました。社員も五十人ほど雇えるようになったのです。コンビニエンスストアが各地に広まったころで、惣菜や弁当がどんどん売れました。
　六十歳になったときのことです。「社長。広島からお電話です」と事務員が電話をとりついできました。
　もう何十年も広島に電話も手紙も出したこともありません。私のことを知っている人がいるはずはないと思っていたのです。電話口に出てみると、元気のよい声で「川本、おまえ生きてたんか。

みんな心配して探しとったぞ」。あのとき一緒に寺に疎開していた仲間でした。「帰ってこいや。被爆五十年の慰霊祭一緒にしようや」と誘ってくれました。「自分の人生の最後は、広島にしよう」。そう考えて、広島に帰る決意をしました。

その後、経営していた会社の整理などもあり、川本さんが広島に戻ったのは七十歳のときだった。広島平和記念資料館を訪れた川本さんは衝撃を受ける。さまざまな原爆関連の資料があるのに、原爆で孤児となった子どもたちについては、靴磨きをしている少年の写真一枚と、「二千人から六千五百人の孤児がいたといわれている」というたった一行の説明しかなかった。これを機に川本さんは自身の境遇に照らし合わせながら「原爆孤児」問題に真正面から取り組むことになる。

広島平和記念資料館に行って、原爆孤児たちの資料が余りにも少ないのに驚きました。施設に入れず町に放り出された孤児にとって、最大の問題は食料の調達でした。食べるものをどう手に入れるかです。孤児たちは、食べられないゆえに暴力団の世話になるしかありません。そうした事実が捨て去られているのです。暴力団を賛美するものでもなく、その存在を容認するつもりもありません。ただ、孤児たちが生きる術として、暴力団との間に切っても切れない関係があったという事実はなくなるものではないと思うのです。

私はいま、ピースボランティアとして活動を開始しました。自分が経験したこと、町で暮らしていた孤児のことを資料館で語るようになりました。ところが、袋町小学校の同窓生たちから私に非

難の声が上がったのです。岡山にいた私に「広島に帰ってこい」と勧めてくれた旧友たちさえ、私の活動に異を唱えるようになりました。

「いまは結婚して子どもも孫もいる。子どもや孫は私が孤児であったことは薄々は知っている。でも、どんな生活をしてきたかは具体的には知らない。川本が話すことで私の忌まわしい過去が知られてしまう」

「川本は、家族がいなくて、一人だけだからいい。子どもや孫のいる元孤児の立場を考えてみろ。そんな証言は、頼むからやめてくれ」

私は、原爆を理由に結婚を反対されて以来、もう二度と嫌な思いをしたくないと結婚はしていません。しかし、ほかの仲間は、皆、結婚して子どももでき、孫もいます。

「わしは、自分の子どもにも話してない。あのときどのようにして生き延びたのかを。話せない……。まだ十歳くらいだった。助けてくれる人などいなかった。自分で生きる道を探すしかなかった。生きるためには何でもやった。他人の食べ物を腕づくで奪ったこともあった。生きるために、しかたがなかった。そうやって生きてきた」仲間は、こう言います。私が証言することで、それを聞いた子どもたちが苦しむというのです。「そんなひどいことをしてきたのか……」と。

みんな忘れたいのかもしれません。しかし、忘れることはできません。なかったことにはできないのです。これからの子どもたちに、本当の戦争の姿を知ってもらうためには、辛くても話さなければいけないと思っています。

孤児で生き延びた人の多くは施設に収容されていた人たちでした。施設にいたおかげで学校に行き、人生設計ができたという人が多いのです。この事実も重要です。施設にいたおかげで学校に行き、人生設計ができたという人が多いのです。この事実も重要です。いっぽうで、街に放り出され家畜同然の生き方を強いられた孤児もいたのです。知ら

れていないばかりか、忘れられようとしています。暴力団の世話をうけて生き延びるしかなかったということも、まぎれもない事実でした。

それは善悪の問題ではありません。戦争そして原爆投下の結果、町中にあふれた孤児たちはどうやって生きてきたのか。語る私も、それを聞く人も辛いことです。でも、それが戦争の本当の姿です。戦争のもつ残酷さを身にしみて感じてきた一人として語る義務がある。私はいま、この事実を伝えておきたいと強く思うのです。原爆孤児を二度と出さないためにも。

証言13

子どもの笑い声が永遠に続くように

伊藤 皎 さん

いとう・きよし　一九三七年（昭和十二年）三月生まれ。原爆投下時、三次市に疎開中。当時八歳。爆心から九百メートルの小町（現・中区小町）に住んでいた父母を原爆で亡くし、原爆孤児に。親戚宅を転々とする少年時代を過ごした。山口県下関市役所勤務を経て、定年退職後帰郷。七十六歳。山県郡北広島町在住。

私には家がない
たらい回しにされた少年時代

伊藤さんは、学童疎開していたため、直接の被爆は免れている。しかし、原爆は彼から家族を奪い、原爆孤児として生きるしかなかった。

もともとわが家は何不自由ない生活でしたが、さすがに一九四五年（昭和二十年）になったころから窮乏生活が始まりました。

当時、私は八歳。甘いものなどほとんど手に入らない時代でした。「学童疎開の児童たちが疎開先のお寺で、おはぎやぜんざいを食べてご満悦」という新聞記事を見て、無性に甘いものを食べたくなったのを覚えています。私はそのとき二年生。疎開は任意でしたが、私は行くことにしました。

疎開先は三次市のお寺でした。ホームシックになって蚊帳を吊った布団のなかで泣く子もいました。「おはぎやぜんざい」のあの新聞記事は嘘でした。食事は味噌汁とたくあん、麦飯。どれもごくわずか。ひもじい毎日が続きました。夜、友達とこっそり寺の台所に忍びこみ、盗んだ生米を布団のなかでかじります。そうやって空腹をしのいでいました。

「学童疎開をしたのは、六月ごろだったのではないか……」と伊藤さんは言う。疎開先で、田植えを手伝った記憶があるからだ。伊藤さんは、そのまま疎開先であの日を迎えた。

八月六日を過ぎても「ピカドン」の話は聞かされませんでした。ただ、先生から「広島に行って君たちのお父さんやお母さんに会ってきた。順番に迎えに来るそうだからおとなしく待つように……」と、言われただけでした。

数日たつと、皆の両親や肉親が、疎開先の寺まで迎えに来始めました。仲間は次々にいなくなってしまいました。しかし、私には一向に迎えが来ません。だんだんと寂しくなり、不安が募っていきました。

八月の末。もう残っているのは、私を含めて三人だけでした。そんなとき、ひょっこりと父方

133　[証言13] 伊藤皎

の従兄弟の禎さんが訪ねてきてくれました。白米と缶詰を持ってきてくれました。飯盒でご飯を炊き、豆と肉の缶詰を食べさせてくれました。やっと迎えが来てくれたという安堵感と、ご飯のうまさ、嬉しさ。それまでの不安が一気に吹っ飛んだことを覚えています。禎さんは、原爆のことは何も言いませんでした。私も禎さんが迎えに来てうれしさで、父母のことを聞くことを忘れてしまっていたようです。

禎さんは呉市の実家に行きました。のちに聞いた話では、禎さんは原爆投下の二日後、私の自宅を訪ね、父たちの遺骨を確認したそうです。茶の間のあったところに、父と母、そしてすぐ上の兄の骨があったそうです。三人の遺骨はそれぞれの座っていた位置そのままのところにあったのです。

私が真実を聞いたのは、九月に入ってからのことでした。禎さんと、京都の大学に行っていた次兄の敏兄さんに連れられて、広島に行きました。広島駅に着いて、町を見たときの驚きは表現できません。足がすくみ、何も考えられませんでした。実家も隣の国泰寺も、跡形もありませんでした。わずかに寺の池の跡だけが残っていました。両親の葬式もできず、両親が死んだということさえ、しばらくは実感できませんでした。

その後、私は禎さんの呉市の実家で暮らしました。私の居場所などありませんでした。禎さんは六十九歳で肺気腫で亡くなっています。私の両親の骨を拾うため、入市被爆したことも影響があったかもしれません。そこには三カ月ほどしかいませんでした。

その後、敏兄さんに連れられ、ぎゅうぎゅう詰めの汽車を乗り継ぎ、神奈川県の大船に行きました。父の弟・謙三叔父さんの所です。国鉄職員の謙三叔父さんは真面目一方の人でした。育ちざか

りの子どもが五人もいるのに、決して闇米を買おうとしないのです。わずかな配給米を、私を含めた家族八人で食べました。当然、毎日の食事もままなりません。一週間、ほとんど何も食べないこともありました。動けばお腹がすきます。私も五人の兄弟も、一緒に部屋の隅でただ寝ていました。みんな栄養失調状態でした。謙三叔父さんは、声が父とそっくりでした。私の寂しさを少しでも紛らわそうと思ったのでしょう。「おまえの父さんの声でしゃべるから目をつぶれ」と言われたことがありました。目をつぶると「元気にしよるか？」と。まったく同じ声でした。父に言われたような気がして泣き出してしまいました。謙三叔父さんのところでは、学校に行くことはできませんでした。

伊藤さんは初対面だった。

伊藤さんは一九四六年（昭和二十一年）四月から、山口県下関市に住む母の兄を頼ることになる。それまで母の実家とは行き来がなく、従兄弟たちとも伯父は土建業を営み、四人の子どもがいた。

経済的には何も困っていない家でしたが、私は見知らぬ家族のなかに一人、放りこまれた感じでした。いつも一人ぼっちでした。四人の子どもたちには、皆、家庭教師が通ってきていました。そのころ、家庭教師がつく家などほとんどない時代でした。従兄弟たちは家庭教師を囲んで楽しそうに騒いでいます。私はいつも彼らを羨ましそうに横目に見ていました。夜中に便所に行ったとき、家族はまだ起きていて、奥さんと子どもたちが仲良く饅頭を食べている光景を複雑な思いで見たこともありました。疎外感ばかりの日々でした。そして私はだんだんと卑屈になっていきました。

[証言13] 伊藤 皎

家には、おトキさんという女中さんがいました。私を不憫に思ってくれたのか、おトキさんは私が学校から戻ると、「ここにお入り！」と女中部屋に呼んでくれましたが、いつも女中部屋にいるのも嫌でした。仲間はずれにされているのを意識しているようで苦痛だったのです。だからいつも、暗くなるまで学校に残っていました。家では言いたいことも言えない反動で、学校では荒れていました。喧嘩をしたり、弁当を横取りして食べたり、家庭科の鯨尺（物差し）をチャンバラ遊びで壊すといった毎日。先生から「もう学校に来ないでほしい」と言われたこともあります。運動会でも辛い思いをしました。昼休みになると、友達は皆、両親とお弁当を食べています。私だけはお弁当がありません。昼休みが終わるまで、ずっと誰もいない教室のなかで時間を潰していました。

一九四六年（昭和二十一年）秋。伊藤さんの長兄・健さんが中国から復員。広島の実家は跡形もなく、あちこち消息を尋ねた末、下関市まで訪ねてくる。長兄に伊藤さんは引き取られる。

健兄さんは私を引き取り、ほどなくして結婚。小学四年生の私を連れての新婚生活が始まりました。健兄さんは私をよく殴りました。軍隊帰りだったことと、奥さんに対する気兼ねもあったのだと思います。いっぽうで、私もかなりの「ワル」になっていました。隣の家の仏壇に供えてあったリンゴを盗んだのがばれて、兄に竹の棒が砕けるまで殴られたこともありました。しかし、そんなに殴られても兄を恨む気持ちはまったくありませんでした。親戚の家での疎外感の方がよっぽど、子ども心にはこたえていたのでしょう。

兄嫁の実家は、うどんの製造をしていました。私は中学生になると、製麺所の二階に住み込みで

働き、他の従業員と一緒に寝起きしました。一人暮らしの始まりです。毎日、朝の三時に起きて働きました。高校と短大は、働きながら夜学に通いました。

肩身の狭かった呉市の禎さんの家。食べる物がなかった大船の謙三叔父さんの家。豊かだがずっと一人ぼっちだった下関市の家。そして、嫁と暮らす健兄さんの家。

原爆が投下されて以来、ずっとたらい回しにならざるを得なかったのです。面倒をみてもらっていましたが、どこも自分の家ではありませんでした。戸棚ひとつ勝手に開けることはできません。窮屈さに耐えかねて鬱積したつらい思いを誰かに話すこともできませんでした。高校生のころ、健兄さんから言われたことがあります。

「お前は、自分は他人と変わらないと思っているかもしれないが、普通の人とは違う。本来、両親から受けるはずのもの、有形・無形のものをお前は何も受けとらずに育ってしまった。そのことを肝に銘じておけ。そして努力を怠るな」

その言葉の意味が理解できたのは、成人してからでした。成人するまで、母を思い出したことはありません。薄情な息子だと思われるかもしれませんが、生きるだけで精いっぱいの日々でした。およそ思い出に浸る余裕さえありませんでした。

短大卒業後、私は下関市役所で働き、一九九七年（平成九年）に定年退職するまで勤め上げました。その後、縁あって広島に戻り、現在は北広島町で妻と二人、趣味の川柳を楽しみながら、平凡ながら楽しく過ごしています。隣の公園から、毎日、ジャングルジムやすべり台で遊ぶ子どもたちの笑

137　［証言13］伊藤皎

い声が聞こえてきます。戦時中、子どもの笑い声はありませんでした。私は小学二年生と三年生まで、ほとんど学校に行くことができませんでした。原爆孤児になり、少年時代の大切な時間を失ってしまったように感じます。

平和とは、子どもたちの笑い声が聞こえる社会だと、ふと気がつきました。

だから、子どもたちには「平和」を大切に守っていただきたい。そして、私は子どもたちの笑い声が永遠に続くように、平和を祈り、平和のために、戦争の恐ろしさ、原爆の悲惨さを語り続けていかなければならないと強く感じています。

　　子どもらの　　笑顔に平和　　教えられ

　　いまになり　　平和の喜び　　生きた道

証言14

母の一言「戦争だきゃ絶対しちゃいけん」

田島忠美 さん

たしま・ただよし 一九三九年（昭和十四年）五月生まれ。広島市内にいた祖母、弟、父、妹を次々に亡くす。助かった母に育てられ、東洋工業（現・マツダ）等で働いた。七十四歳。広島市安佐南区在住。爆心から約七キロの中須村に疎開中で被爆を免れる。当時六歳。

あの原爆が祖母、弟、父、妹を次々と奪った

私は三人兄弟の長男で当時六歳。妹の弘子が五歳、弟の昭夫は三歳でした。原爆の一年ほど前から、私だけ中須村（現・安佐南区中須）の父の実家に預けられていました。長男の私だけでも、安全なところに移そうと考えたのだと思います。戦火が激しくなってきていた時期でもあり、私と同い年の従弟もいました。

田島さん一家は、広瀬北町（現・中区広瀬北町）に住んでいた。その広瀬北町の家は、建物疎開

139　［証言14］田島忠美

で取り壊される予定になっていた。八月六日、田島さんの両親は、家から家具や荷物を運び出していた。小さい弟は鷹匠町（現・中区本川町）の祖母の家に預けられていた。三人兄弟のうち妹だけが両親と一緒にいた。

あのとき、中須の家では朝ごはんが終わったばかり。私は仏間で伯父の膝の上で遊んでいました。「ピカ」も見えなかったし、大きな音も聞こえませんでしたが、家のなかの戸という戸が全部吹き飛びました。中須村には倒壊した家もありましたが、けが人などの被害はなかったそうです。建物疎開の労働で市内に行っていた人が帰り、あるいは中須に身内がいる広島の人たちがやってきます。皆、顔や体が焼けただれ、着衣もぼろぼろ。そのなかに私の両親と妹がいました。
「わーっ！お化け！」
私は思わず叫びました。
母は右正面から熱線を浴びて顔が焼けただれています。顔の右半分がやけどでずるずるになり、右耳も溶けてなくなっているのです。手もやけどを負っています。優しかった母の面影はもはやありません。父と一緒でなかったら、それがどうして母とわかったでしょう。父も背中に大きなやけどを負っていました。妹は額に小豆大の穴が空いていました。不思議に血が出ておらず、泣いてもいませんでした。
父も母も妹も髪の毛から顔まで川を泳いで渡ってきたというのです。朝、被爆して、途中の橋が落ちていたので、着の身着のままで川を泳いで渡ってきたというのです。朝、被爆して、途中の橋が落ちていたので、伯父のところに

着いたのが夕方の五時ごろ。皆、九時間以上歩き通しだったことになります。

翌日、田島さんは伯父と母と一緒に祖母と弟のいた鷹匠町に向かった。鷹匠町は、爆心地のすぐそばに位置している。町は火災でほとんどが焼けていた。そして、祖母の家の焼け跡には、大人と子どもの焼死体があった。それが祖母と弟だと思うほかなかった。悲しみは続く。

父のやけどはひどいものでした。背中のやけどのため仰向けになることができません。うつ伏せに寝たまま、ただ「痛い、痛い」と唸っているだけです。八月九日に父が死にました。享年三十四歳。安川の河川敷で、消防団と伯父たちがうずたかく廃材を積み、父の遺体を焼きました。何時間もかかりました。妹は額の穴のほかは、体のどこにも傷はありません。しかし、妹もだんだんと動かなくなってきました。八月十六日には妹が死にました。

母も体の不調を訴えるようになってきました。食欲がなくなり、横になっていることが多くなりました。親類が「ドクダミ草が体にいいから」と届けてくれました。母もよくドクダミ茶をやかんで煮出して飲んでいました。やがて髪の毛が抜け、丸坊主に。ケロイドを隠す髪さえなくなってしまいました。

母の弟の正さんが、いつも見舞いに来ては母を励ましてくれていました。

「姉さん！　絶対、仇はとったるけえ！　安心しんさい！」

母の人生は、原爆でめちゃくちゃにされたのです。若いときの母の写真を見ると、とても美人です。残された数枚の写真は、私の娘たちの自慢です。被爆当時、まだ三十歳になったか、ならないか。

141　［証言14］田島忠美

まだ若かった母には辛かったでしょう。そのまま一年ほど、父の実家に母と二人で世話になっていました。体調が悪く寝ているときは、伯父さんの奥さんがいつも世話をしてくれました。夜中に何度か、母が泣いているのに気づいたこともありました。起き上がれるようになってからは、鏡を立てて薄化粧もしていました。

のちに、母の髪が生えるようになりました。ケロイドのある右側は髪を長く垂らして、なるべく隠していました。ケロイドは何年たっても、元の皮膚には戻りません。右側は眼鏡の蔓を髪にピンで止めていました。

になったのですが、右耳がありません。

ほどなく、田島さんの母は、中広町（現・西区中広町）の佃煮屋の家政婦として働き始める。そして翌年、田島さんも小学校にあがった。母は中須村から中広町へ、田島さんは中須から二十分ほどの大須国民学校へ通う日々が続いた。その後、古市の分家の土地をもらえることになった。当時は、廃材やトタンの焼け残りを使って、一日でバラック小屋を建てることを請け負う人たちがいた。その土地に六畳一間と三畳の台所付きのバラック小屋を建てた。ようやく母子二人、水入らずの暮らしが始まった。

当然、母は家政婦なので、朝早くに家を出ます。帰るのは夜遅くになります。私は一人ぼっちでした。いつも一人でご飯を食べ、一人で寝ました。このころは、母に怒られてばかりいたものです。「洗濯物を取りこんどいて！」「食器を洗っといて！」。私は、あまり家事を手伝わずに遊んでばかりいました。母が帰ってくると「何でやらん

かったん！」と叱られます。母も切なかったと思います。
　母からは愚痴や恨みがましい言葉を聞いたことがありません。いつだったか布団から上半身だけ起こしていて、ぽつりと「戦争はいけんよ。どんなことがあっても戦争だきゃ絶対しちゃいけん」。そんな独り言を言っているのを聞いたことがあります。
　そんななかで一つの転機があった。田島さんの母が真面目でよく働くので、佃煮屋の主人が気にかけてくれた。「佃煮の製造機の修理に来る人で、奥さんと赤ん坊を亡くした人で、ほかにも小さい子どもがいて、たいへん不自由しとる。その人と再婚せんか」。佃煮屋の社長の紹介で、母は再婚した。

　母の再婚は、私が小学五年生のときでした。再婚相手には男の子が四人、そして女の子が一人いました。三人の義兄は年齢が離れていましたが、女の子は死んだ妹と同じ。そして、その下の義弟も死んだ弟と同じ年齢でした。母の再婚先の家族に会ったのは、一九五一年（昭和二十六年）の元日。双方の親に連れられて、「己斐駅」（現・西広島駅）で待ち合わせをして、皆で宮島に行きました。「これから家族になるんじゃけえ」と、記念写真を撮りました。写真のなかの母は、やはり髪を垂らして右側のケロイドを隠しています。母の再婚で思ったことは「もう自分一人の母ちゃんじゃない」「もう甘えられん」ということでした。私には一歳下の妹と三歳下の弟ができたのだから。
　母の再婚により、母と私は義父の家のある呉市に行くことになりました。そこは農家でした。二頭の黒い牛を飼っていました。子牛を飼育して肉牛にして売るのです。学校から帰ると、二頭の牛

143　［証言14］田島忠美

のために餌の草を刈ります。草のほかにわらも食べるので、わらを小さく刻んで釜で煮ます。そして、糞まみれの敷きわらを替えてやると、牛たちは飛び跳ねて喜びました。田植えと稲刈り、まきにする木の切り出しなども手伝いました。母と義父は毎日、棚田の水田で草取りや畑の作業をやっていました。

その家には、義理の祖父がいた。体は大きいが、すでに腰が曲がりかけていた老人だった。長年、石の切り出しや石垣造りの仕事をし、腰に大きな負担になっていたのだろう。義祖父はやがて寝たきりになった。田島さんの母は、慣れない畑仕事にくわえて、七年間ずっと義祖父の世話をし続けた。義祖父は「美代子、美代子」と、たいへん母を気に入っていた。

中学を卒業すると、私は木型職人の親方のところに住み込みで働くことになりました。「田島家の後を継ぐのは、もう自分しかおらん！」という独立心のようなものがありました。実子の私がいては母が気を使う、ということも考えました。父の記憶はほとんどありませんが、父が木型職人であったことは知っていました。五歳から伯父さんのところに預けられていたし、母と二人きりの生活になっても、いつも母は働いていて、十五年間一緒にいたにもかかわらず母の記憶があまりないのです。

広島には東洋工業があって、車のエンジンを作る前に、必ず鋳物で模型を作ります。その鋳物を流しこむ木型を作るのが仕事です。丁稚奉公は十五歳から八年間続きました。辛い修業時代でした。理不尽だろうが何だろうが朝から晩職人の世界では、丁稚は決して褒められることはありません。

まで怒鳴られっ放しの生活。職人は十人ほど。朝は職人さんたちが来る前に必ず仕事場に入らなければなりません。帯のこぎりの歯を研いだり、接着用のニカワを煮たり、こまねずみのように働きました。そんな生活でも、食べ物があり、階段の下に一畳の寝るところがあります。ほんのわずかですが小遣いももらえました。私にはそれで十分だったのです。

丁稚時代にはときどき、呉市の母のところに帰ることができました。義祖父が必ず言いました。「他の娘を嫁にもらうんじゃったら、和子を嫁にしたほうがええ」。母にも私にも優しくしてくれる再婚相手の娘である和子に、私も次第に心を寄せるようになりました。休日には映画に誘いました。二十一歳のとき、私と和子は呉市の公民館で結婚式を挙げました。家族、親族の他に私の会社の社長や友人が三人来てくれました。質素ですが心温まる披露宴でした。母は「仲ようやってね!」と言ってくれました。

その後、母は体も丈夫になり七十六歳まで生きました。亡くなったのは心臓病で、原爆との関係はわかりません。ただ、あの戦争がなければ、原子爆弾がなければ、きっと母は美しい顔のまま、別の人生があっただろうと思います。どんなに嫌なことが続いても、母から一度の愚痴も聞いたこともなければ、暗い顔も見たことがありません。妻から見ても、そうだったと言います。寝たきりになった義祖父を介護していたときは、義祖父が飲み込むのを待って、ひと匙ひと匙、ほんとうに根気強く時間をかけて食べさせていました。

生活の苦しいなか、妻を洋裁学校に通わせたのも母でした。母には口癖がありました。「言いたいことは明日言うたらええ」。これは母が祖母から教わった言葉だそうです。長い年月のなかで母はきっと辛いときも嫌なときもそのように耐え忍んだのだと思います。

145　[証言14] 田島忠美

妻はいまでも言います。
「実の母が生きとったら、私にしてくれたじゃろうことを、お義母さんは精いっぱいしてくれた。本当に感謝しとる。お義母さんのことを思うといまでも涙がこみあげてくるんよ。小学四年生から一緒に生活してきて、あんなに素晴らしい人を義母(かあ)に持ったことを誇りに思うとる」

むすびにかえて

本書は「男たちのヒロシマーついに沈黙は破られた」とのタイトルで編まれた被爆証言集です。証言者十四人のいずれもが、七十代から八十代の方々です。これまでの人生で被爆に関しては多くを語ることはなく、最近になって重い口を開いて体験を語るようになった方々がほとんどです。被爆後どのような人生を歩み、なぜ沈黙を破ったのか、少しでも思いが伝えられるように留意しながら証言を収録したつもりです。また、こうした貴重な証言が、日本国内のみならず世界各国の方々にもお伝えできればとも考え、証言内容を英訳しました。被爆者の生の声は意外に海外には伝わっていないことも日ごろから感じていましたので、証言の英訳は意味が大きいと考えます。

広島発の被爆証言集はこれで八冊目となり、「二〇一一・三・一一福島原発事故」以降、初めての被爆証言集です。福島原発事故は衝撃でした。原発がいかに危険なものであるか、まざまざと知りました。福島から広島をあらためて考えさせられました。広島の果たすべき役割の重要性も一層増したように思います。本書が福島の被災者への励ましになるのだろうかについても、編集作業の合間によく論議を交わしました。原爆被爆者の放射線被曝は、一瞬の出来事であるのに比べ、福島の放射線被曝は放射能汚染に伴う慢性的な低レベル被曝です。被爆地・広島がこれまで蓄積した知見を持ってしても、低線量被曝の危険性はよくわかっていません。こうしたことも含めさまざまな違いはあるにしても、十四人の広島の被爆者が悩み、苦しみながらも何を支えにどのように生きてこられたのか、その赤裸々な証言は必ず福島の人たちの希望にもつながることを信じています。

「二〇一一・三・一一福島原発事故」をふまえ、何ゆえに広島県北広島町・中国平和記念墓地公園内に「世界平和祈願之碑」が建立されたのか、あらためて考えてみたいと思います。「世界平和祈願之碑」は、戸田第二代会長の「原水爆禁止宣言」から四十周年の一九九七年六月、全世界の「すべての被ばく者」を追悼する意義を込め、人類初の被爆の惨劇を受けた広島の爆心地の真北に当たる東経一三二度二七分に建立されました。

その除幕式に来賓としてお招きした核問題の専門家である熊田重克さん（当時・広島大学平和科学研究センター客員研究員）は、次のようなコメントを寄せてくださいました。

「創価学会が、被曝者を含む『核文明』の犠牲者を悼む『世界平和祈願の碑』を建立されたことは、誠に意義深い。この碑が私の目には『人間賛歌』の素晴らしい群像に映った。そこには二十世紀の愚行の歴史に終止符を打ち、来るべき二十一世紀を『人間の尊厳を謳歌』する時代にしようという、学会の皆様方の並々ならぬ熱意と鋭い洞察とが、ひしひしと伝わってきた。だが、この思想を実現するのは容易なことではない。青年の優れた理性と、情熱に支えられた行動力に、期待するほかないであろう」

世界に類例を見ない核文明の犠牲者を悼む「世界平和祈願之碑」です。広島、長崎の経験は核被害の恐怖を世界に教えました。しかし、それ以降に核開発、核実験、原発事故等々によって、おびただしい数の犠牲者が生まれたのです。いま、世界には苦しむ核被害者が三千万人以上いるともいわれます。もうこれ以上、悲惨かつ理不尽な核被害を繰り返させてはなりません。もうこれ以上、核文明の犠牲者を次々と出すようなことをさせてはなりません。そうさせないために、私たちほどのように核権力と対決し、核権力を封じ込めていけばいいのでしょうか。分厚く高い「壁」を乗り

越えるには、本当に戦わなくてはならない相手とは何かをしっかり見定めなくてはなりません。無知、無関心を払いのけ真に戦うべき相手は、自己の欲望を満たすためには相手を殲滅することも辞さない「核兵器を容認する思想」ではないでしょうか。さらに、打ち倒すべき相手は、自己の欲望を満たすためには相手を殲滅することも辞さない「貧困、格差、差別等に起因する戦争や地域紛争、テロリズムを容認する思想」ではないでしょうか。

この真に戦うべき相手と戦って勝利を収めるカギは、「対話」にあるのではないかと思います。「対話」「対話」「対話」のキャッチボールを通して、志を掲げた人たちが社会のあらゆる分野で意識啓発にうまずたゆまずいそしみ、連鎖反応的に世界のすみずみにまで、民衆の善なる連帯の輪を広げていくしかありません。

声を上げたり、行動を起こすということは、何も特別な人間にしかできないということでは、決してありません。〝平和で安穏な暮らしをしたい〟〝私たちにとって、大切なものを守りたい〟〝子どもたちに苦しい思い、悲しい思いをさせたくない〟といった人間としての当たり前の感情さえ持ち合わせていれば十分だと思います。

最後に、本書の上梓にあたり資料提供、証言取材、内容検証等々を通じ、多くの皆さま方にご協力賜りましたことを深く感謝申し上げます。

二〇一四年三月

創価学会広島平和会議議長　久保泰郎

Lastly, I would like to express my heartfelt gratitude to all the people who gave us their support, shared their experiences, provided us with historical data, and helped us verify the facts. Without their invaluable cooperation, this book would not have been possible.

Yasuro Kubo
Chairman
Soka Gakkai Hiroshima Peace Conference

March 2014

to the human follies of the twentieth century and open the twenty-first century as a new era where there will be respect for the dignity of life. Although easily said, I am aware that it will be an enormous challenge to promote this way of thinking. We will have to depend on the young people's passion, action and wisdom."

The Prayer Monument for World Peace stands as a rare monument dedicated to the victims of the nuclear civilization. The experiences of the atomic bomb survivors of Hiroshima and Nagasaki have conveyed to the world the horrors of nuclear weapons. However, even after this tragic history, there have been more than 30 million victims who suffered from negative consequences of nuclear development, testing and nuclear power plant accidents. We must unite to make sure that there are no more victims from nuclear disasters.

In order to realize a nuclear-free world, should our main goal be to challenge and pressure the nuclear powers? To overcome the enormous hurdle in front of us, it is necessary to understand the root cause of the problem. The real enemy that we need to confront is not just ignorance and public apathy, but the ways of thinking that justify and accept nuclear weapons as a necessary means to annihilate others who become threats or impediments to realizing one's agenda. The same way of thinking today accepts violent conflicts, war on terrorism, poverty and inequality as something justifiable.

I believe that the key to fighting our real enemy lies in "dialogue." Through dialogue, we can raise awareness, create solidarity amongst like-minded people and expand the momentum for action at all levels of society. Voicing opinions and advocating causes are not activities restricted to particular groups of people. Our efforts to realize a nuclear-free world can be driven by our simple desires like "I want to live in a peaceful and safe world," "I want to protect what matters to me," or "I don't want my children to suffer and be sad."

the disaster-stricken areas of Fukushima. Compared to the powerful and instantaneous radiation exposure that comes with an atomic bomb blast, the people of Fukushima must deal with persistent chronic low-dose radiation exposure from nuclear contamination. Even with the knowledge we have accumulated through studies conducted in Hiroshima, experts cannot make any conclusive assessment of how low-level radiation will impact human health.

Although, the nature of the nuclear crisis may be different, we hope that the experiences of the fourteen men who survived the atomic bomb in Hiroshima—how they lived through the ordeal and struggled to live with hope—will offer courage to the people of Fukushima.

Following the March 11, 2011 nuclear disaster in Fukushima, I had the chance to reflect on the significance of the Prayer Monument for World Peace that was erected in the Chugoku Peace Memorial Park in Kitahiroshima-cho, Hiroshima. The monument was built as a tribute to the victims of the atomic bomb and nuclear disaster throughout the world. It is located directly north (137°27'east longitude) of the hypocenter of the first nuclear blast in the history of humankind. The monument was erected in June 1997 marking the fortieth anniversary of the Second President of Soka Gakkai, Josei Toda's impassioned public call for the abolition and prohibition of nuclear weapons.

Shigeyoshi Kumada, a visiting researcher on nuclear issues at the Institute for Peace Science at Hiroshima University, made the following comment at the unveiling ceremony of the World Peace Prayer Monument: "It is truly significant that the Soka Gakkai erected this Prayer Monument for World Peace to pay tribute to the victims of the atomic bomb and the "nuclear civilization." I see this monument as a wonderful "celebration of humanity." The statues symbolize Soka Gakkai members' firm commitment and resolve to put an end

Acknowledgements

The book "Hiroshima — A Silence Broken" is a collection of testimonies of fourteen men who experienced the atomic bombing of Hiroshima. All of them are today in their 70s and 80s and have kept their silence about their lives only until recently. We have tried to record their accounts as accurately as possible, so that the readers can understand what kind of lives they led, how they struggled after the bombing and what made them break their silence now.

It has always been my concern that the experiences of the atomic bomb survivors have not been widely heard outside Japan. For this reason, we have decided to publish this book with the English translation added at the end. It is our sincere hope that this will help the survivors' messages to reach not only the people of Japan but throughout the world.

This book is the eighth volume of the collection of Hiroshima atomic bomb survivors' testimonies we have compiled over the years, and the first one to publish after the Fukushima nuclear disaster on March 11, 2011. The nuclear crisis in Fukushima was a shocking event for all of us, a wake-up call to the rethink the huge risks associated with nuclear power operations. The nuclear accident reminded me of the horrors the people of Hiroshima have experienced over the years. I believe that Hiroshima should play an increasingly active role in realizing a nuclear-free society. During the editing process, we often asked ourselves whether the atomic bomb survivors' experiences will be of any help to the victims of the nuclear power plant accident. However, it is our genuine wish that the messages of these survivors will somehow bring hope to the people of teeth of band saws to boiling glue. I worked like a dog. Although my life was hard, I was served meals, provided with a space to sleep, and given a small allowance. That was enough for me.

During my apprenticeship, I was sometimes allowed to return home to Kure. Whenever I came home my grandfather said, "If you want to marry someone, marry Kazuko." Kazuko was a daughter of my stepfather. She was nice to my mother and me, so I gradually fell for her. I asked her to the movies on my days off. When I was 21, Kazuko and I held our wedding at the city community center in Kure City. My family and relatives, the president and three friends from my company were there. It was a simple but touching reception. "Make a happy family!" my mother admonished us.

After this wedding, my mother improved physically and lived to be 76. She died of heart disease. I do not know if it was related to the atomic bombing, but if it hadn't been for that war or the atomic bomb, she would have lived a completely different life because of her beautiful face. Even during a string of bad luck, I never once heard her complain or even make a gloomy face. I believe she was a good mother to my wife. While she was taking care of my bedridden grandfather, she fed him spoonful by spoonful, patiently waiting for him to swallow each one.

My mother sent my wife to a dressmaking school, even though she herself was struggling to make ends meet. She always said, "Say what you want to say tomorrow." This was a phrase she had learned from my grandmother. I think this helped her endure all the hardships over the years. Even today my wife says, "Your mother did her best to do for me what my mother would have done if she had lived. I'm deeply grateful to her. When I think of her, tears come to my eyes even now. Living with her since I was in 4th grade, I am proud that I had such a wonderful mother-in-law."

Hiroshima August 6, 1945

calves jumped for joy. I helped my stepfather plant the rice paddies, harvest rice and cut trees in the hills for firewood. My mother and stepfather weeded the terraced paddies and worked on the farm every day.

A step-grandfather also lived in the house. He was well built but an older man who already had a bent posture. He was a stonecutter and built stonewalls for many years, which was probably hard on his back. Soon after the marriage, the grandfather became bedridden. Besides doing unfamiliar farm work, she looked after her father-in-law for seven years. Her father-in-law liked her very much, and often called out her name saying, "Miyoko, Miyoko."

After graduating from junior high, I apprenticed myself to a master wood mold craftsman. I lived and worked at his house. I wanted to become independent, saying to myself, "I am the one who will carry on the family name!" I also thought that my mother would care more about other children if her own child stayed with her. I had almost no memories of my father, but I knew that he had been a wood mold craftsman. I was sent to live with my uncle when I was 5, and even after we lived together my mother was always working so I have few memories of my mother despite living with her for 15 years.

There was an auto manufacturer called Toyo Kogyo in Hiroshima. They manufactured a cast model before creating a car engine. My job was to make wood molds to pour the cast in. I served my apprenticeship for 8 years starting when I was 15. I had a tough time learning the skills. In the world of craftsmen, an apprentice is never praised. He is yelled at all day, sometimes for no reason. About 10 craftsmen worked in the shop. In the morning, I had to be at the shop before they arrived. I did all the minor chores, from sharpening the remember when, but one night, I saw her sitting up on her bedding talking quietly to herself. "War is wrong. No matter what, war is wrong."

Eventually, their lives came to a turning point. As Tadayoshi's mother was honest and hardworking, the owner of the store was concerned about her. "There's a man who comes here to repair our processing machine. He lost his wife and baby but he has small children and is having a hard time raising them. Why don't you get remarried?" he asked her. Tadayoshi's mother remarried through this introduction by the storeowner.

When I was a 5th grader, my mother remarried a man with four boys and a girl. Three of the step-brothers were much older than me, but my step-sister was the same age as my late sister and the youngest step-brother was the same age as my late brother. On New Year's Day in 1951, I met my stepfather's family for the first time. We met at Koi Station (now, Nishi Hiroshima Station), and then went to Miyajima Island. "We're going to be a family," he told us and took a souvenir picture. In the picture, my mother has her hair hanging over the right side of her face to hide her keloids. What I thought of my mother's remarriage was, "She is no longer just my mother. I shouldn't depend on her." I now had a sister a year younger and a brother 3 years younger than me.

After her remarriage, my mother and I moved to my stepfather's house in Kure. He was a farmer and had two black calves, which he raised to sell the meat. When I came home from school, I cut grass to feed the calves. They ate straw besides grass so I also chopped straw in small pieces and boiled it in an iron pot before I fed them. Sometimes I replaced dung scatter straw with new straw, and the leave her bed, she began to put on light makeup in front of a mirror.

Eventually, my mother's hair began to grow back. She grew her hair long on the right side to cover her keloids. She tried to hide them as much as possible. No matter how many years pass, once skin turns into a keloid scar, it will never become normal skin.

Later on, my mother began to wear glasses but she didn't have a right ear. She fixed her glasses to her right temple with a hairpin.

Before long, Tadayoshi's mother started working as a housekeeper at a food processing store in Nakahiro-machi (now, Nakahiro-machi, Nishi-ku). The following year, Tadayoshi started elementary school. Every day his mother commuted to Nakahiro from Nakasu, and Tadayoshi walked 20 minutes from Nakasu to Osu Elementary School. Later on, Tadayoshi and his mother were given some relative's land in Furuichi. In those days, workers built makeshift shacks from wood scrap and burned galvanized iron sheets in a single day. They had built a hut with a six-tatami-mat room and a three-tatami-mat kitchen in that land. Finally, mother and child started their livelihood on their own.

My mother was a housekeeper, so she left home early in the morning. She came home when she finished cleaning up after dinner at her employer's home. She would get to her own home late at night. I was often by myself at home. I ate alone and went to bed alone. I used to be scolded by my mother frequently. She yelled at me to "take in the laundry!" or "do the dishes!" I did little to help with the housework. Mostly I would just hang around and do what I wanted to. After coming home, she would angrily say, "Why didn't you do what I told you?" My mother must have been in agony.

I never heard my mother hold a grudge or complain. I don't

house were the burned bodies of an adult and a child. They were forced to the conclusion that these bodies were his grandmother and his brother. His grief continued.

The burns my father suffered were so severe he couldn't lie on his back. He lay on his stomach, groaning, "Ouch! Ouch!" On August 9, he died at the age of 34. On the bank of the Yasukawa River, some members of the local fire brigade and my uncle piled up some wood scrap and cremated my father's body. It took long hours. My sister had no injury except for the hole in her forehead. But she gradually stopped moving. She died on August 16.

My mother started to complain that she wasn't feeling well. She lost her appetite and spent more and more time lying down. Our relatives brought my mother some Saururaceous plants like Lizard's-tail and Water-dragon. They told her, "Saururaceous plants is good for your health." She often drank a concoction made from Saururaceous plants by boiling the plant in a kettle of water. Soon my mother's hair fell out, and she was bald. She lost the hair she was using to hide her keloid scars.

Tadashi, her younger brother, often visited her and encouraged her. "I'll avenge this tragedy. I promise! There's nothing to worry about!"

Her life was utterly transformed by the atomic bombing. In her pictures as a young woman, she looks very beautiful. My daughters take pride in the few pictures that are left of my mother. My mother was only about 30 years old when she experienced the atomic bombing. She was still young. She must have gone through tremendous pain. For about a year, my mother and I stayed at my father's parents' house. When she wasn't feeling well and had to stay in bed, my uncle's wife looked after her. I noticed my mother weeping late at night several times. After she became well enough to

Hiroshima August 6, 1945

My family in Nakasu had just finished breakfast, and I was playing on my uncle's lap in the room with the Buddhist altar. I neither saw the "Pika (the flash)" nor heard a loud sound, but all the doors in the house were blown off. Some houses in Nakasu were destroyed, but no residents were hurt. That night, the Nakasu area was flooded with people fleeing from Hiroshima. Some were Nakasu residents who had been demolishing houses in the city. Others were Hiroshima residents who had relatives in Nakasu and were taking refuge. They all had badly burned faces and bodies and were wearing tattered clothes. My parents and my sister were among them.

"Oh no, ghosts!" I shouted without thinking.

My mother was exposed to the heat ray from the right front, so her face was hideously burned. The right half of her face was burned, its skin peeling, and her right ear had melted off. Her hands were also severely burned. My gentle, kind mother had changed beyond recognition. If she had not been with my father, I would not have recognized her. My father, too, was seriously burned on his back, and my sister had a hole about the size of a bean in her forehead. Strangely, it was not bleeding, and she wasn't crying.

Their hair and faces were dirty, and their clothes were tattered. They said that on the way they had swum across a river with their clothes on because a bridge had collapsed. They were exposed in the morning and arrived at my uncle's house around 5:00 in the evening. That meant they walked through for more than nine hours.

The following day, Tadayoshi, his uncle, and his mother headed for Takajo-machi where his grandmother and his brother were. Takajo-machi was right by the hypocenter. Most of the town was burnt out. And at the fire-devastated site of his grandmother's

Document 14

My mother's word "No matter what, war is wrong"

Tadayoshi Tashima
Born in May 1939. Avoided atomic bombing being evacuated to Nakasu-mura, seven kilometers from the hypocenter. At six years of age, lost grandmother, younger brother, father, and younger sister who were in Hiroshima. Was brought up by his mother. Worked at Toyo Kogyo (now, Mazda) and several other companies. Seventy-four years old; lives in Asa Minami-ku, Hiroshima.

That atomic bomb killed my grandmother, younger brother, father, and younger sister

I was six years old and was the oldest of three. My sister Hiroko was five; my brother Akio was three. My parents sent me to live with my father's parents in Nakasu one year before the bombing. My parents may have been hoping to keep at least their oldest child in a safe place. The war was becoming more intense, so a cousin my age was there as well.

The Tashima family lived in Hirose Kita-machi (now, HiroseKita-machi, Naka-ku). Their house was scheduled to be demolished to make way for a fire lane to prevent the spread of fires resulting from incendiary bombs. On August 6, Tadayoshi's parents were moving their furniture and belongings out of the house. His little brother was at his grandmother's house at Takajo-machi (now, Honkawa-cho, Naka-ku.) Only his sister was with his parents.

anger and frustration to anyone. Takeshi told me once when I was in high school, "You may think you're no different from others, but you are. You've grown up without things tangible and intangible that you were supposed to get from your parents. Always keep that in mind, and work hard to overcome it."

It was not until later that I understood what he meant. I never thought about my mother until I became an adult. Some may think me coldhearted, but back then, all I could do was make it through the day. I didn't have the time to reminisce about the past.

After graduating from junior college, I was employed by the Shimonoseki City Office, where I worked until retirement in 1997. I came back to Hiroshima by chance. My wife and I now live an ordinary but happy life together in Kita Hiroshima-cho. Composing senryu poems is my favorite pastime. Every day I hear children laughing as they play on the jungle gym and the slide in the park next to our house. During the war, no children were laughing.

One day I suddenly realized that peace can be defined as a society in which we can hear the laughter of children. I hardly went to school at all when I was 2nd and 3rd grade. I was an A-bomb orphan, so I feel that I missed out on my childhood.

This is why I hope that children today will cherish and maintain peace. I pray for peace, that is, for the laughter of children to continue. I feel strongly that I should contribute to that peace by telling my story about the horrors of war and the tragedy of the atomic bombing.

A child's smiling face / Always tells us / The importance of peace

Looking back / I find the joy of peace / in the thorny path of life

[Document 13] Kiyoshi Ito

In the fall of 1946, Kiyoshi's oldest brother, Takeshi, returned to Japan from China, having been discharged from the military. Takeshi discovered that his parents' home in Hiroshima was gone. He started searching for his family and finally found his way to Shimonoseki. He took his brother in.

Takeshi took me in, and soon, when I was in fourth grade, he got married. I lived with the newlyweds. Takeshi often hit me. I think it was because he was hot-blooded and violent after coming back from the military, but it was also out of consideration for his wife. Meanwhile, I became a rebel. Once I stole an apple from a Buddhist altar inside the house next door. Takeshi found out and beat me with a bamboo stick until it split into pieces. However, I did not hate him for beating me. The sense of alienation I felt at my relatives' house was much harder on me emotionally than his beatings.

My brother's wife's parents ran a noodle shop in their house. When I was in junior high school, I worked at that shop and lived with other workers on the second floor. I was living on my own for the first time in my life. I woke up at three every morning and worked all day. I went to night school for high school and junior college.

At Tei's house he felt uncomfortable. At Uncle Kenzo's house in Ofuna, he was hungry all the time. At his relatives' house in Shimonoseki, the family was wealthy but he was left out. At Takeshi's house, he lived with his brother and his wife and received harsh discipline.

After the atomic bombing, I was passed around from one relative to another. I was taken care of, but it was never home to me. I couldn't even open a cabinet without permission, nor could I vent my

In April 1946, Kiyoshi had to move to Shimonoseki in Yamaguchi Prefecture, where he lived with his mother's brother. His uncle ran a construction company and had four children. Kiyoshi had never met this side of his family so he was meeting his cousins for the first time.

My uncle's family had no problem economically, but I felt as if I had been tossed into a house of strangers. I was always alone. Each of the four children had a private tutor, though almost no households could afford to hire tutors back then. My cousins looked like they were having fun with their tutors. Watching them from the corner of my eye, I always felt jealous. I once saw my uncle's wife and her children happily eating sweet bean cakes in the living room when I got up to use the bathroom in the middle of the night. I felt nothing but alienated, and gradually became subservient.

They had a housemaid named Otoki. She probably felt sorry for me, so when I came home from school, she always invited me to her room. However, I didn't like being in the "maid's room" all the time. It hurt to think that the others knew that I felt like I wasn't welcome. This was why I always stayed at school until dark.

I couldn't say what I wanted to at home, so I behaved badly at school as a reaction. Every day I would pick a fight, take somebody's lunch, or have "sword fights" with measuring sticks in home economics, often breaking them. My teacher once said, "Don't come to school anymore."

On sports days I had a particularly tough time. My friends ate lunch with their parents during the break. Since I had no parents and no lunch, I had to kill time in a classroom by myself until lunch break ended.

their own chairs.

It was not until the beginning of September that I learned the truth about what had happened. Tei and my older brother, Toshi, who was in Kyoto at university, took me to Hiroshima. We arrived at Hiroshima Station, and I cannot describe terror I felt when I saw the city. My legs gave way and I lost the power of thought. My parents' house and Kokutaiji Temple next door had disappeared without a trace. Only the remains of the temple's pond could be seen. We were unable to hold a funeral for our parents. For some time, I couldn't believe they were dead.

I started living at Tei's parents' house, but I felt there was no place for me. Tei died of pulmonary emphysema at the age of 69. He may have gotten that because he went to gather the remains of my parents and became an indirect victim of the bomb. I lived at his house for only about 3 months.

Soon afterwards, my brother Toshi took me to Ofuna in Kanagawa Prefecture. We travelled on very crowded trains. I found myself at our uncle Kenzo's house. He was my father's brother and worked for the Japan National Railways. He was a man of honesty. Although he had five growing children, he never bought rice on the black-market. His family of eight, including myself, shared a small amount of rationed rice. We did not have enough to eat. There were times when we ate almost nothing for a week. My five cousins and I lay down in a corner of the room because if we moved, we got hungry. We were all malnourished. Uncle Kenzo's voice sounded like my father. "I'm going to talk like your father, so close your eyes." he once said. I closed my eyes and he said, "How're you doing?" He sounded exactly like my father, I broke out in tears. While I was staying with my uncle, I couldn't go to school.

netting. Much to my disappointment, the newspaper story about plenty of sweets turned out to be a lie. We were served small portions of miso soup, pickled radish, and rice cooked with barley. We were always hungry. At night, some of my friends and I would sneak into the temple kitchen and steal some raw rice. We nibbled on it in bed to keep the hunger pangs away.

"I think we were evacuated from the city around June," says Kiyoshi, adding that he remembers he and his friends helping to plant rice out there. "That day" came while he was living at the evacuation site.

Even after August 6, we were not told about the "Pika-don" (lit., flash-boom, the common name for the bomb). Our teacher said only, "I went to Hiroshima to see your parents. They said they'll come get you soon. Let's wait."

Several days later, my friends' parents and families began arriving to pick them up, but nobody came for me. Watching them leave one after the other made me feel lonely and uneasy.

In late August, only three children were left. I was one. A few days later, Tei, my cousin, suddenly turned up with a bag of rice and some canned food. He cooked rice and served me canned beans and meat. I was relieved that he finally had come for me. Because of the tasty rice and happiness he brought, I no longer felt anxious. He didn't mention the atomic bombing, and I was too excited to ask him about my parents.

Tei took me to his parents' home in Kure City, Hiroshima Prefecture. He later told me that he had visited my home two days after the atomic bombing and found the bones of my father, mother, and older brother in the living room. Their bones were still sitting in

[Document 13] Kiyoshi Ito

I pray for peace so the children's laughter will continue

Kiyoshi Ito
Born in March 1937. On the day of the atomic bombing, he had been evacuated to Miyoshi City. Parents lived in Ko-machi (now, Ko-machi, Naka-ku), 900 meters from the hypocenter. Killed by atomic bombing, they left him an A-bomb orphan. Spent boyhood being sent from one relative to another. Worked at Shimonoseki City Office in Yamaguchi Prefecture; returned to birthplace after retiring. Seventy-six years old, lives in Kita Hiroshima-cho, Yamagata-gun.

I had no house
Sent from one relative to another

Because Kiyoshi had been sent out of Hiroshima City, he escaped direct exposure to the atomic bombing. However, the atomic bomb took his family, leaving him an A-bomb orphan.

Although our family had always been well off, we found ourselves living in dire poverty by 1945. I was 8 at that time. Sweets were very hard to come by. Once I saw an article in the newspaper that talked about children being delighted to receive plenty of sweets at the temple to which they had been evacuated. I remember that this article gave me an irresistible urge to eat something sweet. I was in second grade. Although evacuation was optional, we had decided to join the evacuation program. I couldn't get this newspaper story out of my mind.

My friends and I were evacuated to a temple in Miyoshi City. Some of them were homesick and cried on their beds under mosquito gangsters.

This is not a matter of good or evil. This is simply the reality, the way orphans on the streets lived as a result of the war and the atomic bombing. Talking about the past is painful for me and also for those that listen. But this pain is a real aspect of war. As a person who has survived the cruelty of war, I believe I'm now obligated to speak about my experience. I need to convey the facts to the future so we will create no more A-bomb orphans.

[Document 12] Shoso Kawamoto

Some have objected to my activity.

"I'm married with children and grandchildren. They are dimly aware that I was an orphan, but they don't really know how I survived. I'm afraid that my children and grandchildren will find out about my horrible past because of your talk."

"You've got nothing to worry about because you don't have a family. Think about former orphans who have children and grandchildren. Think how they feel. Please stop telling that story."

After I was rejected as a marriage partner because of the atomic bomb, I never got married because I didn't want to be rejected again. My classmates, however, are mostly married with children and grandchildren.

One of my classmates said, "I have never told even my children about how I survived those days. I don't think I can. I was 10. I had no one to depend on, so I had to find ways to live on my own. I did what I had to do to live. I have even snatched food violently away from a stranger. This was how I survived."

My classmates are afraid that if I speak, their children will hear my story and be tormented thinking, "What sort of terrible things did my Grandpa do!" They may all want to forget the past, but it's impossible. We cannot ignore the past. I have to tell the truth even if it's painful because children in the future must understand what war was really like.

Many of the orphans who managed to survive were those who were placed in orphanages. This fact is also important. Many of them were able to continue their education because of those orphanages. Many were able to make plans for their future. In contrast, the orphans who were thrown out into the streets were forced to live like "livestock." This fact is not known to the world; it has been forgotten. The undeniable fact is that many orphans survived in the care of fiftieth-anniversary memorial service." Hearing the voice of an old friend brought back a lot of memories. "I'll spend the rest of my life in Hiroshima," I said to myself. I decided to go back.

Shoso put his affairs in order, closing down his company, and returned to Hiroshima at the age of 70. In Hiroshima, he visited the Hiroshima Peace Memorial Museum and was astonished to find a paucity of information about street children. Although the museum featured a wide variety of exhibits and displays on the atomic bombing, there was only one photo of a boy shining shoes, with one line stating, "It is said that there were 2,000 to 6,500 orphans living in the city." Shoso has been addressing the issue of "A-bomb orphans" head-on utilizing his own experience.

After returning to Hiroshima, I visited the Hiroshima Peace Memorial Museum, where I was surprised to find that almost no material on A-bomb orphans. For the children who were thrown out on the streets because they were unable to get into an orphanage, the biggest problem was food. Most had no choice but to rely on gangsters because they simply couldn't live by themselves. These circumstances have been completely ignored by the museum. I have no desire to glorify gangs. I do not approve of them. However, we must not deny the facts—that orphans on the streets were associated with and cared for by gangs. This was how they survived.

I now work as a Peace Volunteer. I tell visitors to the Hiroshima Peace Memorial Museum about my experience and the orphans living on the streets. I have been criticized for my story by some of my classmates from Fukuro-machi Elementary School, including some of those who encouraged me to return to Hiroshima from Okayama.

[Document 12] Shoso Kawamoto

company because this friend put in a good word for me. At night I went into town and frequented the local gambling house. I was attracted to the gang because of my friend's influence, so I asked him if I could join. He said, "You're not cut out to be a gangster. You're too nice, so no." Sometime later, my friend died in a fight.

I led a rebellious life for about 10 years. Then one day, when I was 30 or so, I was fined 2,000 yen for a traffic violation, and I couldn't get the money. I felt miserable. I no longer had the will to live. I couldn't be bothered to borrow money to pay a fine. I began to believe my life was not worth living. "I'm going to kill myself!" I thought, "But I don't want to die in Hiroshima. I'll go some place where nobody knows me and die there." I decided to leave the city.

I only had 640 yen with me and could only make it to the next prefecture, Okayama. I got off at Okayama Station and started to walk. Still wondering which way to go, I saw a noodle shop with a notice saying: "Live-In Help Wanted".

"No one in Okayama knows me. Maybe I can start my life again," I thought. I went in and asked the owner to hire me. "If you're really serious about working here, you're hired," he said. I was hired on the spot. I worked hard at that shop. I ended up working in Okayama for 30 years, and even started a small food company with about 50 employees. Around that time, convenience stores were popping up across the country, so our prepared food and boxed lunches sold well.

One day, when I was 60, an employee told me I had a phone call from Hiroshima. I had not called or written to anyone in Hiroshima for decades, so I was sure nobody knew where I was.

I answered the phone and heard a cheerful voice say, "Hey, Kawamoto! I'm glad you're alive! We were worried about you. We've been looking for you!" It was one of my friends from when I had stayed at the temple. "Come home, Kawamoto! Let's hold a future," I was told. Under these conditions I was allowed to live in the house of the Kawanaka Soy Sauce Store. Since I had nowhere else to go and didn't want to live with my uncle, I worked hard at the shop. I did everything I could, from looking after cows early in the morning to mowing to cutting rice stubble in the paddies and farming. I also learned how to brew soy sauce. I worked there for 10 years without taking a day off. When I was 23 years old, as promised, they built me a house of my own. I also became leader of the local youth association.

I then fell in love with a girl from the village and asked her to marry me. Her parents, however, strongly opposed our marriage, saying: "You were in Hiroshima at that time, weren't you? Those who were there were contaminated with radiation. You probably won't live long, and if our daughter marries you, she will give birth to a disabled child. We can't allow you to marry her!"

This made my blood boil. "There's no point in having my own house if I can't marry anyone. From now on, I'm going to live my life the way I want to," I said to myself.

Shoso ran away from the village in anger and returned to Hiroshima. He visited the city for the first time in 12 years and found that it had changed completely. By chance he met a man who had been a grade lower than him in elementary school and had also been an orphan. This man was a "full-fledged gangster." Little is known about the street children who managed to survive with the help of gangsters and about how they grew up afterwards.

I met a friend on the street with whom I had stayed at the temple. He was swaggering along in his territory with some young men in tow. Since I had a driver's license, I soon got a job at a trucking

[Document 12] Shoso Kawamoto

made from cigarette butts that occupation soldiers threw down on the streets. The gangsters taught the children how to work, then pocketed all the money. Even so, the children didn't run away because they were given food and a place to sleep. This was how they managed to survive.

Not many know these things. The stories of the orphans abandoned to the streets are never told. When people hear the word "orphan," they think of children whose parents have died and are in orphanages. The fact is, in Hiroshima, the street children greatly outnumbered orphans in institutions.

The city was full of street children, who died one after the next, starting with the younger ones. When older children caught younger ones with food in their hands, they snatched it away from them. I even heard about a small child who was mumbling, so a bigger child held him down and opened his mouth only to find he was sucking pebbles. If a child fell ill and lay unconscious on the street, nobody paid any attention. As soon as a child died, other children stripped off his or her clothes, which is why most children found dead on the street were naked. On the other hand, orphans taken in by gangsters survived.

Eventually his father's brother wanted to take him in. All the orphanages were full, but he didn't want to stay with this uncle. At the end of February the following year, he was placed in the custody of the Kawanaka Soy Sauce Store in Numata. The shop owner was the village mayor, and Numata was where his grandparents on his father's side had lived.

"We can't afford to send you to junior high school, but we'll give you food if you help out around here. We'll build you a house in the

Hiroshima August 6, 1945

orphanages. The exact figures are unknown, but it is reasonable to think that at least 2,000 orphans were left abandoned to become street children.

I was the only one in my family of six to survive. People around me worked hard to send me to an orphanage, but those facilities were full to overflowing. I even couldn't go to an orphanage. The month after the atomic bombing, the powerful Makurazaki typhoon hit Hiroshima, washing away many of the street children who were sleeping under bridges.

The people who took care of most of the neglected street children were young gangsters. They built a two-story shack, where they lived upstairs and the street children slept downstairs crowded together like livestock. The gangsters provided the children with food and shelter, in return for which the children had to work and pay kickbacks. Only orphans who were teenagers or older were able to form groups with leaders that could live on their own, as in Barefoot Gen. The younger children could only commit petty crimes like pickpocketing, so they could not make it on their own.

The gangsters gave the children work. The children were divided into groups of five and provided with shoeshine kits. Two of the five children worked as shoeshine boys, with the other three recruiting customers. They returned to the shack at night and gave the money they made to the gangsters. The group that made the least amount of money was replaced with another group and was sometime made to go without meals. For this reason, all the children worked hard, and the groups would often fight with each other.

Besides shining shoes there was plenty of other work. For example, they sold glasses of methanol diluted 10 to 1 with water for 10 yen each. They sold stimulant drugs and "rebuilt" cigarettes

[Document 12] Shoso Kawamoto

gradually became accepted by the orphans. It was easy to tell whether a child was a "street orphan" or not by looking at his or her clothes. Street orphans wore clothes that were obviously different from the children who had parents or lived in institutions.

At night street orphans had no place to go so they slept under bridges, in corners of burnt-out buildings, and in air-raid shelters. They slept together in groups of five or six, with their clothes on. But the groups did not mean they were friends or comrades. They were collections of individuals gathering because it was better to sleep together than separate. In the morning, they went their separate ways looking for food.

Street orphans targeted open-air food markets trying to get food. The markets were mostly run by women or elderly people. A street orphan would make off with a rice cake. While the shopkeeper chased after that orphan, other orphans appeared and instantly stole the remaining rice cakes. Stealing was a frantic struggle. Having food in hand was often dangerous. An orphan with food became a target for other orphans, who would immediately try to grab the food. So stealing and eating had to be done at the same time. Older orphans would even pry open the mouths of the younger ones to take food before it could be swallowed. The term "hungry little devils" described them perfectly.

About four months after the bombing, Shoso's sister fell sick. Blisters on her feet broke and bled continually. Her hair fell out. A week or so later, she died. Shoso was then taken in by the mayor of Numata (now, Numata-cho, Asa Minami-ku) in February the following year. Before the bombing, about 8,600 elementary school students in Hiroshima were evacuated to the countryside. Of those students, 2,700 became orphans, and only 700 were admitted into she burst into tears. She said that she had visited the site of our house in Shioya-cho the day after the bombing and had found the burned remains of what appeared to be our mother, younger sister, and brother. She found them holding onto each other in the living room. Although their faces were burned black and were difficult to recognize, she was sure the bodies were those of our family members because of where she found them. Our father and eighth-grade sister had been out helping to demolish houses for a fire lane and were missing.

Shoso and his sister returned to burned-out Hiroshima. Their house had burned to the ground. So, with the boxes of their family's ashes, they were passed from one relative to another. None of their relatives could afford to keep them. Eventually his sister, who had just turned 16, rented a room, and they moved in.

When my sister and I stood on the platform at Hiroshima Station, I was stunned. The sight from there was beyond belief. No buildings stood in front of us. I could look over the city out to the islands in the Seto Inland Sea. And the whole city was dead silent. It made me sick. My sister rented a room in the building where she worked, so we started living there together. My sister worked for the management bureau of Japan National Railways. I had nothing to do, so I walked around the streets every day. There were many orphans in the city. Having lost their parents, they had nowhere to go. Some of them were my classmates from Fukuro-machi Elementary School. We went to the fire-ravaged sites to collect iron scrap and cigarette butts.

Hot meals were provided twice a week. I desperately wanted to make friends, so at soup kitchens I often traded places with orphans standing in the back of the line. I collected iron scrap with them. I

[Document 12] Shoso Kawamoto

growing on the roadside near rice paddies. It wasn't about the taste. I just wanted something to eat, something to stave off hanger.

What I liked best was Japanese leopard frog. I pulled the legs wide apart and easily stripped its skin. The cook at school deep-fried it for me. It tasted like white chicken meat and was a precious source of protein for me. I believe that I am able to build my body today because I ate those frogs. I also ate locusts, grasshoppers, anything that could be eaten.

At the temple, we didn't have time to study. Instead, we had to fill bamboo tubes with resin from pine trees by scraping the bark. We also collected pine root oil. This oil was used for airplane fuel. We cultivated unused land, planting potatoes and sweet potatoes.

On August 6, we had been working in our field since early that morning planting vegetables. Then, I noticed the sky looking so odd. A gigantic column of white cloud was rising in the direction of Hiroshima City. I had never seen such a sight so I was eager to know what was happening. "The way the clouds are forming is not normal," I said to myself.

At that time we were more than 50 kilometers away from the city, so we did not see the flash or hear the roar, but how the clouds were forming bothered me greatly. Our teachers had clearly heard news from the village office by evening, but they didn't tell us what had happened in Hiroshima.

Later, I heard different stories from families who came to pick up their children. Even when I heard that Hiroshima was totally destroyed by a "special" bomb, the reality had not hit me. Many families came for their children and took them away, eventually leaving only a few of my classmates and me.

On August 9, my five-year-older sister finally came to the temple from Hiroshima City to pick me up. As soon as she saw my face,

Hiroshima August 6, 1945

Document 12

To create no more A-bomb orphans

Shoso Kawamoto
Born in March 1934. Entered Hiroshima from evacuation site in Kamisugi-mura, Futami-gun three days after the atomic bombing to return home in Shioya-cho. Five members of his family died or went missing, making him an A-bomb orphan. He was 11 years old. Now seventy-nine years old, living in Nishi-ku, Hiroshima.

A forgotten A-bomb orphan
No choice but to live as street children

Shoso was born the eldest son in a family of seven in Shioya-cho (now, Ote-machi, Naka-ku) near the hypocenter. In April 1945, all the six-graders from Fukuro-machi Elementary School were sent to four villages for school evacuation. His group went to Kamisugi-mura, Futami-gun (now, Miyoshi City). A total of 45 boys and 32 girls stayed at a temple called Zentoku-ji.

A meal was a bowl of rice, miso soup and some pickled vegetables at the temple. It was not enough for growing children, so we were hungry all the time. At lunchtime, the lunchboxes local students opened looked like feasts to me. Fully packed with white rice, they made me envious. I sometimes bartered for some, saying, "For some of your lunch, I'll give you a pencil and an eraser too!" I wanted anything I could put in my mouth. Children from farms in the area told me which plants were edible. I even tried raw wheat, pulling off the kernels and rubbing them between my hands. I picked soybeans

[Document 11] Takanobu Hirano

the spirit of Hiroshima to the generation to come. Last year I read in the newspaper that Hiroshima City had launched a project to train younger people to convey the experiences of the A-bomb victims. I was immediately interested in the project and applied. My testimony was recorded and released on a DVD entitled "A-Bomb Survivor Testimony from Hiroshima." In my community I was president for the Regional Development Association for 4 years and am now a board member. I am also a member of the executive committee of the Yachiyo Sports Association. Spreading hope in our local community, I intend to devote the rest of my life to peace.

Hiroshima August 6, 1945

I decided to apply for an Atomic Bomb Survivor Health Book, although it took me a long time to do so. People who had entered the hypocenter area within two weeks of the atomic bombing were recognized as atomic bomb entry victims. The health book allowed free physical checkups. I needed a witness to prove that I entered the city. My grandmother had already passed away, so I looked for the sister of my stepmother. I met her and persuaded her to become my witness.

I have suffered a sharp ringing in my ears since I was young. I often get dizzy. I went to see a brain surgeon, who said he had no idea what caused the condition and couldn't prescribe any medication. I can't help but think that it's because I entered into the bombed area. When I'm not feeling well, I get so worried that I can't sleep.

Sometimes my son ran a fever or got a nosebleed because of the heat. This is not a big deal for most children, but with my son, I wonder in fear if it is related to radiation. The slightest thing made me uneasy. My heart freezes with fear even about things that don't seem to upset others.

My sister also married without telling her husband that she had been exposed to radiation. "If I talk about my experience, I may not be able to get married," she said. Since then, she and I have never talked about Zaimoku-cho. We both wanted to keep it a secret as much as possible. It saddens me to think about how much she suffered without being able to talk to anyone.

Probably many people in Fukushima are now experiencing the same grief my sister and I have gone through. I wonder if some of them will have to endure the same pain in the future. This is why I cannot consider the suffering of people in Fukushima to be "someone else's problem."

Soon I will turn 80. I have come to believe that I have to pass on as a barber. His wife continued to run the beauty shop, and he started working at an aluminum window frame company run by his wife's brother. He later opened his own window frame business, which he managed for 20 years. "A-bomb survivors have mixed feelings," he says. Almost 70 years since the bombing, he feels the atomic bombing continuously tortured him.

A part of me says, "Leave me alone," while another part of me says, "I need to tell people about the suffering I've gone through." I have been tormented by these conflicting emotions. As a matter of fact, when I got married, I didn't tell my wife that I was a hibakusha. I was afraid to talk about it. "I will never tell anyone all my life," I thought. In those days, it was said that Hiroshima would be bare of vegetation for the next 75 years. When the atomic bomb was dropped, I was in Yachiyo-cho, a town not directly affected by the bombing. I became an entry victim when I went to gather my father's ashes. I thought that unless I mentioned it, nobody would notice.

Despite this, three years later after our marriage, my wife got pregnant with our first son. She was diagnosed with placenta previa at the hospital in Yoshida-cho, and was told that the hospital could not handle the case. We somehow managed to get a referral to the Hiroshima Prefectural Hospital, where she gave birth. The baby was born two months premature, weighing 1,800 grams.

I was restless for days, thinking, "Is it because I was exposed?"

When our son was one and a half years old, he had a hernia. I could not bear to see him suffer from so many physical disorders, so I confessed to my wife that immediately after the atomic bombing, on August 14, I went to Zaimoku-cho, which was near the hypocenter. She simply said, "Don't worry." Fortunately, our son grew up healthy without any serious illness.

Hiroshima August 6, 1945

After serving his apprenticeship at the barber's for 4 years, Takanobu worked there without pay for a year. When he was 20, he returned to Yachiyo-cho, where he opened a barber shop. He spent the money he had made from his job to marry off his two sisters.

Soon after I started working as a barber, I met a boy at the nearby lumber shop whose owner I made friends with. My friend said, "He's a war orphan. I'm thinking of hiring him." The boy was 15 or 16, and always had a lonely expression on his face. I now think that without our grandmother, my sisters, brother and I would have met the same fate.

Several years after that, when Takanobu was 26, he married a woman introduced to him by one of his friends. She was 2 years younger and was a hairdresser. After getting married, they built a beauty and barber shop along the national highway, where they both worked. After three years of marriage, they had a son.

Four years after our marriage when I was in high spirits enjoying my family, in 1965, I suddenly got a backache. Then, I had a slight fever for a while. My family doctor said, "I have no idea what disease this is." He eventually referred me to the Hiroshima University Hospital. At the hospital I was diagnosed with tuberculosis and was told that I would be admitted to the hospital as soon as a bed became available. I was worried because I had a son to look after. Instead of being admitted, I went to the hospital regularly as an outpatient and took streptomycin.

Although Takanobu recovered, people in the neighborhood found out about his disease. As a result, he could no longer work

[Document 11] Takanobu Hirano

were only the four of us left—two sisters, a younger brother and me. Helplessness filled my heart. I felt I had nobody to rely on.

If we had not had our grandmother, we would have had no choice but to live as A-bomb orphans. We are still very grateful to our grandmother. The four of us continued to live with her. Now that I think about it, our grandmother grew her own rice and vegetables but had no other source of income.

Back then, everyone was hungry all the time. We mixed minced radish in a small amount of rice to make our food go further. Day after day, we only ate a small amount of rice mixed with chopped radish or sweet potato. Since we had no shoes, we wore sandals to school. When it rained, sandals splashed mud on our clothes, so we were always barefoot on rainy days.

This is a story I heard long afterwards. One day, an elementary school teacher came to our house and wanted to adopt my younger sister. My older sister firmly opposed the offer, saying, "I don't want to part from my sister or brothers at any cost!" Our grandmother objected, too, and said, "I'll take care of my grandchildren myself." This is how my younger sister was able to remain in the house.

After that, Takanobu graduated from a junior high under the new educational system. He apprenticed himself to a barber when he was 15. Why did he choose this job?

There was a barber shop on the national highway. When I passed by the shop, it was always brightly lit and looked so beautiful. Since we used lamps and lanterns at that time, my heart danced at the sight of the shop's bright electric lights. That was why I wanted to become a barber.

machinery. They also found my father's body on the staircase.

Takanobu's grandmother asked the relief squad to dispose of his father's body. His stepmother and her younger sister had gone out early on the morning of August 6. They remain missing. His grandmother and the sister of his stepmother turned back to Yachiyo-cho.

A week later, on August 14, my grandmother, my sister, and I got a ride from a truck to go to Hiroshima and went back to our house in Zaimoku-cho. I will never forget how shocked I was when I got off the truck. The town had been reduced to a field of ashes. The tobacco shop and the clog shop were gone. I had never seen such a sight. I couldn't stop my knees from shaking.

I saw a dead horse floating on the river. There were almost no people in the neighborhood. We looked for a burned sewing machine and entered the house and there were the ashes of cremated remains heaped up on a burnt galvanized iron sheet.

"Soldiers cremated the body for us," our grandmother said quietly. I looked around and found a burnt kettle on the ground. We put the ashes into the kettle, and I carried it as we went home. To this day I still treasure the kettle. I resolved to keep it for the rest of my life.

After our father's funeral, my grandmother, my sisters, my brother, and I held a memorial service in Zaimoku-cho on August 19. Two months later, the wife of our father's brother remarried, took her son and left, saying: "My husband has been missing since he was drafted into the military." This was shocking news to me, for she had cared for us like a mother at our grandmother's house. "She, too, has left me," I said to myself, feeling abandoned.

Our grandmother was so old that I excluded her. To me, there

[Document 11] Takanobu Hirano

returned to Zaimoku-cho. I was later told that before leaving, he said, "I've got a little more work to do."

On the morning of August 6, I was playing in an empty lot in front of the house with the boys from next door.

"WHAM!"

"BOOOOM!"

A tremendous rumbling came out of the ground. I looked to the south and saw a giant mushroom cloud rising high. Since our grandmother's house had no electricity, she had no radio. I only heard a rumor that something serious had happened in the area of Kabe. I went to bed as usual that night.

The following day, I heard the news from a neighbor. "It seems Hiroshima has been destroyed!" That evening, my sisters and I started for Route 54 to meet our father when he came home. We left my youngest brother with our grandmother. My older sister led my younger by the hand. Yachiyo-cho was about 30 kilometers from the city center, and very few trucks were running on the road. Feeling tired, both of my sisters squatted on the road.

When we saw a truck approaching from a distance, we got up and peered inside. The truck was carrying a lot of injured people. Some were bandaged. Some were burned and sooty. Every time a truck passed by, we strained our eyes, hoping that it would pull over and our father would get off. We waited for him until it got dark. He didn't come home that night. Our grandmother tried to cope with the situation. "Don't worry. He'll soon be back!"

The next day and the day after that, my sisters and I went to Route 54 to welcome him home, but he never came back. On the fourth day, my grandmother and the sister of my stepmother went to Zaimoku-cho. They told me they soon recognized the site of Hirano Sock Merchants because of the burned sewing machines and other

Hiroshima August 6, 1945

In March 1945, when the war got more intense, the four children in the Hirano family were evacuated to their father's mother's house in Yachiyo-cho.

We had not been close to our grandmother, so we felt quite nervous at her house. The four of us huddled together all the time. When people are insecure, the loneliness of not having a mother is beyond words.

Our grandmother's house had no electricity. At night, we had to carry a lantern when we went to the outhouse. We also needed it when taking baths. It was inconvenient, and that also made us uneasy. Even during the war, the Yachiyo-cho area had a relatively laid-back atmosphere. There were 3 boys about my age next door. In summer, we used to go swimming in the river. The wife of my father's brother and our younger cousin also lived at our grandmother's house. She took good care of us like a mother.

Meanwhile, Takanobu's father and stepmother lived together in the factory-house in Hiroshima. Hearing sad news that many cities were being destroyed by air raids, Takanobu's father decided to evacuate the factory to the countryside. He found a factory site in Yachiyo-cho and started to move there. Takanobu's uncle went to pick up some luggage by horse-drawn carriage in the early morning on August 6. Takanobu's father usually went right back into the factory after seeing people off at the entrance. On that particular day, however, he watched until his uncle turned the corner of the street, as if he were reluctant to see him go. Perhaps he had a feeling that it would be the last time he would see his brother.

On the day before the atomic bomb was dropped, my father

[Document 11] Takanobu Hirano

Probably when I was 4 years old or so, my father was away from home on business, and I fell down the stairs and cut my lower lip near the right corner of my mouth. My mother quickly lifted me up in her arms and hurried to a nearby clinic. I still remember vividly the warmth of my mother at that time. In later years, when I was going through a tough time, I used to look at the scar on my lip in a mirror. That would bring my mother's warmth in my mind.

After my mother's death, my father decided to remarry a female relative who worked in the factory. He introduced her to us and said, "This is your new mother." She looked after my youngest brother.

During the war, we had an air-raid shelter under the living room in our house. When the air-raid warnings sounded, my sisters, my brother, and I quickly put on our air-raid hoods, opened up the floor and climbed down into the shelter. There we all held our breath and waited. The air-raid warnings were intense and sounded more frequently. The all-clear sirens were nonchalant. They made me feel relieved even though I was merely a child.

It happened when I was a little older. I was waiting for a bus to go back to Yachiyo-cho (now, Yachiyo-cho, Aki-Takata City), my parents' birthplace. All of a sudden, an air-raid warning sounded. All the people waiting for the bus hurried down to the air-raid shelter at the Western Drill Ground nearby. I jumped in with them. With a blanket covering us, we all sat still. I lifted one end of the blanket and looked up at the sky through a gap of the shelter. I saw B29 bombers flying in formation, and antiaircraft guns busily firing toward the bombers. Not one of the shells hit a B29. The bullets totally failed to reach the bombers. The B29s flew magnificently away. Even as a child, that made me wonder if Japan was actually going to win the war.

Hiroshima August 6, 1945

well. I had a sister two years older, another sister two years younger and a brother four years younger.

On the other side of our house was a big mansion owned by a family who ran a kimono fabric shop. The view of the garden from the second floor of their house was breathtaking. There was also a movie theater in the neighborhood, and I often watched movies through a knothole.

There was a bridge called Honkawa over the Honkawa River. In summer, we often dived into the river from the bridge. The water was clear, and there were crabs and shrimps on the sandy riverbed. The road to the bridge was a slight up-slope, so a horse-drawn carriage carrying a heavy load often got stuck before the bridge. When we saw such a carriage on the road, we helped push it.

On the other side of the river was Honkawa Elementary School. I went to Nakajima Elementary School, and the two schools were rivals. When we jeered at them saying, "Honkawa is run-down and old. It's insides are worn out." They called back, "Nakajima School is even worse." This competition is one of my good old memories.

After Takanobu's mother gave birth to her youngest son, she had difficulty recovering and was bedridden. Although the house was used for the factory and residence, his mother lived in a room in front of the house while recuperating. She passed away when Takanobu was 7 in 1943.

On the day my mother died, my teacher came to me and said, "Go home right away." When I got home, Mother took her hand out of her bed and held my hand silently. That was my final parting from my mother. I don't remember much about the days my mother was sick or about her funeral.

Document 11

I resolved to pass on the spirit of Hiroshima before turning 80

Takanobu Hirano
Born in November 1935. His house was in Zaimoku-cho, 300 meters from the hypocenter. Entered Hiroshima a week after the bombing when he was 9. His father was killed by the bomb; his mother died of an illness during the war. He was raised by his grandmother. Having worked at a barber shop and at a construction company, he now engages in community service activities. Seventy-eight years old; lives in Akitakata City.

My house was at the hypocenter; I am an entry victim

Hirano family's house was at 25 Zaimoku-cho (now, Nakajima-cho, Naka-ku.) That is near where the Cenotaph for the A-bomb Victims now stands in the Hiroshima Peace Memorial Park. Before the bombing, the area was a busy shopping district. Takanobu lived there until March 1945. His family ran a sock factory called "Hirano Sock Merchants," where several male and female workers knitted threads into socks using six or seven sewing machines every day.

There was a tobacco store next to our house. I was often sent there to buy cigarettes for my father. He always let me keep the change, so I looked forward to this errand. Next to the tobacco store was a wooden clog store. The lady there was talkative, and whenever she saw me, she talked to me by starting to say, "Hello! Little master." My family was wealthy, and I remember our neighbors called my sisters "Young ladies" and called me "Young master." They treated us company had confidence in me. I was nominated to be secretary of the union.

There was a single woman in her 40s at my taxi company. She was beautiful but seemed to be having trouble getting married.

"She was exposed to the bombing." That's what I heard. She had no keloid scars nor was she weak, but many people at that time could not get married because they were discriminated against due to their A-bomb experience. For this reason, my sisters hesitated to receive Atomic Bomb Survivor Health Books.

I suffered burns on the back of my hand, but they neither swelled nor turned into keloids. The burned skin looks like a bruise, though it still cuts and bleeds easily. I don't know whether this disorder has anything to do with the atomic bombing, but I also have trouble with my prostate. I still take medicine for it.

How much more pain is the atomic bomb going to cause us? Is it trying to keep us in hell? This whole talk is truth about war. No matter how often people turn their faces away from me, I am determined to speak openly about my experience about the atomic bomb. I believe this is my mission, the best thing I can do for world peace.

Station only to find that a button on her blouse had come off. She headed home to fix her blouse. She missed the train to work and was saved. Most of her coworkers, she told me later, were killed.

My other sister was missing for 2 days. We were certain that she was dead, but she came home in tatters. Her monpe work pants were burned and looked like underpants. She was in the city for 2 days in that miserable state, but she was fortunate never to suffer from A-bomb disease.

Kaoru's work in the military ended and he lost his job. He and his friends started dealing black-market goods for Occupation soldiers, who gave them Lucky Strike cigarettes, the artificial sweetener saccharin, and other desired products. However, his sister worried about him dealing in the black market, so she found him a new job. He worked as a live-in salesman for medical appliances.

After visiting clients, I always stopped by a noodle restaurant called "Marumatsu" in Matoba-cho on my way home. A bowl of noodles cost 15 yen. I fell in love with Emiko, who was working at the restaurant. Soon, we got married. I was 23; she was 18. Seven years had passed since the end of the war. I changed my job and became a life insurance agent. We were quite slow to be given a child, but after 11 years of marriage we had a daughter.

The Olympic Games were held in Tokyo in that year, and Japan entered its era of rapid economic growth.

The year after the Olympics, I thought I should make money on my own to adapt to the coming age, so I became a taxi driver. There were not many cars and the roads were not crowded, so it was easy to drive, and I got have my day's fare. I worked feverishly and made a good income. My sales performance was excellent, so the taxi mountains of ash with rakes, then carried off the ashes and the skulls.

I cremated the dead day after day—three to four hundred bodies a day. This means I burned nearly 8,000 bodies in 20 days. A huge crowd of people who had lost their relatives gathered where I was working. Some said their mothers were gone, and others said their children were missing.

Some said, "Give me some ashes," and took unidentified remains home with them. They used them for memorial services for their missing family members. Gradually, cremation sites increased until they filled every corner of the city. Smoke was seen rising up from each neighborhood.

The corpses decayed rapidly. If we had buried dead bodies without cremation we would have needed far more land. A cremated body was less than one tenth the size, so we had no choice but to burn them.

Around the time when the autumn breezes began to blow, Kaoru and his fellow civilian workers were each given an empty gun and 1,000 yen in cash. A thousand yen at that time was equivalent to about 800,000 yen today. At the end of October, Kaoru finally went home.

My mother was a nurse. She looked for tiny pieces of broken glass in my head and arms, removing them one by one with a pair of tweezers. She found about 30 pieces in all. By that time, 3 months had passed since the bombing. I heard that if you leave glass in your body for more than half a year, they cannot be removed.

My 2 sisters, both of whom worked at the Senda-machi branch office of the Hiroshima Postal Savings Bureau, were safe. In the morning of August 6, my oldest sister had arrived at Akinakano

the vicinity of Furue, Nishi-ku.

The job of disposing dead bodies included meals. The remains were pulled up from the rivers here and there and carried in trucks. There were 7 rivers running in Hiroshima, and the victims jumped into the rivers because they were thirsty and hot. Most died. There were countless corpses floating in the rivers. Because the tide would take them out, then bring them back in, the corpses were not washed out to sea. This, too, was a scene from hell, with the mouth of each river full of corpses where it poured into Hiroshima Bay.

Corpses that had been in the water for a week or 10 days had swollen bellies, and their rotting flesh was spongy and easily torn. When I pulled the arm of one corpse, it came right off. I had no time to worry about the horrible smell or feel disgusted. Thinking about it now horrifies me, but we were not even given gloves. We did this work with our bare hands.

Furue is full of rice paddies. Farmers built "dig-down fields," and the ridges were raised 50cm above the surface after harvesting the wheat. By laying old railroad ties over the ridges, we could line up 6 or 7 bodies at once. The spaces between the ties helped the bodies burn well. The National Railway gave us the old ties, which we carried in a truck owned by the Ordnance Depot. Farmers nearby provided sheaves of straw.

To burn the bodies efficiently, we alternated heads and feet. We poured on the heavy oil and lit fire. Bodies that had been soaking in water and were rotten were first inflated in the heat. Then they hardened like chinaware, and "Pop!"—their heads burst open. We put a large quantity of straw over their heads to keep them from flying into the air. We would hear the heads exploding one after another as the bodies turned to ash. Senior military workers scraped together severe burns or bleeding from their faces and bodies. However, no children, women or fatally injured people were allowed to ride in the military trucks. Kaoru was told to help form a treatment line in the cave.

I put a white paint-like medicine that was mercurial ointment mixed with zinc oil on the injured, who arrived one after another. They were glad to receive the treatment, and said, "This will save my life." It was cool in the cave, and I found it a relatively comfortable place to stay. Even so, it was summer, so the cave was filled with the stench from the victims' festering wounds. Their bodies were so swollen they were unable to move. They lay on the ground in their own excrement.

One time a young military officer got overexcited and lost his mind. All of a sudden, he shouted out, "I'll kill all American soldiers!" He began to shoot his gun in the cave.

Anybody who could walk was taken to Ninoshima Island in Hiroshima Bay. Those who couldn't walk were left in the cave. They lost their hair three or four days later, and most eventually died. Even under such circumstances, people with burned skin hanging from their bodies were continually being carried into the cave.

"Give me water! Water, please!" many cried out.

But the officer ordered us not to give them any. "If they drink water, they'll die! Don't give them water!" he said. We could do nothing but watch over them.

"I don't care if I die, just give me water!" Many shouted this, then passed away. One worker, who felt pity for the injured and gave them water, was hit by an officer.

Around August 10, Kaoru was ordered to dispose of corpses in

[Document 10] Kaoru Hashimoto

Department at the Army Ordnance Supply Depot. I was treated well, as my teacher had promised. I always brought home food like frozen tangerines and dried horsemeat, which made my family happy.

On August 6, I was 2 months shy of 16. I was on the night shift and was released from work at 8:00 in the morning. I was on my way home with Hayashi, a friend of mine. When we came to an area called Danbara, we heard a deafening roar and were instantly blown down by the blast. It was pitch dark. The next thing I knew, there was no one around us. The hypocenter of the explosion was on the west side of Hijiyama Hill, and Danbara, where we were, was behind the hill. In other words, the Hijiyama Hill protected us. However, the pressure of the blast from the sky was still monstrous.

Danbara Elementary School was blazing up with tremendous force. Some children were trapped under the collapsed school building crying, "Help! Help me!" Not knowing what to do, we did nothing. We just watched as the children were engulfed in flames. The children were still alive but we could not rescue them from the fire. I am still filled with regret. The children were burned alive in a hell on Earth, and all we could do was watch hell unfold.

I saw bodies of people who had dived into a fire cistern by the street. I saw people lying motionless on the roadside. I even saw a dead horse still standing. Some shards of glass propelled by the blast had pierced my field cap and were stuck in my head. My arms were covered in blood, but I felt no pain at the time.

In the evening on August 6, Kaoru was taken in a military truck to a cave in Niho-machi (now, Kita Okou-cho, Minami-ku). There were hundreds of victims with white, sludgy ointment painted on them. Without receiving any emergency treatment, victims were carried in trucks to the cave one after another. They were all suffering from

Hiroshima August 6, 1945

Document 10

I want to tell the truth because this is my mission for world peace

Kaoru Hashimoto
Born in October 1929. Was exposed to the atomic bombing at 15 on a street in Danbara-cho, 2.8 kilometers from the hypocenter. Eighty-four years old. Resides in Higashi Hiroshima City.

A gun and a thousand yen in cash
Twenty days I burnt the dead

There were 7 people in Hashimoto's family. His father ran a barbershop. His older brother worked as a civilian worker at the Army Ordnance Supply Depot in Kaita (now, Kaita-cho, Aki-gun). His 2 older sisters both worked at a branch office of the Hiroshima Postal Savings Bureau. Kaoru was the second son and the fourth of five children. He had a younger sister. He continued his education at an elementary school in Nakano (now, Nakano, Aki-ku).

When I was a second-year student in a higher school, my teacher told me, "Working as a civilian for the military to serve the country will make your parents proud. You'll get better rations, too. You can eat what others can't!" Six or seven of the 58 students in my class joined the Youth Pioneer Volunteer Army of Manchuria, and most of the others went to Japan National Railways.

In March 1944, I graduated from elementary school. Then as of April 1, I was assigned to the Repair Team in the Ordnance

the difference in destructive power.

The purpose of the Atomic Bomb Casualty Commission (ABCC) set up by GHQ on Hijiyama Hill was not to treat the survivors but only to collect the data from them. The survivors, who went there expecting medical treatment, were stripped naked, had their keloid scars photographed and their blood tested, and were then asked how their physical condition had changed. They were then sent home. I believe that the U.S. used the A-bomb survivors as guinea pigs.

Two years ago, in front of Hiroshima Station, I was asked about a train by a couple from Tokyo. They told me that they were temporarily evacuating to where their children were because the radiation emitted from the Fukushima nuclear power plant accident had increased in their neighborhood due to a change of wind direction. Radiation flows on the wind. On that day in 1945, my family headed for Mount Mitaki but thinking about it now, we were going in the same direction as the black rain and the radiation fallout.

At the urging of a member of the Hiroshima Peace Volunteers, I spoke for the first time in front of people I didn't know, about my experience. My wife was there and kept her head down while I spoke. I do not know how much longer I can live, but I'm going to talk about my experience as long as I can. That's what I have decided.

People from around the world visit Hiroshima with interest. I learned that the largest number of non-Japanese visitors is Chinese. Some time ago, my first son, who is living in the city of Fukuoka, said, "The era of China is coming. You better learn Chinese, I guess." Also encouraged by one of my friends, I am attending a Chinese language course in a lifelong learning program provided by the Open University of Japan in Hiroshima University. I go almost every day. I hope that someday I will be able to talk about my experience to Chinese people in their language.

Hiroshima August 6, 1945

bandaged up to his head. I was horrified. It reminded me of myself.

Although I have lived in Hiroshima, I never entered the A-bomb Museum (Hiroshima Peace Memorial Museum) until I was 71 years old. I didn't want to remember. I didn't want let anyone know my past. I avoided talking about the atomic bombing in every way possible. Every year when August 6 approached, I made myself turn off the TV news.

It was when I visited a peace exhibition that I started to think I should investigate a little about the atomic bomb and peace. I learned many things for the first time when I visited the A-bomb Museum. Japan failed to predict that the United States would drop an atomic bomb on Hiroshima.

"We won! We won a battle, and another battle!" The Imperial Headquarters announcements to the people were nothing but lies. A week before the atomic bomb was dropped, several adults were digging an air-raid shelter near my house. I followed my mother when she went out with cups of tea to serve them. They were talking and laughing.

"Hiroshima has never been hit by any air raids. This is really a good place to live!" On the day of the bombing, the military sounded an air-raid warning because of the reconnaissance planes that had come earlier, but no such warning was issued against the bomber that dropped the atomic bomb on the city. If an air raid warning had sounded, I would not have been on the school playground. I might not have had to suffer so much from the atomic bomb. I regret it so intensely.

"To bring an early end to the war" was an excuse. Obviously, the United States used Hiroshima and Nagasaki as sites to conduct nuclear tests. Worse still, the U.S. dropped a uranium bomb on Hiroshima and a plutonium bomb on Nagasaki in order to examine bombing. When walking with someone, I unconsciously but consistently walked on his or her right side. I always tried to keep people from noticing the keloid on my right hand. Only once did I tell a coworker I became close to in Osaka that I had experienced the atomic bombing.

"What about the A-bomb disease! Isn't that contagious?" That's what he said. There must have people who noticed the keloid scars on my hands and legs, but I never mentioned them myself.

In those days, most people married with the help of a matchmaker and arrangements made by their parents. Moreover, they referred to "background investigations" as "inquiries." Whenever Hiroatsu had an offer of marriage, he was refused as soon as the "inquiry" revealed that he was a survivor. "I'll never have a chance if I have an arranged marriage," thought Hiroatsu. But in 1966, he got married.

My wife was exposed to the atomic bomb in Ujina when she was 15 months old. I have never asked her anything about it. I'm afraid to ask. Even if I did, I could do nothing for her. Neither has my wife asked me anything about my experience. I have never told even my wife about my experience, and she never asked because of her sweetness.

My wife became pregnant when she was 30 years old. I was filled with anxiety. I had heard the rumor that women who exposed to radiation from the A-bomb were likely to give birth to children with disabilities. I couldn't sleep at night. When our first son was born healthy, I was so happy I wept alone.

When our second son was 2, he developed herpes. He had what looked like keloid scars on his face and had to have his neck

Osaka alone.

My mother became ill and spent a lot of time in bed. She ended up in the hospital with liver cancer. She spent the following 2 years there. Due in large part to her hospitalization, I quit my job in Osaka and returned to Hiroshima. I was 21 years old at that time. When I visited my mother in the hospital, she said, "You were exposed to radiation from the atomic bomb, so take good care of yourself and live a long happy life, Hiroatsu."

"You've been the nicest to me of all my sons." This was my last conversation with her. She was only 49. For 15 years after the atomic bombing, my mother went through continuous hardship. Although she was exposed to the bomb herself, she tried desperately to do everything she could think of to heal my burns and cure my keloids. Soon after my mother's death, the aunt who had always been mean to her also passed away. When I was at her bedside before she died, she apologized to me by saying, "Forgive me, Hiroatsu, for having been so hard on your mother."

Hiroatsu applied for an Atomic Bomb Survivor Health Book in 1956, and has since had a physical checkup once a month.

I have been exposed to radiation once, so I never know when I might get leukemia. I still can't get over the fear that I will develop some A-bomb disease. And, I don't have any short-sleeved summer shirts. No matter how hot it is, I always wear long-sleeved shirts. While I worked for a trucking company or a taxi company, I always found excuses not to participate in company retreats. The mere thought of taking a bath with my fellow workers made me miserable.

I never brought up the fact that I had experienced the atomic happily. When I touched my head, I could feel the rough stubble and was overjoyed. As my burns healed, they started to itch horribly. When I scratched the skin around the scabs, pus oozed out, and scabs formed again. Fortunately, I was managed to get my right hand moving by the time I entered junior high school.

Since I have keloids on my right hand and the backs of my legs, the skin there does not respire. The skin in those areas are cold even in summer. I am also unable to sit cross-legged. Even today, the keloid scar on my right leg twitches when I sit this way. I feel sluggish all the time. I get tired easily and often can hardly keep standing. I soon have to lay down to rest. On sunny days, I feel sick, as if I had sunstroke. I have suffered with these conditions ever since the bombing and to this day. I also have an irregular pulse, but I don't know if this is related to the atomic bomb.

My father's family was mean to my mother and me because we had been exposed. I couldn't stand to see them saying unpleasant things to my mother. My father's brother and other relatives had been discharged from military service and were living in the house. My family of five just landed in their house, so it was inevitable that we were treated as a burden. Several times I saw my mother watching the fire on the hearth with tears in her eyes after being bullied by my aunt. "Get out of this house!" my aunt once told us.

That was the last straw. I replied back, "My mother had to be in the bombing because she went to Oshiba because she was no longer allowed to live here. If she were never kicked out of the house, it would never have turned out like this!"

Hiroatsu graduated from high school and started working at a transport company. After about 2 years, he applied for a transfer to the Osaka branch. His request was quickly accepted, so he left for

Hiroshima August 6, 1945

off. He started going to school again in the 4th grade.

Most of the houses around my grandparents' house were tilted at least a little by the blast. I had keloid burns on my right arm and legs, and people around me treated me cruelly, saying, "Hey, Mr. stinky! A burn!" At that time, it was thought that A-bomb diseases were contagious. "The son of the Taniguchi family has A-bomb disease!" People often spoke ill of me behind my back, which was so distressing.

I especially disliked sports day. All the students had to wear short-sleeved shirts and shorts, so everybody saw my keloid scars. My scars had twisted up tight causing me to move awkwardly. No matter how much I was bullied, I never told my mother. I didn't want to make her unhappy. However, there were times when people openly abused me in front of her. My mother would remain silent with a stern look on her face pretending she didn't hear anything.

My right hand, with which I had shaded my face from the atomic bomb, hardened into a fist; with my little finger, third finger and middle finger curled inward, I could barely move my thumb and forefinger. When I forced my fingers to move, the skin between my little finger and third finger tore and blood gushed out. When I tried to tear my curled, fused fingers apart, I always ended up tearing the skin. Nevertheless, I kept pulling my fingers apart after the blood and pus dried.

When I heard about skin grafted from areas like the buttocks and thighs to replace keloid scars to make faces smooth, I went to consult a doctor about the treatment. I was told that operating on fingers was not possible because they constantly move. When I was a 6th grader, my hair finally began to grow.

"Your hair is beginning to grow, Hiroatsu!" said my mother

[Document 9] Hiroatsu Taniguchi

"Peeling it off slowly hurts a lot more," my mother said as she jerked it off in a stroke. Every time I had to cry out. There was no remedy available even in hospitals. There was no other way to treat my wounds. Later, we were able to get some grease paper from a pesticide plant, and we used that instead of the cloth to treat my wounds.

The open sores on my burned skin smelled so horrible that my brothers kept away from me. Only my mother came to me saying, "Don't worry. You are going to get better, for sure!" She made a concoction from Saururaceous plants like Lizard's-tail and Water-dragon. These were believed to work as an antibiotic. She had me drink the stuff every day. My family worked hard picking the plants. Soon, all around my house the plants were gone, so my mother started learning to ride a bicycle just to go around looking for Saururaceous plants. As soon as she learned how to ride, she went to pick the plant deep in the mountains more than an hour away.

For two and a half years, my life was nothing more than repeated inflammations of the burns and the scabs. I stayed in my house, sitting all the time. I used my hands and my rear end to move. Because I festered so badly I couldn't use bedding even in winter. In summer, flies gathered on my wounds, which were soon infested with maggots. My mother always removed the maggots with chopsticks. To make matters worse, my hair fell out.

Hiroatsu's father was demobilized and returned home. His father was a military man by nature and always had a stern look on his face. Hiroatsu hardly ever went to school after the atomic bombing. His father always scolded him for not doing well in school. Before each meal he made his son say his multiplication tables up to the 9's. By the time he finished the 3rd grade, all the scabs had fallen

Hiroshima August 6, 1945

potatoes in our restaurant.

The Taniguchi family decided to go further out to Hiroatsu's father's parents' house in Nishihara (now, Nishihara, Asa Minami-ku). Five family members—grandmother, mother and 3 boys—walked about 4 kilometers. Hiroatsu was forced to walk bent forward due to the twisted skin on his burns. He moved forward unsteadily and slowly.

Dead bodies were lying right in the street all along the way. We had to step around them. I saw many people who had thrust their heads into fire cisterns seeking water and died like that. At the foot of Shinjo Bridge, people had gone down to the river where they died and were floating on the river. I was desperate to drink water and tried to go to the river several times, but every time, my mother grabbed my hand and pulled me back to her. "Don't drink the water! If you do, you'll die!" My mother never let my hand go until we got to my grandparents' house. As soon as we got there, my grandmother could no longer move. She was bedridden for 3 months, then died.

The burns I suffered were severe. In particular, the backs of my knees down onto my calves, which were not covered by my shorts, were seriously burned. My legs seemed permanently bent. I couldn't stretch them out. I slept on my back with my knees up. There were times when the back of my knee got stuck, my calf to my thigh, and peeling them apart was excruciatingly painful. My mother cut her kimono into strips and wrapped my knees.

She put medicine that looked like talcum powder on the burns. The next morning, the cloth was hard with blood and pus. Peeling the cloth off was also extremely painful. Each and every morning I used to groan and sweat oily sweat.

that she had been watering the yard in her black polka-dot blouse. The black dots turned to burns, leaving black spots on her skin. My mother had been covered with dust and was waiting for me. I arrived home in tears and as soon as I saw my mother I clung to her. She couldn't stop crying and saying, "I'm glad you're back! I'm so glad!" I was so fearful I kept holding onto her kimono sleeve. I followed her wherever she went.

My grandmother had been in the room on the second floor where we kept our family Buddhist altar. She was unhurt. My brother, who was three years older than me, survived in a classroom at his school, and had returned home.

Many neighbors began to flee. We heard that fire had broken out in the city. Everyone headed for the hills of Mitaki, where there was no fire. In the bamboo grove there, families and friends were sitting in small groups. Some were burned; others badly injured. A mother carrying a baby with its head hanging backward lifelessly on her back was wandering around like a sleepwalker. I couldn't tell whether the baby was alive or not. There were people whose clothes had burned leaving them covered in soot and naked. Some just sat down, uttering incomprehensible phrases, while others remained standing like ghosts.

Soon black rain started to fall. The coldness of the rain felt good on my burns. People bathed in the rain, faces up, opening their mouths to drink. I, too, turned my face up and went around with my mouth open to catch raindrops. My mother came rushing over and said, "Don't leave my side without my permission!" She then took me back with her. One family picked up a piece of burnt galvanized tin roofing to keep themselves from the rain. My mother went back home to collect things we needed. Since our house was completely destroyed, however, she could find nothing more than some steamed

Hiroshima August 6, 1945

first graders near the platform on the playground used for morning assembly.

Out of nowhere, I heard the faint sound of a bomber. I looked up at the sky, shading my eyes with my right hand. The summer sun was so dazzling I squinted, when all of a sudden, a sharp flash blinded me. In the next instant, there came a deafening roar—"Ka-boom!" Just as I was squatting down as trained to do, I was carried off by the blast. I came to in an eerie silence. I opened my eyes slightly and saw a cloud of sand enveloping everything. Ten or so children, with whom I had been playing, were lying or sitting on the playground crying. Our classroom shack had been completely destroyed.

One boy was standing and crying out loud. His shorts were burned to tatters. I quickly looked at my navy blue shorts and was relieved to see that they were not damaged. However, when I looked at them later, I found that the back right side was burned dark brown. I didn't notice it because it was in the back.

I was wearing a white, open-necked shirt with short sleeves, my head, and my right arm and both legs were burned where they were not covered by my clothes.

Fortunately, my face was not burned. That was probably because I had held my right hand over my eyes to block the sun while looking for the bomber. Most of my face was in the shade of my hand. However, my right arm was badly burned. My head was the most seriously injured. I had close-cropped hair, which instantly burned off, leaving my head covered with what seemed to be hot coal tar. My head must have looked terrible because when I touched it, the skin peeled off.

I started to walk toward home crying. I lost my shoes, which were blown off by the blast, so I had to walk barefoot. My house was tilted over, and my mother was waiting for me out in front. She said

[Document 9] Hiroatsu Taniguchi

Document 9

Someday I want to talk about my A-bomb experience in Chinese

Hiroatsu Taniguchi
Born October 1938. At six years of age was exposed to the bombing on the playground of Oshiba Elementary School, 2.3 kilometers from the hypocenter. Worked at a transportation company until he was almost 70 years old. Currently studying Chinese so he can talk about his experience to people all over the world. Intends to do so as long as he can. Seventy-five years old, resides in Higashi-ku, Hiroshima.

My mother took desperate care of me; she was exposed, too

Hiroatsu's mother had a son from a previous marriage who was his older brother. His father was serving in Dalian, China, as an aeromechanic. While his father was away, his mother probably felt uncomfortable in her husband's house. She went back to her parents' home in Oshiba-cho with her 3 children and helped out at her mother's restaurant.

That morning, an air-raid warning sounded, and my family of five took refuge in an air-raid shelter. The air-raid warning was cleared at around 7:30. I walked to Oshiba Elementary School, which was about 10 minutes from my house. In those days, soldiers were stationed in the school, so we couldn't use the classrooms. We studied in a shack built in front of the school building. The upper-class students were mobilized to work in factories, and the soldiers had gone out on a mission. Only lower-class students were left in the school. With a little free time before class started, I was playing with other develop symptoms of an atomic bomb disease.

The members of my family who returned to Korea lived truly miserable lives. My father died less than 10 years after returning to his homeland. My brother suffered a ruptured aneurysm. My younger sister had acute leukemia, and another brother developed liver cancer. They all died young, leaving my mother behind. Obviously, they were affected by radiation from the atomic bombing.

From the time I started working at Musica in Enkobashi-cho, I've worked in coffee shops for a total of 60 years. I came from Korea to Japan when I was 4, and 80 years have passed since then. I was able to live without feeling the uneasiness of living in a foreign country because I have been supported by the people around me. I've never experienced any Japanese making discriminatory remarks about me, nor have I been treated unfairly because I am a Korean. Because I happened to live in Hiroshima I encountered the atomic bomb, an experience very few human beings have had.

If a nuclear war were to occur again, it would eventually lead to the extinction of human beings. These days I hear growing calls for a military buildup or a national defense force. This is totally unacceptable. If a war starts, the killing will be terrible. People will kill each other with no hesitation. After the war, people like us will be left to suffer. Two or three generations will suffer.

The absence of war is better. Peace is the best. I've lived a full and happy life. Japan is a beautiful, wonderful country. I hope that Korea, where I was born, and Japan, where I've spent most of my life, will trust and cooperate with each other to pave the way for lasting peace, like my wife and I have found.

The Monument in Memory of the Korean Victims of the A-bomb stands in Hiroshima Peace Memorial Park. Every year on August 6, I pray at that monument from 4:30 to 5:00 in the morning.

[Document 8] Toshio Morimoto

Toshio worked at Musica as the manager for 10 years. The Café was increasingly thriving and the annual year end concert became so popular it attracted as many as 200 people. Many regular attendees were music fans, including the mayor of Hiroshima and famous residents in the city, such as writers, artists, poets and students; they all enjoyed classical music during those years.

Toshio later became independent and opened his own coffee shop. After that, his life was focused on managing his coffee shop for 40 years, until he closed the shop. Toshio has concentrated all his life on overcoming the sufferings of the atomic bombing. However, the aftereffects remain present in himself and his family.

I was exposed to the bombing in Matsubara-cho (now, Matsubara-cho, Minami-ku), 1.7 kilometers from the hypocenter. Over the years, I have had many health problems. I have persistent diarrhea from time to time. I used to go to the hospital frequently to get vitamin shots. I have also suffered from gastric ulcer, kidney trouble and other internal disorders. I collapsed from a heart attack and have been taken by ambulance to the hospital a total of seven times. My wife is also a hibakusha. On the day of the bombing, she was sleeping in the basement of her boarding house. The radiation from the bombing may have had adverse effects on her as well.

Our first daughter suffered uterine cancer. Our second daughter has gone through three operations for tongue cancer and is now being treated for thyroid cancer. Experts have said that the second generation would not be affected by the atomic bombing, so none of them even have an Atomic Bbomb Survivor Health Book. However, the fact is, two of my daughters have contracted and are suffering from cancer. I cannot help worrying that our grandchildren will obtained this record on the black market in Osaka, and only with great difficulty. I still vividly remember that day. It was snowing. The shop only had seating for 30 people. Outside the café, a large crowd of people stood and listened attentively to the music. Music knows no boundaries. At a time when people were short of food, it was a moving sight to see so many people healing their hearts with Beethoven's music. That Ninth Symphony record concert continued to be enjoyed by the local community for many years.

Musica was in the black market for 10 years, then moved downtown to Ebisu-cho in Naka-ku. It moved into a wooden three-story building and was the only music café in Hiroshima. On moving to the new location in January 1955, I was officially assigned as the manager of Musica and was entrusted with all responsibilities regarding the management of the café. Café Musica was quite prosperous and had nearly 20 waitresses. I married one of the waitresses. She was a year younger. Here name was Mariko, and she is still my wife.

At the time, however, her parents and relatives strongly opposed our marriage. It was probably because I was both Korean and exposed to the bombing near the hypocenter. Also, Mariko's family had already chosen a marriage partner for her. All of her relatives were furious and did everything they could against our marriage.

"What a silly affair you have!" her relatives would say, attacking her. "I'm in love with him, and that is not a silly thing!" she answered back—an episode that she and I still talk about. She also told me that there was even a rumor going around in her neighborhood that she had eloped with a Korean man. We married despite the opposition of her relatives, so her parents disowned her for some time. Despite all this, these days her relatives say, "You married the most affectionate man of our family. You must be happy, aren't you?"

[Document 8] Toshio Morimoto

However, my brother's life after that was complete misery. When I helped him sit up, I saw that the wounds on his back were infested with maggots. We went so far as to make him take powdered human bones as medicine, as we were told that human bones worked wonders on wounds.

On New Year's Eve that year, my family and two other Korean families talked about returning to Korea. It was decided that my family would return first. At that time, I already had a job in Hiroshima, and I couldn't speak any Korean. I had grown up in Japan since I was 4. What worried me most was that I couldn't speak, read, or write Korean. The mere thought of this made me hesitate to go back. Some of my relatives and friends decided to stay in Japan. I, too, decided to stay in Hiroshima.

I started to work at an eatery in front of Hiroshima Station. A relative, also a Korean resident in Japan, had started a coffee shop and restaurant right in front of Hiroshima Station. The owner's wife was my father's sister, which was why I was able to work there. At that time, the Enkobashi-cho (now, Enkobashi-cho, Minami-ku) area right by the station was a black market district that had rapidly recovered after the war. There were intense battles over territory. The conflicts between crooked peddlers and gangsters became nationally known due to a hit movie series called "Battles Beyond Love and Justice," distributed by Toei Production Company.

That coffee shop and restaurant was later born again as a music café called "Musica" and continued to do a fairly good business. The owner acquired classical music records on the black market and opened a music café because he wanted to use music to energize people in Hiroshima. "Musica" is a Spanish word for "music hall."

On New Year's Eve in 1946, the year the café opened, we offered a concert playing Beethoven's Ninth Symphony. The owner machi (now, Kawara-machi, Naka-ku). His house was completely destroyed. He then headed for a house where his family had decided to gather in an emergency. There, he found his mother, younger sister, and youngest brother. But another younger brother, who had gone out to play, was missing.

My family had decided to gather at a friend's house in Kouchi-mura (now, Itsukaichi-cho, Saeki-ku) in case of emergency. We had already taken a wooden chest and other household necessities to that house. My mother, younger sister, and youngest brother were already there. My father, who worked at a cannery for the Army Provisions Depot in Ujina, came and joined us. He had a few cuts on his head from broken glass.

Only my younger brother, who seemed to have been playing outside near our house, was missing. We searched for him everywhere but kept failing to find him. I went mainly to look in schools used as shelters. I called his name out loud, but no answer came. I continued to look at the face of each injured person.

Three days after the atomic bombing, I was told that a boy who looked like my brother was at Kusatsu Elementary School. I hurried over there. Hundreds of injured people filled the classrooms. Among them, I found a badly burned boy lying on the floor. He had hideous burns all over his body, which was almost naked. His head and face were so severely burned it was hard to tell who he was. I recognized him only by the belt buckle he wore with his trousers. It was one I had made but had given to my brother because he wanted it so badly.

I then remembered that my brother had a scar on his right ankle. When I checked the boy's right ankle, I found that scar. I shook the boy and called out his name. He nodded slightly. I was finally convinced he was my brother. Thus, all of my family was still alive.

[Document 8] Toshio Morimoto

Station, its power dropped to near zero. "I wonder if an oil is leaking. Check it," the driver told me. I went under the truck to see about the oil.

The instant I crawled under the truck, a dazzling flash so bright that I couldn't open my eyes, filled the air.

Then, booooom, a tremendous explosion like nothing I had ever heard. Then, a powerful wind. Pieces of wood and all sorts of things flew all around. A huge cloud of smoke rose high into the sky, then things like dust and dirt started falling down like rain.

Fortunately, I was saved because I was under the truck. The driver was also uninjured because he was in the truck. We immediately decided to walk back to the branch office in Ujina. On the way to Ujina, we saw incredibly horrible sights on the streets along the Hijiyama streetcar line. Pieces of wood and roof tiles from collapsed houses were scattered all over the ground. The streetcars were standing still. People were walking around with their hair burned and frizzled, wearing nothing but rags for clothes. Many were barely able to walk; many could not.

Although the Ujina branch office building was not damaged, we were told to return home immediately to check on our families. We all had no choice but to walk home. After crossing Miyuki Bridge, I passed the Hiroshima Red Cross Hospital and came to Takanobashi shopping arcade. There, crowds of people were running around nearly naked, trying to escape. When I crossed Meiji and Sumiyoshi Bridges, I looked down the rivers and saw hundreds of people floating the water. No one dared to rescue those people. Most of them were probably already dead. All I could do was watch and pray for their safety.

In desperation, Toshio approached his house in Kawara-

Hiroshima August 6, 1945

Document 8

Every year on August 6, I visit the Monument in Memory of the Korean Victims of the A-bomb

Toshio Morimoto: Korean name Kim Sugabu
Born in Pusan, South Korea in 1929. Came to Japan at 4 years old. At 16, was exposed to the bombing under a truck in Matsubara-cho (now, Matsubara-cho, Minami-ku), 1.7 kilometers from the hypocenter. After the World War II for 60 years, he has worked in coffee shops, including managing a music café called "Musica." Eighty-four years old; resides at Nishi-ku, Hiroshima.

Coming from South Korea, exposed to the bomb
Focused on surviving and living my life in Hiroshima with my family

Toshio was born in South Korea. He came to Japan with his parents when he was 4 and lived in Hiroshima. His father's younger brother, who had come to Hiroshima earlier, ran a laundry. Toshio says that many South Koreans lived near his house. In 1939 when he entered junior high school, his family was forced to change their family name from "Kim" to "Morimoto" because of the order from the Japanese government. When he was 16, Toshio worked as an assistant truck driver transporting military supplies.

That day we were carrying 60 bales of rice on the truck. I say "truck," but it was a charcoal-driven vehicle that gave us nothing but trouble with the engine and electrical system. On that day, as always, the engine was not working properly. When we got near Hiroshima

[Document 7] Yoshiharu Nakamura

One aspect of the bombing that I will never forget has to do with my best friend from Hiroshima Commercial School, Goro Mitsuda. He was an excellent athlete, especially good at kicking up on the horizontal bar. He was the class hero. His family sold baby chicks at their store called "Mitsuda Chicks". When I moved to Saga with my mother, I had nowhere to work so I wrote Goro a letter saying that I wanted to raise chicks and have them lay eggs. He never replied. Instead, I received a letter from his older brother informing me of his death. It was a short letter but I was devastated.

On August 6, Goro left home at 8 in the morning to get a special cadets medical checkup at the Hiroshima Chamber of Commerce and Industry Building, which was only 260 meters from the hypocenter. Goro was so strong and fit, but he died young. I am skinny and not very strong, but somehow I am still alive. This makes me believe that our lives are intertwined and ruled by fate or destiny. This is why I have pledged to always do my best do whatever I can for peace.

under the Station to have their bags checked. My rice was safe because I always put the vegetables on top of the rice.

At some point I came across a friend from Hiroshima Commercial School. He came from a wealthy family and lived in a big mansion. Everything was burnt out by the bomb so he built a shack over the ruins of his house and was living in Nagarekawa. When I asked him, "Do you mind if I build a shed next to you?"

He said, "You are more than welcome."

I quickly built a 40-square meter shack next to his and moved in. The walls were made of wood. The roof was made of bark sliced off tree trunks. It had two small tatami mat rooms with a kitchen and a toilet. I lived there with my brother and sister for nearly three years.

My oldest sister, who had lived with my mother, got married. Our life became easier when we were able to get our mother back from Saga. We moved to Rakurakuen in Itsukaichi-cho (now, Itsukaichi-cho, Saeki-ku), where the four of us lived together. Later, I married and left home. I was 34 and my wife was 26. She was from Hiroshima, but she had not been there at the time because of school evacuation. Her family did not complain about me being a hibakusha.

Yoshiharu's sister got a job at a trading company under the Mitsubishi Corporation. The company treated its employees well, so Yoshiharu went to work at the same company. It delivered goods like furniture and refrigerators to occupation families in Kure City. The company's task ended when the occupation ended, so the company was dissolved. Yoshiharu then worked at a security firm, based on an introduction by his brother. He was later headhunted by Hiroshima Sugar, which was partially owned by that security firm, and worked there until retirement.

[Document 7] Yoshiharu Nakamura

My mother's parents' home was in Kashima (now, Kashima City) in Saga Prefecture. The West Japan Newspaper I read in Saga said that Hiroshima was totally ruined by a new type of bomb. My mother's relatives thought we were all dead. When my mother, my two sisters and I showed up, they were shocked.

My older brother was discharged on the day the war ended, so he also visited us there. My oldest sister found a job at a noodle factory across the street from my mother's parents' house, but the rest of us had no way to make a living. Eventually, my other sister and brother went back to their former workplace in Hiroshima, the Telephone Bureau. I was also able to work there, thanks to my brother and sister. Due to the war and the atomic bombing, they were understaffed, so they gladly hired me.

We rented a room from my father's parents in Atago-machi so the three of us could work in Hiroshima. My mother and my oldest sister stayed in Saga. Thus, my family lived separately for some time.

The following spring, the lymph gland in my neck started swelling but almost no doctors or hospitals in Hiroshima were able to treat me. I went to Saga to look for a doctor. At the hospital in Saga I was told to have surgery right away. I took some days off work and had an operation. Eventually I recovered but I had to return to Saga once every two months. One of the reasons was food. There was still a lack of food in Hiroshima, but in the Kashima countryside we could get plenty of rice and potatoes.

My mother always worried if we were eating enough and would make me take home rice and vegetables. I hid the food in the bottom of my backpack. Even after the war the government prohibited the trading of food and other goods. If the police discovered rice out of the rationing system, they would confiscate it. At Moji Station, passengers had to line up in four rows in the underground passage

happening." Four or five days after we arrived in Kabe, I got a high fever the cause of which was unknown. I was so weak I couldn't even stand. All I could do was crouch down and focus in staying alive. It was about half a year later when I found out that this weakness was one of the symptoms of the A-bomb disease.

On August 15, the Emperor announced the end of war. Just a week before, speaking the word "Emperor" made people stand at attention, but when we heard the broadcast we just listened in a daze.

It was the first time that ordinary people ever heard the voice of the Emperor. People were saying, "Is it true? Is the war over?" But many simply said, "I couldn't understand what the Emperor meant."

The day the war ended, my family left for my mother's hometown in Saga Prefecture. Since my health had improved a bit, my family helped me get onto a train. We had Disaster Certificates, so we didn't have to pay for the ride. Disaster Certificates were distributed by soldiers along with dry biscuits on the day the bomb was dropped on Hiroshima. People living in the same neighborhood were gathering together and fleeing in groups, heading to the same designated evacuation area. The soldiers didn't bother checking the identity of each person. Although it was a certificate, it didn't even include a name or birthdate. It was just a piece of paper with the words "Disaster Certificate" written on it. We were later able to exchange our certificates for "Atomic Bomb Survivor Health Books."

We left Hiroshima Station and arrived at Otake Station. Beyond Otake the railroad tracks had been ruined by air raids. We then crossed a railway bridge over the Oze River and made our way to Iwakuni on foot. From there we got on a train to Saga Prefecture.

safe. My whole family was lucky to be alive.

Four of the Nakamura family headed for Ochiai-mura (now, Ochiai, Asa Kita-ku), the designated evacuation area for their neighborhood. On their way, they met crowds of people with burnt and blistered skin.

I had no ability to feel horror or pity on seeing those people. I must have been emotionally numbed. Telephone poles had fallen. Electric wires were scattered here and there. Burnt bodies were everywhere. We stepped over tremendous numbers of bodies, avoiding actually stepping on them, and escaped. Floating dead bodies filled the river. Two soldiers were distributing dry biscuits so we got some. We passed by some refugees, while others went ahead of us, but we kept going until we passed Higashi Ohashi Bridge.

We arrived at Ochiai-mura in the evening. It received no damage from the bombing, and the atmosphere was quite peaceful. I remember that when we got there, my strength left me all of sudden. We had already found a farmer who said we could stay the night. That night, the family we stayed with put up mosquito nets for us. I remember feeling so strongly, "I am really lucky".

However, the Nakamura family had no house to go back to. This meant that they would have to rely on a distant relative. The next day, they proceeded to Kabe (now, Kabe, Asa Kita-ku) where their late father's sister-in-law lived.

On August 6, the people in Kabe saw a giant mushroom cloud in the direction of Hiroshima. They were saying things like, "I have no idea what happened, but it seems there's something horrible was what caused the "black rain."

About then, I realized I was covered in blood from my shoulders to my arms. Countless pieces of broken glass had pierced me through my navy blue hard-collar railway uniform. I had just become a conductor, so my collar badge was white. My white badge was red with blood.

The area in front of Hiroshima Station was in chaos, filled with a tremendous crowd of people. The extension of the station building was totally destroyed.

I shouted to my boss, "May I go home to see if my family is all right?"

"Go ahead!" So I left with permission.

I ran out of the station and ran with all my might. My house was about a 20-minute walk away. The Dambara Elementary School in front of our house was on fire and burning furiously. My house was totally smashed. My mother and older sister were bloody. They had been blown around by the blast were standing dazed in front of the house. They had both crawled out from the collapsed house, but they were badly hurt. I could only imagine how they had managed to escape the ruined house with no place to step. Their hair was a mess; their faces black with soot.

Behind our house, three combat medics started putting up a medical aid tent. They offered first-aid treatment, putting oil on the burns and wrapping bandages around open wounds. I had my wounds cared for there. Then, my oldest sister, who was working for the Army Ordnance Depot as a Women's Volunteer Labor Corps, came home. She said that the Ordnance Depot was crushed by the blast but she was unhurt. My brother, who previously to worked for the Telephone Bureau, was drafted and assigned to the communication corps in the Ozuki Unit in Yamaguchi Prefecture. We assumed he was cargo trains coming to Hiroshima were either to or from Himeji or Shimonoseki. We were not in charge of the district beyond these cities, so it was impossible to go to Saga.

Yoshiharu's main job was switching the cargo train couplings. Switching the couplings sounds easy but it was quite a difficult job. He had to consider the horsepower of the train, then, make a plan for the number of cars to connect. He also had to think about the order of cars that would be decoupled according to station orders. The cars for the first stop had to be connected at the end, with the ones for the second stop coming before them, etc.

Locomotives at that time were the steam, mostly D51 and C31. The D51, equipped with 4-by-4 drive wheels, was a high-powered train that could pull 30 cars. "D" is the fourth letter of the alphabet, which meant it had four sets of drive wheels. "C" meant three sets of drive wheels, so the C31 was a locomotive with 3-by-3 drive wheels. Fifty-one and thirty-one were model numbers. I had to take a test to become a cargo conductor, so on my days off, I studied for the test.

On that morning, I was studying as usual with 12 of my coworkers. We were on the second floor in the wooden Conductor Building next to Hiroshima Station. I was by the window at 8:15 am. In that instant, just as I became aware of a bright flash like the spark from a train, my body was lifted and carried away. I heard nothing. Thought it had been a clear sunny day, my surroundings turned pitch black. I groped for the handrail of the stairs and went down to the first floor following that handrail. I went outside.

I saw a gruesome sight. As the darkness lifted little by little from the ground up, it seemed like black dust was being vacuumed into the sky. It didn't rain where I was, but I always thought that black dust

Hiroshima August 6, 1945

My father's job was recruiting and managing craftsmen to deliver window frames and other fittings to the Navy, but he fell ill and spent his days in bed. Fresh fish was out of reach for ordinary people, so I often brought home braised mackerel served at the dining in the shipyard. My father was always happy to see it. It was a time of severe food shortage, and we could hardly get any food. When we heard Eba dumplings made from rice bran were to be sold in Eba (now, Eba, Naka-ku), I quickly ran out to buy some. If I was lucky, I would be able to get some. If I was unlucky, I would go home empty handed.

There was also a shortage of medicine. My father had bronchitis, so when he started coughing hard my mother would rub his back. Other than that, all he could do was rest. That was his "treatment," the best we could do. My father got weaker and weaker. He passed away in 1944, at the age of 56.

In March the following year, Yoshiharu turned 18 and graduated from Hiroshima Prefectural Commercial School. He got a job at the National Railway.

There was almost no work other than military-related companies. Most of my classmates remained the shipyard. However, there was also work at the National Railway, which needed conductors for trains carrying military supplies. In those days, no one could freely choose a job.

My mother wanted to move back to her hometown in Saga Prefecture after my father died. One of the reasons I entered the National Railway was because I thought that I might be able to have a chance to go to Saga. But I found while working there that the

My fate is to do my best for peace

Yoshiharu Nakamura
Born in May 1927. After graduating from Hiroshima Commercial School, worked for the National Railway. Studying to be a train conductor when the bomb exploded. Exposed to the bomb in a building within the Hiroshima Station Conductor Section, 1.9 kilometers from the hypocenter. Fled to Ochiai-mura, then evacuated to his mother's home town in Kyushu, Saga Prefecture. Eighty-six years old, resides in Saeki-ku, Hiroshima.

No reply from Goro
My best friend, departed

I had 2 older sisters and 1 older brother. I was the youngest of 4 siblings. We used to play soccer in a vacant lot until sunset with three boys who lived in the neighborhood. I remember New Year's Day when my father was still healthy. He would use a wooden mallet to pound steamed rice to make cake. My mother would turn the rice in the pestle between each whack. My sisters would roll the rice pasted into cakes. My father loved sumo wrestling. Whenever he could, he listened to sumo with his ear glued to the radio.

While Yoshiharu was in elementary school, the war grew increasingly intense. He studied through the first semester of second grade, but after that he was called out to student mobilization. Day after day he welded and bent pipes at Mitsubishi Heavy Industries, Hiroshima Shipyard. School lessons took place only once a week. A teacher would come on Saturdays and students would listen to the teacher in the shipyard dining room.

Hiroshima August 6, 1945

recognized for his calligraphy ability and was mainly asked to write certificates and addresses on business envelopes. He worked at that until retirement age, but his clients continued to request his hand-brushed calligraphy. In 1995, he started his own company called Kihara Kikaku, where he still works as a calligrapher.

When I was young, I hid the fact that I was an atomic bomb survivor. After turning 65, I resolved to tell my story to future generations. First, I told my friends and people I knew. Then I started my public storytelling activity. What shocked me most was that young people were not interested in the A-Bomb. I don't want to let them forget that terrible bomb!

To keep that hellish event from happening again, I believe I have to share my story now, and I will do so until I die.

[Document 6] Tadashi Kihara

Ten days after the bomb was dropped, I continued to have diarrhea. Then my hair started falling out. Now I know those were symptoms of A-bomb disease. Long after the bombing, we saw many women in Hiroshima wearing scarves on their heads. I always thought they had lost their hair like me.

Tadashi continued to work at the Hiroshima Railway Bureau until April next year. He then started training at a Japanese confectionary store in Kobe to take over the family business. He later returned to Tsuyama City to help his father.

My father knew only the old way of making sweets was delighted to learn the new technique I brought from Kobe. The new sweets were popular. There were even some shop owners who offered to sell my new sweets. We decided to stop retail sales and concentrate on production. I was 27 or 28. I heard that survivors could obtain a Atomic Bomb Survivor Health Book. With the health book, you could get medical care free of charge. I was within 2 kilometers of the hypocenter, so the book was issued immediately. However, I really didn't want to get it because I thought it would affect my chances of getting married. I wanted to be a "normal person" as much as I could.

But my physical condition got worse and worse. As a result, the health book was very helpful. I had a bladder operation when I was 32. I had an intestinal obstruction when I was 45. When I was 55, I had gallstones removed. After three abdominal operations, my navel disappeared. I was able to survive these serious diseases because of the health book.

Tadashi started working at Sanyo Jimu Koki, a job he found in the classified section of the newspaper in 1967. Eventually he was

Hiroshima August 6, 1945

was already dead. Its body color had changed. It was probably the mother's reflex to keep holding a dead baby. She had particularly severe burns from her face to her shoulder. There was nothing I could do for her. I put my hands together and apologized, and walked away. This still causes pain in my heart.

There were many survivors who died right after drinking water. Therefore, most people did not give water to survivors even when they begged for water. In reality, they would have died anyway.

The Eastern Drill Ground where we were was a huge area of land. Soldiers used it for bayonet practice or marching in file, but after the bombing it was completely full of survivors taking refuge. Some with injuries were lying down. Some families crowded together. There were so many people it was impossible to tell how many were there. But as the day passed, the numbers fell rapidly. Some evacuated to relatives' homes, but many more simply died. The dead bodies were loaded on a cargo train and carried away. One day I looked into one of the empty cargo cars. The stench that hit my nose made me feel like throwing up.

Roofs surrounding wooden houses were bent in waves. The atomic bomb exploding in the sky must have pressed down on them with tremendous force.

During the night, raging flames enveloped Atago-machi, near the Eastern Drill Ground. Firefighters ordered civilians to help put the fires out with manual water pumps. A few days later, I saw heavy oil being poured over lines of army horses that were killed by the heat ray. They were being cremated. The horses killed by the atomic bombing thrust their legs out straight. Their bellies were bloated. They looked like inflated balloons. The stench was horrible.

[Document 6] Tadashi Kihara

I thought I probably got injured when I stumbled over a tie on the railroad track on my way back to Eastern Drill Ground. My white short-sleeved shirt was red with blood from my chest from my shoulders to my waist. My right leg was also bleeding. The wound went all the way down to the bone. I took out some medicine from the first-aid kit and stopped the bleeding.

I waited them for an hour, but no one came back, so I returned to my workplace. A few days later I found out that the children had decided that staying in the city would be dangerous so they made their way back to Niho, walking along the paths in the hills near the drill ground.

A dead baby holding its mother's nipple in its mouth

Since I was in a train, I was not directly exposed to the heat ray. I only had wounds. My colleagues at the electric repair workshop were busy tending to the injured. I was put in charge of night duty and told to spend the night with four assistant stationmasters. We put some boards and straw mats in the front yard and slept in a mosquito net. That night, I connected an electrical cord to a miniature light bulb and made an electric lamp. I used an extra-large battery used to test traffic lights. Using this light we looked for injured people on the alleys or under the collapsed buildings nearby. My workplace had over a 100 employees before the bombing; we were reduced now to around 20.

When I went around on watch, the injured who saw my light would beg for water. In the darkness I saw a woman suffering with burns and naked from the waist up. She held a baby in her arms and said, "Soldier, please give me some water!" She probably thought that anybody coming near her was a soldier. Her voice was feeble but intense. The baby in her arms held a nipple in its lips, but it

out in an instant. At almost the same time, a tremendous roar shook the train hard. All the slate fell off the station roof. The fallen tiles and dust made the world dark.

There had been no air raids in Hiroshima, but I knew that incendiary bombs were being dropped like rain on other cities. I knew the attack wouldn't end with just one bomb. I thought, "We have to get out of here before the next bomb comes." Crying out loud, the children covered their eyes and ears with their hands as they had been trained to do and were lying on the floor. All the children were injured by shattered glass from the windows. I helped each child down from the train onto the track.

Each child held onto the belt of the one in front and followed the track. I headed for the Osuga-cho (now, Osuga-cho, Minami-ku) railroad crossing about 200 meters ahead. I wanted to take them to the Railway Hospital near Sakae Bridge, but a flood of people from the city were rushing down the Sakae Bridge toward us. They all had terrible burns on their faces and arms.

We were engulfed in the whirlpool of people and forced to enter into the Eastern Drill Ground. I had no choice but to gather the children into a corner of the ground. They were all bleeding from their faces and arms, crying and shouting. I said, "Stay here! I'm going to go get some medicine. I'll be right back." I headed for my workplace in Minami Kaniya-cho (now, Minami Kaniya-cho, Minami-ku).

There I found the pillars broken, with the walls and windows shattered. There was no place to step in. Still, I somehow found a first-aid kit and went back to the Drill Ground, but the children were nowhere in sight. I wondered if they had been moved somewhere else for some reason. I decided to wait for them there for a while, and it was only then that I realized that I was injured.

to be right there. The plan was to lay sand on the vacant lot and form a bucket brigade to carry sea water from the beach. Then the sun would dry the field leaving the salt behind.

August 6 was the first day of the salt field construction work. Grade 6 students from Niho Elementary School were mobilized to help, but we couldn't give the children difficult tasks. They were assigned simple chores, like carrying tools here and there. That morning, I was planning to take 10 students to the salt field with 4 colleagues. We were to meet on the Kure line platform at Hiroshima Station.

The train arrived about 10 minutes late that morning. That was a cruel twist of fate. If the train had left Hiroshima on time, it would have arrived in Mukainada or even Kaitaichi at the time of the bombing. If they had gone that far, they wouldn't have been exposed to the bombing.

I saw the B-29 bombers in the sky just before I got on the train, but since no air-raid warning sounded, I didn't think anything of it. I had the children get on the train first, and I followed. I stood near the entrance to the coach and chatted with the children.

The train master always told passengers to close the wooden shutters before departure, but we left the windows open because the children were too excited. For them, it was like going on an excursion, and it was hot, too.

Departure time was 8:15.

All of sudden, I saw a bright magnesium flash, but hundreds of times brighter. It filled the train. I felt as if my eyes had been scooped

Hiroshima August 6, 1945

Hiroshima Railway Bureau. He was 14 years old. The National Railway Company (now, Japan Railways) had 8 bureaus in Japan, one in Hiroshima. His workshop did highly technical work. His main job was regular checks and repairs of the relays that switched the railway signals. He also conducted maintenance checks and repairs of devices like clocks and switchboards.

My workplace was more like a factory than a railway company. My duty was engineering so I handled plating and coiling, woodwork, casting, and lathe work. When my boss wasn't watching, I would sometimes make belt buckles, rings, and ice axes for climbing. At the time, the National Railway transported military supplies and soldiers. Because of a labor shortage, we received assistance from the military. I would see soldiers wearing white military uniforms shoveling coal into the furnace of a freight train. I wonder if the military gave the National Railway exceptional treatment. I felt National Railway employees were slow to receive conscriptions compared to other occupations. Still, 5 of my colleagues received draft notices.

On my days off, I would often go hiking and camping to Mt. Dogo with my colleagues. Mt. Dogo stands between three prefectures: Hiroshima, Tottori, and Okayama. We did not have to pay the train fare as we worked for the railway. We rode on the Geibi line. After 9 p.m. we would switch on our carbide lamps and head for a cottage. One of my fellow workers died because of the bomb, another was never found.

The food shortage became increasingly serious in 1945, so Tadashi and his colleagues decided to make a salt field in a vacant lot by the railroad track near Koyaura Station on the Kure line. Going down a path by the track at that station, the Inland Sea used

[Document 6] Tadashi Kihara

Document 6

I will never let people forget that atomic bomb

Tadashi Kihara
Born in February 1927 to a family that ran a Japanese confectionary store. Was 18 when the bomb exploded and was on a train stopped at Hiroshima Station, 1.9 kilometers from the hypocenter. Worked for Hiroshima Railway Bureau, and after the bombing, took over the family business. Later, started working at a company that recruited him for his skills in calligraphy. At present, is an independent Japanese calligrapher. Eighty-seven years old, residing in Higashi-ku, Hiroshima.

I will tell my story as long as I live.

I was the 4th child of 8. I had 4 brothers and 3 sisters and was the 3rd son. My parents ran a small Japanese confectionary store in Tsuyama City, Okayama Prefecture. My whole family worked for the store. When I was in elementary school I helped by making sweet bean paste with my brothers and sisters. My father was a strict craftsman, so if I did something careless, he would scold me. He even hit me with a piece of firewood.

I was good at making bean-paste-filled wafers called monaka. I placed the wafers inside down on a wet dish towel. When the edges were just the right dampness, I would scoop bean paste onto one wafer and precisely place the other wafer on top. I enjoyed scooping the sweet bean paste and tasting while cooking.

In April 1941, Tadashi was assigned to work in the signal room of the electric repair workshop at the Facilities Department of the years before that recognition are said to be a "empty decade." You can find many monuments all around Hiroshima, but those built early on do not use the words "atomic bomb". People were probably hesitant to use "atomic bomb" because of the press code established by the occupation.

Kazukuni worked as a teacher in public schools in or near Hiroshima until retirement. He then started working on the Board of Education. He also taught at Hiroshima Bunkyo Women's College until he was 70. He chaired his Neighborhood Association and the local Council of Social Welfare. He also served as a probation officer for more than 20 years. His many contributions were acknowledged when he was awarded the Medal of Honor. His father also received that medal, so two generations, father and son were recognized. His face softened for the first time when he told us this. However, when he resumed talking about the atomic bomb, his expression once again became solemn.

I was 15 when the bomb exploded, and now at the age of 83, I feel like my life has been a continuing series of atomic bomb diseases. When I was 25, 10 years after the bombing, I had liver ailment. In my late 40s, I got severe stomachaches from eating anything oily. I was diagnosed with inflammation of the gallbladder and had my gallbladder removed. Now, I'm taking medication for a thyroid gland malfunction and prostate cancer.

This is why the nuclear power accident at Fukushima is not just something happening to someone else. TEPCO and the government have not told us the whole truth. I believe that the peaceful use of nuclear power is a lie. Nuclear power and human beings cannot coexist indefinitely.

[Document 5] Kazukuni Yamada

"Don't believe in rumors. It's not true." My wife's brother was a doctor, and he encouraged me. His words cheered me up.

Kazukuni points out the three types of damage from the atomic bomb. One is burns due to the heat ray. Next is injuries caused by the blast. Like his mother, many survivors were struck by glass shards or trapped under fallen houses. The third type of damage is the radiation.

You can't see radiation. Those who entered the city after the bombing or were in the womb contracted A-bomb disease without even knowing they had been exposed. If I had known about the dangers of radiation, I would never have returned to Hakushima Naka-machi. I would have stayed in the countryside, just like the people of Fukushima who have fled from the power plant.

Soon after the war ended, the US opened a research institute on Hijiyama Hill called the Atomic Bomb Casualty Commission (ABCC). Its purpose was not to give treatment but to conduct medical checkups to collect data on the effects of the atomic bomb. It was a time of severe food shortage in Japan, and if you went for a checkup they would give you curry rice and chocolate. I went there several times. I remember that they even came to pick us up by car.

Radiation is said to be the science of death." We knew nothing about radiation so we built shacks, cultivated gardens and grew vegetables on the scorched land.

Many people were unable to work due to overpowering fatigue. We used to call it the "idleness disease" or "lazy illness." In ten years, many of these people passed away one after another. In 1957, the government announced for the first time that the cause was radiation. This was the first time that A-bomb disease was acknowledged. Ten

many students to the A-bomb disease. "I was exposed, too, but confronting the reality of students being killed was more difficult than my own anxiety."

"Mr. Yamada, your student (name) died because of leukemia last year." Whenever I attend class reunions, I always heard that one or more of my students had died. Even after 60 years, a survivor can still contract an A-bomb disease. It's unbearable. One of my students who was married and living in Tokyo loved being a grandmother. One day she told me, "My hair is falling out, and I don't feel so well." She passed away just the other day.

At the every reunion, I always tell my students, "Let me die first. I won't forgive you if you die before me!"

I have lost about 25 students, including those who died after graduation, to A-bomb disease. For the sake of those children who were killed so young, I have to make the most of my survival by telling the story, getting the facts out. Even as a teacher and after retiring, I have spoken at every opportunity about my experience. My wife and I sometimes encourage each other saying, "We have to talk about the atomic bombing as long as we remember it."

Kazukuni married in 1956. He was within 2 kilometers of the hypocenter, which is designated the "direct exposure area." His wife was 2.3 kilometers away, so they are a survivor couple.

Of course, I worried about the aftereffects. I decided that we should help each other since we are both survivors. If my wife were not a survivor, her family would have opposed our marriage, but no one did. We have three children. I was quite worried when my wife was pregnant our first baby.

[Document 5] Kazukuni Yamada

her moaning. I couldn't open the door and go in until her voice calmed down. Leukemia often causes sharp pain all over the body. When I entered the room, I was relieved to see her smile delightedly.

She had the brand-new 8th grade textbooks right by her pillow. I opened the social studies textbook and told her "We're studying here." She nodded her head many times. Soon after that she passed away.

I couldn't go to her funeral because I had to teach. I visited her family later to pay my condolences. All her classmates knew she was in the hospital due to the bombing and was unable to come to the school. There were many children like Hideko, who were exposed to the bombing when they were very young. Although I knew it would cause those children to feel anxiety, I told them about her death. I can't express how hard it was for me. I had not taught Sadako Sasaki, the model for the Children's Peace Monument, but she was also enrolled at the Nobori-cho Junior High School.

I taught for almost 40 years and was transferred to five other schools. At each school, there were always a few students who had been exposed to the bomb as a baby or in their mother's womb at each school. One I will never forget is Kaoru Hikichi. He was in my 9th grade class and was an excellent student. He took leading role in intramural volleyball tournaments. He was superior in studies and sports. I am sure his parents had great expectations for him. However, immediately after Kaoru was accepted to the most prestigious public high school, I received news of his sudden death. He had leukemia due to radiation exposure as a baby. I was so shocked I couldn't speak.

"As I experienced these incidents one after the next, I realized that teachers must endure grief and loss," says Kazukuni. He lost

Hiroshima August 6, 1945

will to do anything. My gums bled and would not stop. Mosquito bites would remain red and swollen and wouldn't heal. I got my blood checked, and it turned out that my white blood cell count was 100,000 when normally it should have been within 7000 to 8000. It seems I had acute leukemia.

My mother also had acute leukemia so her wounds wouldn't close for a long time. I felt so sorry for her. I now believe that it's a miracle that she survived. I also think it was good we left Hiroshima as soon as we could.

We had no idea what was happening to our bodies at the time. All we knew was that we had been hit with a "new type of bomb." We had no clue that it was the cause of our leukemia. Since information was not available, we didn't even worry about it. Not knowing was our only consolation.

Kazukuni and his mother stayed in Kabe until fall. In October, he was finally able to go back to school. Later on, the school system changed and his school became Hiroshima University. He continued his education there, graduating when he was 21 years old. He became a social studies teacher at Nobori-cho Junior High School. However, he was destined to face the atomic bomb again.

When I started teaching in 1951, I was a 7th grade homeroom teacher. One of my first students passed away due to the atomic bombing. Her name was Hideko Yumoto. She was a quiet girl with white porcelain skin and bobbed hair. At the end of the year, she fell ill and stopped coming to the school. In April the following year, classes changed but she didn't come to the school. We let her move up to the next grade and kept her name on the school register. I went to visit her at the hospital. When I stood in front of her room, I heard became black, though it was mid-day in summer. I later heard that black rain fell nearby. Luckily, the black rain did not come to where we were.

We reached a grove of trees near the village shrine in Nagatsuka at midnight. I looked by chance toward Hiroshima and noticed that the whole city was burning. Even the hill in Ushita was on fire. The light from the fires was so bright it was possible to read a newspaper. We slept outside in the trees.

"It hurts!!"

"Water, water, please!" Moaning, crying voices gave me no sleep at all. The next day, a farmer family of that area offered us a temporary room. I still remember how grateful I was when I lay on a tatami mat. We were finally able to relax and tend to our injuries. We picked the glass fragments from our skin and cleaned our wounds. I felt like a decent human being again for the first time. We were given some tomatoes, and they were so delicious. My mother and I stayed at the farmer's house that night and the following morning, we left for our relative's house.

My father's sister and my three cousins lived in Kabe (now, Kabe, Asa Kita-ku). My three cousins were often mobilized to work at my father's factory, so we knew each other. My mother's wound from her neck to her shoulder suppurated.

"It hurts! It hurts!"

She cried in pain, but I could do nothing for her. School classrooms were used as an Army Hospital in Kabe, so there could hardly be satisfactorily equipment. They couldn't even take the glass shards from a patient's wounds. All they could do was sterilize the wounds with their only medicine, iodine.

Then, before one week passed, my body went through a strange change. My body was so fatigued I couldn't keep standing. I had no

Hiroshima August 6, 1945

"A huge fire ball was flashing!" came the replies.

Those who looked directly at the flash had burns in their eyes and died one after another. Those with burnt bodies were groaning and calling for water. Some crawled down the steps to the river, entered the water and were swept away by the river. While floating down, they reached out their hands as if asking for help. But if you took hold of their hand, the skin on the entire arm peeled off. You couldn't even lift the fallen survivors. It was absolutely a hell.

When you got burned by the heat ray, your clothes would burn off in a matter of seconds. You would be naked with a few rags hanging around your body. But you had no feelings of embarrassment. Those who could flee, did. Those who couldn't, died. Those who fell while fleeing were trampled by those who were determined just to get away faster than anybody else. Many must have been killed by the trampling. Everyone was consumed with fleeing and had no capacity to care for others.

Time passed, but we had no concept what had happened. My mother and I were unable to think any more. We were just pressed on by the crowd and crossed the Engineer Bridge.

Asked for help by an almost naked woman, I got her some clothes from a crushed house. There were many women like her at the foot of the Engineer Bridge.

We crossed the bridge and went further north. We didn't see many with terrible burns or injuries after leaving the riverbank. "Residents of Hakushima Naka-machi will escape to Nagatsuka-cho (now, Nagatsuka, Asa Minami-ku) if something happens." Each neighborhood had designated evacuation areas in case of emergencies.

We rested on a riverbank until noon, and I remember it happened just as we were about to leave for Nagatsuka. The sky suddenly

to the other side. We walked against the crowd. I was pushed back a number of times as I was carrying my mother on my back. We had to give up on getting to the hospital. Soldiers kept shouting, "Run north!" So we headed north picking our way through the crushed houses. We reached the riverbank near the Engineer Bridge that connected the areas of Hakushima and Ushita. That was a scene from hell. People would arrive, then collapse in the weeds on riverbank. Maybe their will was weakened by the smell of weeds and creatures. Hundreds of them fell down and died right there.

Many bridges had fallen under the blast, but the Engineer Bridge, a suspension bridge, miraculously remained intact. This bridge was built to connect an army post near there with the military training grounds. There was a training ground for the Corps of Engineers beneath the bridge. Normally, guards stood at each end of the bridge, and residents were prohibited from entering. To escape the fires pressing from behind, many survivors crossed the bridge that day. "The bridge of life" that saved many lives. Years later, a plan was made to tear the bridge down and replace it, but local residents opposed it. The bridge was strengthened and preserved.

On the other side of the bridge, a group of soldiers sat on the ground. They were all blinded by damage to their eyes. Because they couldn't see, they held onto each other's shoulders. They were constantly moving their faces this way and that trying to find something they could see. Their faces, badly burned by the heat ray, were swollen red and black.
"What did you see?" a voice asked.
"A fire ball!"

turned everything white.

I heard a tremendous roar but before I could even think, I was blown a few meters away with the doors. The ceiling collapsed and the floor caved in with all the tatami mats. I was covered in blood. My mother was hurled into a glass door in the kitchen and was cut by glass from her shoulder to chest. Blood was gushing out of her wound. I carried her on my back and got us outside.

What we saw is the most tragic scene I have ever seen. Telephone poles were down, so electric wires were rolling around on the street. Store signs, pieces of wood and galvanized tin sheets lay everywhere for as far as I could see. Most houses were smashed down, their roof tiles covering the narrow streets. Countless dead and injured were scattered all around. Their bodies were burnt black and so unrecognizable it was impossible to identify even the gender.

And yet, the leather shoes and belts worn by soldiers remained unburnt.

I was shocked by the appearance of the people who were fleeing. When you steam potatoes, the light brown skin peels off. The people looked exactly like that. Their skin hung like potato skin from their faces and hands.

My mother and I headed for nearby Nagayama Clinic, but we found it in ruins, unable to treat patients. I lifted my mother again and headed for the Communications Hospital.

What I saw along the way was gruesome. People who were outside when the bomb exploded had melted faces, arms, and legs. Their hair and clothes were burned leaving them half naked. Those who had been inside a house were trapped under beams or pillars, unable to move. I could hear them screaming for help under the debris, but there was nothing I could do.

The JR Sanyo railroad bridge was destroyed so we couldn't get

Document 5

The concept of nuclear peace is a lie

Kazukuni Yamada

Born in March 1930. Exposed to the bombing at home in Hakushima Naka-machi, 1.7 kilometers from the hypocenter. He was 15. He has worked as a junior high school teacher, on the Board of Education and as a university professor. He contributed to his community as president of a neighborhood association and chairman of a social welfare council. Eighty-three years old, resides in Naka-ku, Hiroshima.

I told my students, "I won't let you die before I do!"

I was a student at Hiroshima School of Education. My father recommended that I become a school teacher, so I went on to higher school. Although it was a school, instruction had been ceased long before; students were mobilized to work every day. My first mobilization task was to fold and carry waterproof tents made at a factory that made such tents. After that, I was assigned to loading munitions at the Munitions Depot run by the Akatsuki Corps (Army Marine Headquarters) in Ujina. I was supposed to go to the Akatsuki Corps that day.

I was at home in Hakushima Naka-machi (now, Hakushima Naka-machi, Naka-ku) with my mother. My father was plant manager of a factory in Yoshida (now, Yoshida-cho, Akitakata City) that made military supplies. He had to stay at the factory and was not home. The air-raid warning was cleared, so I was getting ready to leave for work. While I was leaning on the sliding doors to put on my gaiters, I heard the drone of some bombers. An instant later, a bright light

Hiroshima August 6, 1945

In the fall of 2010, I told my story to children at the Fuchu Elementary School. Later, I participated in an event that announced a new song, We Will Never Forget That Summer. The children wrote it after they heard me and other hibakusha tell our stories. I had wondered if they really understood the bombing, but they clearly grabbed it firmly. I was grateful.

The people in Fukushima are going through hard times. In our day, we had no concept of the horror of radiation. We built shacks and lives on radioactive soil. We resumed living, focused on getting through the day. Then for some of us, nosebleeds would not stop; hair would fall out; people would die without knowing what was happening to them.

Now we understand the ferociousness of radiation, and large numbers of people of Fukushima are still unable to go home. Not being able to move forward is painful and difficult. But no matter what, they must never lose hope or give up. I want them to stand up and display their power. I wish this with all my heart. How can they stand up again? How can they challenge realty? I believe there is always hope as long as you accept the challenge presented by the difficulties.

to think about our marriage. My wife and her mother persuaded him and we were allowed to marry.

I was especially worried when my wife was pregnant with our first baby. A rumor was going around that hibakusha couldn't have a normal baby. Even now, I still feel uncomfortable when talking about marriage. My daughter and sons married around 30 years ago. It was clear that their partner's parents worried about it as well, so I never told them my A-bomb experience. Now, it's my grandchildren's turn to get married and, again, it seems my wife wants me to avoid talking about it, if possible.

In the summer in1945, when it became clear that Japan was losing the war, the Chugoku and Shikoku regions were constantly being hit by air raids. Okayama was attacked on June 29. Three major cities in Shikoku (Kochi, Takamatsu, and Tokushima) were attacked on July 4. Matsuyama in Ehime was hit on July 26. Many cities around the country were being attacked. On August 5, Hiroshima had still not been hit. It is said that the US military intentionally prevented an air raid in order to see how much damage would be done by the atomic bomb.

"The US used the people of Hiroshima in an experiment," says Kazunori angrily. Three aircraft participated in the bombing. The Enola Gay dropped the bomb just after an air-raid warning was cleared. In other words, the US created a situation that maximized the effect of the bomb in order to conduct a test.

I have lived into my 80s. The two classmates who saved my life were killed at14. Had they not helped me, I would have died. For the dead souls of my two friends, I believe that I must talk about my experience.

Hiroshima August 6, 1945

thigh to heal.

My father passed away two years after the bombing in 1947. He was bedridden, and his hair fell out. Eventually he started throwing up blood and became weaker. The doctor had no idea what was causing the symptoms, but in the end he was diagnosed with tuberculosis. We heard that diseases of the lung required nutrition, so I would often go all the way to Saijo to buy milk for him. I now believe that my father had acute leukemia. He went into Hiroshima to look for me right after the bomb was dropped, so he was an "entry victim".

Kazunori graduated and entered Satake Manufacturing Company. He learned about machine coating. The disability in his left leg made him work harder than other employees. After a year, he was independent. He received all the orders for rice milling machine coating. In 1961, he joined Toyo Kogyo (now, Mazda). There he began a career coating cars, moving to product management, and finally into the Personnel Education Center. He retired at 60.

After retirement, he studied the repapering of fusuma (sliding doors) and the hanging of scrolls at the Training Center for the Disabled. He received many orders for repapering fusuma at Mazda's company housing. He was always busy but gracious. He found it extremely difficult to carry his heavy finished fusuma into company housing that had no elevator, but he managed to get them up the stairs, protecting his disabled left leg.

I married when I was 28. I was in my second year working at Mazda. My wife was from Kure City, so she was not affected by the bomb. A friend from the community introduced me to her. When my wife's father found out I was a hibakusha, he said that he wanted time left side against folded futon.

We had cows on our farm, so there were a lot of flies. They would swarm around my wounds. My sisters used a fan to keep them away, but no matter how she tried, the flies came. They were bothersome. Then, white maggots began crawling around on me. It was my body, but it didn't look human any more. My sisters removed them with chopsticks and toothpicks.

Thanks to the devoted care of his family, Kazunori was able to go back to school in February the following year. He thought it had taken him a long time to heal and that his friends would already be well. He was delighted to go back to school to see them.

I did not see Yanagida or Nishikubo in the classroom. I had a bad feeling and asked my teacher, "What about Yanagida and Nishikubo? Why are they absent?"

My teacher said "They're both dead." It was unbelievable. Everything turned white. I thought my teacher was lying. I pulled myself together and looked around the room and noticed that only half the students were present. I later learned that nearly all the rest were dead.

I was survived because of my two friends. If not for them, I would have died. When the bomb exploded we were marching along the Kyobashi River toward Yayoi-cho. The hypocenter was to our right. We were right by the river so nothing shielded us from the flash. All of us were exposed directly to the heat ray.

Yanagida had probably turned his eyes towards the bomb at that instant. That is why his face was charred. I got burns on the right side of my body from my head and right ear to my neck, shoulder, right arm, waist, thigh and ankle. It took the longest time for my waist and

Hiroshima August 6, 1945

The next day, the old lady got on a train with us and took me home to Kodani-mura. When I arrived, my mother's surprise and joy were overwhelming. I must have looked grotesque because half my body was burned and my leg was injured.

"Kazunori, I'm so glad you made it home!" She crouched down and started crying."We heard that a bomb was dropped on Hiroshima and terrible things are happening. We were all worried for you."

My father had been looking for me in Hiroshima and was gone the day I arrived. He came home from Hiroshima that night and was thrilled to see me. I felt nothing but relief that I survived and had come back home. I didn't feel any pain or itching for some time. All I did was concentrate on surviving each day. All my feelings were paralyzed, numb.

After a week, I started to feel pain and itching. We didn't have any clinic in Kodani-mura. If we wanted to go to a clinic, we had to go to Saijo, and it was impossible to go there because of my terrible burns. Nor did the clinics have appropriate medication. There was a shortage of medication in Japan even before the bomb was dropped.

"I cannot leave you as you are. I will do everything necessary to heal you." My mother asked around on how to treat burns and tried various methods. She used steamed chameleon plant, turning it into a paste, but this had no effect. Next, she heard that potatoes absorbed heat, so she mixed mashed potatoes with ground root of red spider lilies and cooking oil. Potatoes applied to my burns absorbed the heat and soon dried. She would remove the dry cream and put on a new layer. She kept repeating this, and eventually my burns turned into scabs. Since I could not take baths, we cooled a towel in the well water and put it on the wounds. All we could do was wait until I healed naturally. I couldn't lie down on my back or stomach. Anything that touched my right side was painful, so I had to lean my

[Document 4] Kazunori Nishimura

walk on the dead step by step. Some of the "dead" were still alive. They grabbed the legs stepping them and screamed out for help.

I have no idea how we got through Ochigo Mountain Pass, but once over it, we reached Nukushina (now, Nukushina, Higashi-ku), and a creek. I was hot so I put my arms into the creek. As soon as I did so, blisters appeared on my arms and shoulders. Yanagida washed his face, and most of the skin of his face peeled off, dangling around his mouth. One eye he couldn't open at all, the other he could, but just slightly. Nishikubo appeared to have few injuries. We found some tomatoes in a nearby garden. We ripped them off and bit into them. Yanagida cried out loud.

"I can't eat this tomato!" The skin on his face was blocking his mouth so he couldn't eat. It was so pitiful.

"He carried me in this condition?" I was filled with regret. Tomatoes still remind me of Yanagida.

My arms were burnt and covered with blisters that hurt in direct sunlight. Whenever I let my arms down, the blood rushed to my fingertips giving them furious pain. I put my arms above my chest like a ghost and advanced, leaning on the shoulders of my two friends. We finally reached Nishikubo's house in Funakoshi (now, Funakoshi, Aki-ku).

As soon as his mother saw her son, she came running out of the house. She cried as she dragged Nishikubo forcefully into the house. Yanagida and I waited vacantly in front of the door. An old lady next door said, "Come to my place." We stayed the night with her. She served us a meal, but Yanagida could not eat. The old lady said, "You have to eat!" and made porridge for him. She lifted the skin that was blocking his mouth and fed him porridge, spoon by spoon. "Oil is good for burns," she said and put cooking oil on the right side of my body.

Hiroshima August 6, 1945

after Shiraichi. Since we always sat in the same seats, we would meet every day on the train and go to school together.

"If they come again, we'll be all killed! Hurry! Let's escape!"

"I can't move. My leg is injured."

"Then I'll carry you!" Tender and big, Yanagida was a boy who took care of his friends. He was kind of a boss among us. Carrying me on his back he started walking toward a school in Onaga (now, Onaga, Higashi-ku). But he was soon out of breath. "Yanagida, let me down. I think I can walk a little!"

So saying, I got down and hopped on my good leg while holding onto what I could for support. Yanagida saw that I could hardly walk and carried me on his back again.

"Yanagida this won't work. You go on ahead and tell my parents." I yelled this at him over and over." Then, I heard someone else call out my name. It was Nishikubo. He was an untroubled son from a rich family who had a lovely face with white skin.

"OK, let's go as a trio!" I borrowed shoulders from Nishikubo and Yanagida; I almost hung on them. We made our way to the school. We thought that once we got to the school, they would have medicine, and we would receive treatment. But our expectations were smashed. The school had burnt down to ashes; nothing remained.

"We're close to Funakoshi. Let's go to my house," said Nishikubo. I started walking again, hanging on their shoulders. When we came to Ochigo Mountain Pass, said to be a difficult peak to pass. What we saw was hell. Most of the people that had fled this point had used up all their energy and had tumbled to the ground. As they died, people fell on corpses already there. A mountain of bodies piled up in layers. Once a person fell down, it seems they could not get up again. Tremendous numbers of people were dead there. All these people had families! Those just arriving would push their way into the crowd and

42

[Document 4] Kazunori Nishimura

desperately, but no one could afford to care about others. "Help! I don't mind losing my leg!" When the fire was a meter away, I was thinking, "No help. My life is over," and I started wondering what it would be like to die. I still clearly remember this moment as I prepared my mind for death.

Just then, I heard someone say, "I'm coming to get you." I think it was a military policeman or a soldier from Hijiyama Hill. Clearing away the rubble, he used a piece of wood as a lever to lift the timber. I pulled with all my strength and was able to dislodge my leg.

"You pulled me out! Thank you! I'm saved!" I was barely avoided burning to death because of this man.

I then noticed that I had severe burns on the right side of my body. I had lost conscious the very instant I was trapped by the flying debris, but it seems the heat ray hit directly on the right half of my body. From face to shoulder, arm, waist, down to the gaiters on my foot—the entire right side was burnt.

The debris spread as far as I could see, so I couldn't tell where the streets were. Some joints in my left foot that was trapped under a timber were broken. I could hardly walk. I collapsed on the ground on my back.

My father would find me when he came to search for me! With this faint hope, I faced upwards because I wanted him to see me. The sun was so bright and harsh it made me dizzy. I don't know how much time had passed, but I heard someone calling out my name. I saw a very black face that got sooty. Some skin was peeled off here and there from the burnt raw face. Do I know this person?

"Who are you?"

"I'm Yanagida."

It was my classmate Yanagida, with whom I had been walking in file. He always got on the train at Nishitakaya Station, the station assigned to clear houses for fire lanes. The train departed from Shiraichi Station, and students got on the train from seven other stops on the way to Hiroshima Station. When we were near Saijo Station, the air-raid warning sounded. The train master notified us that the warning had been cleared before we reached Hiroshima Station. We were to help out in Tanaka-machi (now, Tanaka-machi, Naka-ku).

We reached Hiroshima Station and walked in file heading for Yayoi-cho (now, Yayoi-cho, Naka-ku). All the students wore khaki school uniforms with field caps and gaiters. But the color and the size of our uniforms did not match, due to a lack of supplies. Uniform colors varied and caps differed.

While we were marching along Kyobashi River near Yanagi Bridge, we heard the roar of a B-29. Since the B-29 was a large bomber, the sound was full and loud compared to other bombers. There had been almost no air raids in Hiroshima, so we had no experience escaping into air-raid shelters. We kept on marching.

It was like a TV monitor turning off all of sudden. That was what happened inside me. I don't remember any flash or roar. I suddenly lost my sight and consciousness—for how long I don't know. When I came to, I was buried under timbers and rubble. Buildings in those days were mostly made of wood, so the debris came from surrounding houses. Through a crevice in the pile above me I could see a crowd of people fleeing. I was able to free my upper body, but my left leg was caught under a big piece of timber.

Fire broke out at a house about 50 meters away and headed toward me. The flames were on me in the blink of an eye. "Big sister! Father! Help! Help!" I shouted out without thinking. "I want to go home again!" Many thoughts came and went. My whole life flashed before my eyes. When a person knows that death is approaching, he recall the moments of his life one after the next. "Help!" I kept shouting

[Document 4] Kazunori Nishimura

Document 4

For the souls of my friends who saved my life, I should talk about my experience

Kazunori Nishimura
Born in November 1932. Exposed to the bomb when he was 12, at the foot of Hijiyama Bridge, 1.5 kilometers from the hypocenter. He has been president of his Neighborhood Association and a leader on the crime prevention committee for ten years. He actively teaches children about the importance of life and how to protect it by talking about his experience at community centers and other venues. Eighty-one years old, resides in Fuchu-cho, Aki-gun.

My teacher said, "They're both dead." My friends are gone.

Kazunori was in his first year at a private school, Matsumoto Industrial School (now, Setouchi High School). He was born and raised on a farm in Kodani-mura, Toyota-gun (now, Takaya-cho, Higashi-Hiroshima City), a rural village an hour train ride from Hiroshima City. When asked about his childhood memories, Kazunori sang a number of songs.
"Thank the soldiers I can go to school with my brother."
"Thank the soldiers who fought for our country."
It was a period when people did not question the justice of war.

I was the third child of six. I had two older sisters and was the first son. My oldest sister treated me with affection. I relied on her and always called out, "Hey, big sister!" whenever I wanted her help. On that day, I was one of the 20 first-year middle school students

Hiroshima August 6, 1945

mediated by a friend. After a while, he was able to work as a plasterer. He married in 1974 when he was 44 years old. His wife was from Kure city, so she was not affected by the bomb. He still has aftereffects from the radiation.

It's almost 70 years since I was exposed to atomic bombing. When it rains, the scars on my back start to itch and purple spots appear on my thighs and arms. I've had prostate cancer and heart-related illnesses. Going to see doctors has become a daily routine.

Someone said that countries with nuclear weapons are evil. This explains everything. Unless the US experiences the atomic bomb, they will never understand how hard it was for us. It's not just the US, of course. All countries with nuclear weapons—Russia, China, France, the UK—they're all evil. They hold on to their nuclear weapons while not allowing other countries to have them. I can't understand how they can say, "We have these weapons but you shouldn't." It's unfair.

I still hate the USA for making me like this. I think it's a natural feeling. I can't ignore my feelings because that bomb ruined my life. I have suffered continually from it all my life.

Senji's wife said, "Every year there are fewer people who went through what you did. If you keep quiet, who will speak out?" Strong encouragement from his wife made him overcome his reluctance and caused him to give us this testimony. Still, he expresses mixed feelings about speaking about the bombing. "No matter what I say, those that haven't experienced an atomic bombing will have no idea what it feels like. Only one who is hungry can understand a hungry man's heart. It's the same with this. This is far deeper than words."

[Document 3] Senji Kawai

letting anyone know about my keloids.

The Kawai family lived in Kabe for two years. Senji was concerned about the house and factory so he went to Hiroshima alone. He was surprised to find that his cousins had restarted the factory. "I can't believe you survived!" They were happy to see him. He still remembers that they treated him rice porridge with sweet potato. Around that time, he overheard the local doctor told his mother, "Senji will not probably live past 30."

I was always a competitive boy, but after I heard this, I was scared of nothing. I thought that since I had only ten more years to live, I didn't care if I died. My life grew wild. When I was 19, I spent most of my time in the red-light district. I had googly eyes so people called me "Googly". There were red-light districts on the east and west sides of the city. I was known as "Googly, the playboy of the west".

There was another reason why I was out of control. I wanted to work, and I passed the written exams, but I would always fail the physical checkups. That was because of the keloids on my back. When I got sick and visited to hospitals, doctors saw the keloids on my back and said, "Let me take some pictures" None of them knew how to treat them.

My scars made people uneasy. I bathed at home even in the winter and avoided going to the public baths. I never went on trips either. I was ashamed of myself. But I was never able to become a real gang star. At one point, I heard there was a job carrying flour at Ujina Port (now, Hiroshima Port). I applied, but I didn't have the strength to lift flour so I was told to go home.

Later on, Senji was apprenticed to a plasterer, a position

couldn't move. I just stayed in bed.

My mother had many expensive custom-made kimonos at home in Hiroshima. During the war, she kept the kimonos at the Kasabo's house in Kabe. My spoilt older brother was home, but he showed no inclination to work. My mother started selling her kimonos to keep us alive. She didn't need to go out to trade her kimonos. People around us willingly helped her. It may have been because of her character. Somehow she had always been well liked.

She never had to carry kimonos around to exchange for potatoes. Farmers got together bringing vegetables to our house. My mother would line up the kimonos and show them like a salesclerk. There was even a farmer that had brought a cow and asked for a set of kimono. My mother always drove a hard bargain.

After about a month at the Kasabos' house, my hair started to fall out. I would run my fingers through my hair, and it would come out in clumps. Eventually I lost my eyebrows and all other bodily hair. My gums turned purple and started to rot. They bled easily and pus would ooze out. When I brushed my teeth, pieces of jelly-like flesh would get caught in my toothbrush.

I have no idea why, but after about a year, the blood and pus stopped. My hair started growing back. My whole back was covered with scabs. They itched and drove me crazy. My skin was bumpy like a lizard's. I would scrub my back with a dry towel until the scabs rubbed off. Although it stung a little, it felt good. Then my back would get hot, and pus would appear. After a while the scabs would reappear. Then I would get out a towel and repeat this cycle over and over again.

I had twitching keloids all over my back. They used to make it hard to move my body. I was a militaristic boy, and that made me quite competitive. That's probably why I have lived so long without go.

This was ten days after the bombing. All this time she thought I was dead. She had a bandage around her arm but was alive. A kind young Korean man had saved her. That young man made a simple shelter for her with some burnt galvanized tin under a bridge. He carried her there and told her, "Rest here." However, my father, who had gone off to look for his employees was missing, as was my brother, who I left for treatment at Misasa Bridge.

When I last saw him, my father was alive and well, so I couldn't understand why he hadn't come to Kabe. A month passed in great anxiety. In those days, a fortune-telling game called "Kokkuri-san" was popular in Japan. I used a five-yen coin and chopsticks to find out if my father and brother were alive. The game told me that they were both dead.

My brother was directly exposed, so he would not have survived. Since he was doomed, I still feel I should have given him the water he was so thirsty for. I think my father may have gotten caught in a fire or breathed too much smoke.

Senji stayed at the Kasabo house for a year. His four-year-older brother was discharged and came home from Gifu prefecture. Senji, his mother and brother began to build a new life together.

I developed leukemia and needed blood transfusions. My older brother donated his blood by intramuscular injection to my thigh a number of times. Meanwhile, he got sick with fever and diarrhea. He was diagnosed with typhoid fever and was put in isolation. That put an end to my blood transfusions. I got more and more tired. Eventually I couldn't even lift a teacup. A big typhoon called Makurazaki hit in September. Water flooded in under the floor, but I

Hiroshima August 6, 1945

us in yukata, a summer kimono. She prepared a truck that had old tatami in the bed. We decided to head for Sugita's house in Mibu (now, Mibu, Kita Hiroshima-cho). Sugita's mother had fled to a hat store we visited. His mother went to borrow a large cart from a neighbor. The three of us got a ride on the cart and finally were seen by a doctor. The doctor put Mercurochrome on us and picked out the glass fragments and bamboo splinters in our backs. The backs of the women's yukata we were given in Oasa were bright red with blood and pus. Sugita's mother gave us new shirts to wear. We stayed there for a week, going to the clinic every day on the cart. The wounds treated with Mercurochrome dried and became scabs.

There was a big hospital called Kasabo Hospital near Senji's house at Kami Tenma-cho. It was owned by Mr. and Mrs. Kasabo. They would always tell his family, "Our parents live in Kabe, so if the war gets any worse you're always welcome to stay out there." Senji's parents would reply, "If something happens, we'll evacuate to your parents' house." Recalling this conversation, Senji made his way to the Kasabos' parents' house in Kabe.

I entered the premise from the front gate. As I walked past the garden, I saw a small person sitting on the porch. "That's my mom!" My mother always sat up straight and smart-looking. She sat in the way she always did. "It can't be true! I must be dreaming." But the person in front of me was, indeed, my mother. Without thinking I ran up to her and hugged her. "Mom!"

I didn't know what to say. I cried out loud. The fear, loneliness, hardship, pain—all the feelings I had endured burst out all at once and I kept sobbing. My mother started crying, too. "You're alive! I'm so glad you made it, Senji." She held on to me tightly and didn't let

[Document 3] Senji Kawai

carefully positioned between the injured.

Before we got to Kabe, two young women died. Their skin had peeled off showing black and red flesh. Their faces were burned and unrecognizable. They were so pitiful. They had been lightly dressed because it was summer, so they were almost naked as their clothes were burned by the heat and blown to tatters by the blast.

"These two are dead! Let's get them off!"

The truck stopped and the firefighters lifted them down.

We covered their private parts with leaves and prayed for them to console their souls. We had no tool nor the time to bury the bodies. Removing one dead another injured to get in. There was no point in carrying the dead.

After a while someone on the truck suddenly had a spasm. It was my friend Chuji Sugita. His eyes rolled back, and he began to moan in pain. It looked like he was about to die. I got on top of him and shouted, "Oji! Don't die! We're going to your house!" His calm and mature personality earned him the nickname Oji or old man. I slapped him and he came to.

The police station in Kabe was crowded with survivors. The injured got Mercurochrome on their wounds and bandages wrapped around them. Firefighters came to a vacant lot behind the police station. They used hand hooks on the corpses, dragging them to an area where corpses were piled on the ground. Nobody could afford to treat us here either. Mothers with babies and small children were neglected. They sat on the ground not knowing what to do.

We decided to travel to a friend's house in Oasa (now, Oasa, Kita Hiroshima-cho). We got on another truck filled with injured near death. When we arrived at the friend's house, his mother was surprised to see us.

"I only have women's clothing," she said and put the three of used as a first-aid station. There we saw a soldier who was near death in a crouched position with his head stuck to the wall. His back was severely burned and completely covered with maggots.

"I wonder if he's dead," I said. The soldier turned around and glared at me. "Humans don't die easily," I thought. He had burns all over his back but was still alive. What I didn't know was that my back looked just like his, severely burned and covered with maggots.

One of the classrooms was being used as an examination room. People with burns were waiting in line. Mercurochrome was put on our burns with cotton, and the next person would be called. This was the only type of "treatment" available. I picked some of the glass out of my back; the remaining glass was buried under my skin leaving tiny bumps.

Chairs had been put out in the corridor, and hibakusha were sleeping on them. Many were almost dead; some had already died. Pieces of dry bread were put beside their pillows. Thinking, "It's a waste to leave that there." I stole some of them, and shared them with my friends. It was the first time I had ever stolen from someone.

All the infirmaries were overcrowded. The military were refusing to treat civilians.

I heard someone shout, "Get the badly wounded on this truck! We're going to Kabe (now, Kabe, Asa Kita-ku) where there are doctors!" I saw a truck loaded with severely injured victims. It was not a military truck; it was a private citizen's truck. Someone got the truck to take injured people to Kabe. We got onto the truck with many people who were near death. There were over 20 people on the truck. Most of them were burned black. We couldn't even tell if they were male or female. The injured were lying like a fish on the floor of the truck begging in whispers for water. They were too weak to move. The firefighters and the four of us were the only ones sitting, our legs

[Document 3] Senji Kawai

Mitaki-cho, Nishi-ku). My brother's body was hot, and he shouted for water, heading for the river.

"Don't let him drink the water! He'll die!" shouted a firefighter from a distance. I couldn't let him have any water. At the bottom of a nearby mountain, a relief corps member was giving treatment for the wounded. I left my brother there and walked up the mountain with my friends. Our bodies were covered in blood from shards of glass and pieces of bamboo from the earthen walls that had stuck into them. Meanwhile, it started raining a thick black rain, which got heavier and heavier until it was pouring down. That's when I realized blood was running down my back. Countless small pieces of glass had punctured my back. Washed by rain, the blood was running. I grew cold. The village had a Shinto shrine. We entered the shrine, tore down a banner, wrapped it around ourselves and rested.

The rain stopped. I suddenly wanted to go to the toilet. It was unbearable.

"Go ahead," I told my friends. I stayed back and defecated near a garden. It was amazing. I excreted an enormous amount of black feces. "Is all of this coming from my stomach?" It was an unbelievable amount.

A doctor later told me, "It's good that you relieved yourself. You probably let a lot of the poison out of your body."

After resting a bit, we started toward the house of a friend who lived nearby. But then one of my friends said he was going home to Mitaki. The remaining three of us decided to head for Gion-cho (now, Gion-cho, Asa Minami-ku). We had heard rumors that they were offering treatment there. However, when we got there we found piles of dead bodies and not enough people to treat the wounded.

We walked to Furuichi (now, Furuichi, Asa Minami-ku). Omei Elementary School (now, Furuichi Elementary School) was being roof. All of the surrounding houses were down. I could see the ruins of the Industrial Promotion Hall, a building I normally could not see at all from my house. In the Tenma River, I saw people screaming as they were washed away with window frames, furniture, and horses. It was still morning, but it was dark as night. It felt like I had crossed the River Styx. I thought so because the sights I was seeing were not of this world.

I heard my father said "Senji! Your mother is trapped. Come and help!" Our house was a wreck so I had no idea where things were. I ducked back down under the roof and tried to find the first floor. My mother was lying on her back with her left arm trapped under a door frame. Her arm was torn off and white bone was protruding. My mother was so pale—she looked dead. She didn't utter a sound. "She won't make it!" I knew this by intuition. My father and I dragged her out from under the frame and carried her to the bank of the Tenma River behind our house.

"I'm going back to look for the employees! Take your friends and get out of here," he told me, then ran back to the house.

I realized that my younger brother was lying on the ground right beside me. He looked up at me and struggled to stand up.

"Senji" he said. The hands he stretched out to me had skin hanging from them.

Senji's younger brother was on the school swimming team. He was planning to help clear buildings to make fire lanes, but changed his mind and went to swim in the river. He was on the steps by the river and was directly hit by the heat ray. He was 13 years old.

With my brother and 4 of my friends, we escaped to Mitaki (now,

[Document 3] Senji Kawai

and serve all the guests with sake and zouni (soup with rice cakes) and vegetables served on New Year's Day. People we didn't even know would hear about us and stop by. "Come in!" My mother didn't care who they were. She just invited them into the room where we served food and drinks.

She often took me to the Geisha cabaret. I often saw my mother handing monetary gifts to the younger Geishas. Once I started school at the First Commercial School (now, Hiroshima Commercial High School), a lot of friends came to my house. It was a boys' school so they were all boys. I got a taste for sake at a young age. There was a liquor store next door where I would take home as much sake as I could put on my parents' tab. When my friends came to my house, we always drank sake.

In 1945, I was in my third year of middle school with one year to go before graduation. Middle schools under the old system covered five years, but during the war they were shortened to four years. One of my classmates was accepted to the Naval Aviation Preparatory School, so five of us took him out to celebrate. We partied by drinking and singing at a string of restaurants. The next day, I was exhausted and took the day off from school as we were to work hard clearing fire lanes. Four of my friends who had partied the day before also decided to cut classes while on their way to school, and came to my house. "If you're not going to school, we can't be bothered to go either," they said. We talked about nothing in particular and hung out on the second floor.

An air-raid warning cleared, and we could no longer hear the anti-aircraft guns. "I bet they ran out of ammunition!" we joked.

That instant we saw a blinding flash followed by a tremendously loud roar, and my house collapsed. I felt like my body was being squished into a mold. I used all my strength to crawl out onto the

Document 3

Who's gonna tell folks about the atomic bombing? My wife pushed me to talk

Senji Kawai
Born in February 1930. Exposed to the bomb when he was 15 at home in Kami Tenma-cho (now, Kami Tenma-cho, Nishi-ku), 1.2 kilometers from the hypocenter. Has keloid scars on his back, prostate cancer, heart-related illness, and other aftereffects of the bomb; still undergoing treatment. Until 10 years ago, worked for a construction company. Eighty-four years old, resides in Nishi-ku, Hiroshima.

I still suffer from aftereffects. The atomic bomb is an absolute evil.

"My mother used to be a Geisha, so she was outstanding and big-hearted," says Senji. His father was totally devoted to his work. He studied how to improve rubber-soled footwear for the working man, and his products were eventually commercialized. His parents were total opposites but perfect for each other. Senji was their second son.

Two young employees worked with sewing machines in a workshop on our premises. We also had two housekeepers. My mother was always ordering them to do this or that. My father's business got on track, and we were quite prosperous. Our house was in Kami Tenma-cho (now, Kami Tenma-cho, Nishi-ku). It was a big two-story house about 9 meters wide by 30 meters in depth. I was pampered as a little boy. Every New Year's Day, we would welcome children to carry this burden.

I live near Peace Park and the Cenotaph for the A-bomb Victims. I wake up at five every morning and go there and pray. I have never before spoken in detail about my experience of the atomic bombing.

Katsuyuki changed his mind after the nuclear power accident in Fukushima due to the Great East Japan Earthquake of March 11, 2011. According to the International Nuclear Event Scale, the Fukushima accident is rated at the highest level, 7, which is same as the Chernobyl accident that occurred in 1986. Ichiro Moritaki, the great leader of the anti-nuclear movement, often said that "humankind and nuclear energy cannot coexist". If an accident occurs again, it will be too late. Now, whenever Katsuyuki has the chance, he talks about his experience. He says, "Although the power of a single person is small, if we all put our voices together, we can make a change."

I saw a worker in the Fukushima nuclear power plant on TV. I think I saw a rash on a worker's arm—the same kind of rash I saw on my brother's body. It made me shudder. The situation inside the reactors has not even been confirmed yet, but the government quickly declared the accident to be under control. Radiation is not that simple. The government shouldn't be so vague. We hibakusha know the horror of radiation from the tragic experience inflicted by the atomic bomb. I believe it is time for us to raise our voices.

Hiroshima August 6, 1945

within 3 kilometers of the hypocenter. But to apply for the health book I needed someone to certify that I was there. The president of the Neighborhood Association filled in a certificate to vouch for me. It was the same president who had helped me move our furniture. His face was burnt by the heat ray and disfigured by keloid scars. When I went to get the certificate, I said, "You've been through a lot, haven't you." He replied, "I'm OK. Only my face was burned. It was just fate that this happened to me. You take care of yourself, Katsuyuki."

The Atomic Bomb Survivor Health Book is a small book with a yellow cover. Nobody applied for them in the beginning. At the time people were going around saying, "A-bomb disease is contagious."

A radio drama called The Yellow Book was broadcast to promote the book. By showing the Atomic Bomb Survivor Health Book and your health insurance card, you can get free medical treatment. As people learned more about this system, they started getting the book. Those who cannot find someone certify their presence can advertise on the radio saying, "Anyone who knows Mr. X, who used to live in XX, please contact me".

I married when I was 31. One of the senior dancers used to warn me saying, "If you don't get married by 30, it will get harder to find a partner. You'll be single all your life. If you find someone you like, get married right away!"

My wife was from Tokushima prefecture and didn't experience the atomic bombing. There was a rumor that hibakusha would have handicapped babies, so when my wife was pregnant, I was so worried I couldn't think of anything else. Fortunately, my two daughters are both healthy. At the time, there was talk about issuing Atomic Bomb Survivor Health Books for second generation hibakusha. I was asked if I wanted to apply for my daughters, but I declined. Living with my own A-bomb experience was enough for me. I didn't want my clinic. I was diagnosed with tuberculosis and took streptomycin. Rumor spread that moxibustion (a type of heat therapy) would help if radiation lowered the white blood cell count. After that, moxibustion became a popular form of treatment. When I was not feeling well, I used to go to get a moxa treatment. I can't prove it is related to the bomb, but my father died of liver cancer in 1963 at the age of 58. In 1990, my mother passed away from colon cancer when she was 80. My sister married, but later lost her sight due to hemorrhages in the eye and other complications.

In 1946, my friend's sister died in an accident. I heard he was planning to dance at her memorial service. I went to watch my friend practice. That was how I first encountered Japanese classical dance.

Lessons were held on the 8th floor of Fukuya Department Store. "You can borrow my fan and sandals, so just order a yukata (summer kimono) and I'll teach you," the teacher told me. I thought dance might make me stronger, so I decided to become an apprentice under Master Mitsuyuki Hanayagi of Hanayagi School. I was 17 years old. When I first started, I didn't have enough strength. I fainted during practice several times. But dancing worked. I gradually became stronger.

In June 1953, I became master of the school. My teacher gave me a new name using a Chinese character meaning happiness (幸). He called me Kojiro Hanayagi (花柳幸次郎). My teacher's name was Mitsuyuki Hanayagi (花柳光幸), but he later changed his name to Kaji Hanayagi and became one of the best dancers in the Chugoku Region. I continued dancing for 60 years.

In 1956, I received an Atomic Bomb Survivor Health Book. I was convince herself.

His shoulders and arms got thinner and thinner until they were like chopsticks. My mother massaged and encouraged him continually, but he died on August 29. He had been a mischievous, very masculine boy. Our personalities were quite different but we always played together. I remember I could never beat him in sumo wrestling, marbles in the alley, or most other games. After watching a samurai movie, we wore wooden swords on our waist and fought like the heroes in the movie. My brother was dominant in that fighting as well. For the harvest festival in early winter, he always made himself up as a red or blue demon and chased other children around the neighborhood. Sometimes he played too much, but if I tried to stop him he would just get wilder and wilder. He loved military drills and always said, "I'll go to Naval Aviation Preparatory School as soon as I turn 15."

My mother's grief and suffering were so deep, I couldn't stand to see her. Every day she cried, losing her voice, holding tight to a can of ointment she had applied on my brother's burns. My brother was only 13 but he looked like an old man when he passed away. His skin was tattered, and his arms and legs were so skinny he looked like a skeleton. I later heard that his friend Nakamura passed away on the same day.

Although I was only 1.2 kilometers away from the hypocenter, I had no burns, nor did I experience acute A-bomb disease. My doctor thought it was strange. He said, "You were well shielded." I think that being indoors was the main reason. Still, I have gotten sick easily the rest of my life. I always feel tired. I used to get vitamin injection shots. I always observed physical training class at schools. I didn't have the strength to participate.

Right after the war, I developed a strange cough and went to a were shielded by the adults all around them.

The fire had not started yet so the two of them managed to make their way home. My brother had worn a hat at the time of the bombing, and it was burned to his head, a deep, black burn. He looked as if he were sick.

I could not believe that despite the horrible disaster Hiroshima had suffered, my entire family had survived and reunited. I could not help smiling when I thought about this simple reality. We told each other how fortunate we were.

That day we ate fried rice using the rice rations my mother had saved aside for emergencies. The kitchen was destroyed, so we built a stove using an oilcan on the earth floor. My mother put a pan on it and made fried rice. All of us, including Nakamura, surrounded the oilcan and watched how my mother cooked. Thinking back, I know it was simple rice fried with cooking oil and a little soy sauce, nothing else, but that was a great feast at that time. I remember that taste even now.

The next day, the fire had died down in most of the city, except Atago-machi (now, Atago-machi, Higashi-ku). Nakamura spent the night with us, and I walked to Tokaichi-machi Station with him. We saw a scorched streetcar that was burned brown.

"You were on that thing!" I was impressed by the fact that my brother and Nakamura had both survived even in such a completely destroyed streetcar. We noticed the ruins of the Industrial Promotion Hall as we crossed the Aioi Bridge and headed for Tokaichi-machi (now, Tokaichi-machi, Naka-ku), following the streetcar track.

After about 20 days, my brother's hair started falling out and red spots appeared all over his body. "You'll be fine! It's just the poison coming out of your body. Be strong!" My mother encouraged him, but he just lay there looking weak. It seemed like she was trying to to work at the Asahi Arms Factory in Jigozen-mura in Saeki-gun (now, Hatsukaichi City).

When he saw the mushroom cloud above Hiroshima, he came to look for us by boat from Jigozen. He was thinking, "There are no houses on Hijiyama Hill so it won't catch fire. My family will take refuge there." On this assumption, he had walked to the hill.

After reuniting with my father, we decided not to go to Hijiyama Hill. We headed for a house we had rented in Katako (now, Onaga-cho, Higashi-ku). It took probably thirty minutes, crossing Kojin Bridge, which had lost its handrails to the blast. There were charred, coal-like dead bodies lying everywhere. We couldn't tell the men from the women.

I saw so many miserable people. I saw one whose clothes were burnt out from the back by the heat ray, and the skin on his back was hanging down to his feet. Another was walking along dragging the skin of his back. Another was hit by heat ray from the front so his or her face was red, black and terribly swollen. All of them walked like sleepwalking ghosts with their arms out in front of them, their skin hanging from their fingertips.

My mother and younger sister Rumiko (then, 5) had previously evacuated to our house in Katako. Although the house was ruined by the blast, they were both safe. However, many people in Katako had severe burns and other injuries. When my mother saw us coming back safe she was overjoyed and said, "I was so afraid, seeing so many people fleeing!"

Then my younger brother Akio came back. He was 13 and mobilized at Toyo Can Manufacturer. He was at Nagarekawa on a streetcar at the time of the bombing. He told us that most of the people around him died instantaneously because of the heat rays and blast. Because my brother and his friend Nakamura were small, they spread from mouth to mouth. The people on the riverbank stood up and started heading toward Hijiyama Hill. I followed the crowd. When we reached Yanagi Bridge, it ignited and started burning right before our eyes. The fire spread, and in a minute or so the whole Bridge was burning. Nobody could put it out. We couldn't do anything but stare at the burning bridge.

Yanagi Bridge had been frequently washed away in the past by floods. This time, the bridge was under repair and building materials were piled up around it. They say that those materials caught fire and spread to the bridge.

The bridge was burnt out. If we wanted to get to the other side, we would have to wade and swim. We were fairly near the Inland Sea so we had to wait for the tide to go out. Besides, a strong wind whirled through the air, and the waves were quite high.

In Dote-machi (now, Matsukawa-cho, Minami-ku) on the opposite side of the river, the fire was raging bright red. I could feel its heat in a hot wind all the way from the other side. The fire was so strong I felt as if it would spread to my side. We felt so hot we went into the river to cool down. We brought tatami mats from a collapsed house and put them in the river. We put the heavily wounded on them. Then we just waited for low tide.

Finally the water was low enough and we were able to cross. Everything in Dote-cho was burnt out, but the fierce fire had subsided. We crossed the river pushing the tatami. The severely injured were shivering, though it was midsummer. By strange good fortune I found my father on the other side. It was a miracle. My father was not a soldier. He was in the National Volunteer Corps in charge of building demolition. He also went to factories to help. He had been on his way careful!"

I breathed in a lot of dust and dirt from the walls lifted up by the wind. I got sick, and before I knew it I was vomiting a lot. Still throwing up, I managed to crawl over the roof and escape. It was summer, so I was wearing shorts and an open-necked shirt. My clothes were torn to pieces while I was trapped under the house. Roof tiles and debris were all over the road, making it difficult for me to walk with my bare feet.

Because I was in a room, I had taken off my shoes. I walked on the road, then on top of roof tiles from roof to roof. I found some sandals in what looked like a shoe closet in a fallen house. I put the sandals on and headed for Kyobashi River, dragging my left leg in pain.

I passed a community kitchen on the way and saw an old lady trapped under a telephone pole. She couldn't move and was screaming "Help!" I pulled her out from under the pole. Apparently she thought I would leave her there and clung hard to my waist. Taking her with me, we got as far as a field on the riverbank.

By the bridge was a group of eight to ten women. They were all at a loss. Fire was breaking out here and there. They didn't know where to go. Their hair and clothes were all burned; they were essentially naked. They crouched down trying to cover their bodies with wood and newspapers. The old lady I was helping saw someone she knew, so she joined that group. Many people had fallen to the ground. Countless bloated and black-scorched bodies were tossed everywhere.

I ran up to the river bank and looked over the town. All the houses were leaning or crushed. Of all the tall buildings nearby, the Chugoku Newspaper and Fukuya Department Store were the only ones still standing, and smoke was coming up from both of them.

"There must be a first-aid station on Hijiyama Hill!" This thought

[Document 2] Katsuyuki Shimoi

My body fell down, as if being vacuumed into an abyss. At that time, nearly all houses had earthen walls, and the president's house was among them. They were fragile and fell apart immediately.

It was pitch dark. I was trapped between a wall and a pillar. I tried with all my strength to move my body, but I couldn't. My left leg was wedged under a fallen beam. I was in pain. It seemed I had injured my ankle.

"Help! Help!" I shouted.

"I'm stuck as well! Who can help you!" a voice came back in a rage.

I heard someone nearby saying, "Somebody's caught down here." Hearing that voice, I calmed down a bit. I waited for a while. A part of the rubble shifted, and I was able to move a little. If I crawled under the pillar above my left shoulder, I thought I might be able to get out. But I couldn't get my head under the pillar. With all my might, I bent my neck as if willing to break it. Finally I was free! I started to crawl, little by little. I fought my way out by crawling toward a ray of light in the roofing. I was assuming that only the president's house was destroyed, until I passed the roof.

I pushed my face up over the roof, then stood up. I was stunned. The blast had toppled every building in town, all in the same direction, like dominos. All I could see were roofs. Debris was everywhere. I could see the Fukuya Department Store and Chugoku Newspaper buildings in the distance. I later heard that the president's wife, his daughter, and some others were found on the first floor burned to death. I couldn't find the president or the person that yelled back at me. Suddenly I felt the wind and instinctively felt that a fire had started somewhere.

I had heard from my aunt, who survived the Osaka air raid, "When a fire turns a corner, it creates a wind as strong as a tornado. Be

the morning, he made engine parts for airplanes at the Hiroshima Factory of Kurashiki Aviation in Yoshijima (now, Yoshijima, Naka-ku). He was in charge of inspection. He dipped the finished parts in liquid to make sure there was no crack in them. He then chiseled anchor marks on the parts that passed the inspection. In addition to male students, housewives and female students were mobilized at the factory. They didn't have enough strength to use chisels so they used drills to cut the anchor mark. Katsuyuki later heard that all the window glass in the factory was blown out by the blast. The inspectors always worked by the windows where there was plenty of light. All the housewives and female students who were at work were pierced by glass shards in their faces and heads. They died in pools of blood.

On August 6, I took the day off. I had submitted a medical certificate from my home doctor to the factory. The day our house would be demolished was approaching, but we had not found a new place to live. We had no choice but ask to the president of the Neighborhood Association to keep our property temporarily in his house in Shimo Yanagi-machi (now Kanayama-cho, Naka-ku). As soon as I confirmed that the air-raid warning had cleared, I changed into my work clothes and went out. The president's house was about 50 meters from ours.

He agreed to keep our property on the second floor so we were bringing his furniture down to the first floor. I used a rope to let the tilted furniture slide down a ladder. The president and some neighbors received it at the bottom. It happened just after we started this work.

Suddenly I saw a brilliant light, thousands of times brighter than the flash of a camera. Then I heard a tremendous loud booming roar. In an instant, the second floor room I was in rumbled and collapsed.

Document 2

I talk about the horror of radiation since I saw the accident in Fukushima

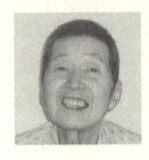

Katsuyuki Shimoi
Born in January 1930. Exposed to the bomb when he was 15 at the house of a Neighborhood Association president in Shimo Yanagi-machi, 1.2 kilometers from the hypocenter. At 17, served apprenticeship under a master of the Hanayagi School of Japanese traditional dance. Was an accredited master and given the name Kojiro Hanayagi when he was 23. The character for "Ko" in Kojiro is a character he received from his master. Now 84, resides in Naka-ku, Hiroshima.

My brother was exposed in a streetcar.
Despite being only 13, he died with the face of an old man.

I lived in a row of apartment houses on a narrow alley. Hiroshima City planned to force us out and demolish our building to expand the alley. My family was informed by the City that we had to move out and demolish the house by the end of September. Air-raid warnings sounded frequently in those days. People living in densely built areas were required to leave their homes to make fire lanes that were supposed to keep the fire from spreading and provide a way to escape.

Katsuyuki was 15. He graduated from higher elementary school and enrolled in Second Shudo Middle School. However, instead of studying at the school he was mobilized to work in a factory. This was called "labor service". Every day beginning at 7:00 in loved ones at once and took such good care of me through her grief, tears come to my eyes.

Shigeru has come this far without talking about the atomic bomb to anybody, but his grandchildren went to Peace Park and asked me about the atomic bomb. I decided to share his story. And finally, in Italy...

In 2011, I told my A-bomb experience to an audience in Italy. I was in Rome on January 30, then Florence on February 1. I was invited by some peace groups, including the Pugwash Conference and International Physicians for the Prevention of Nuclear War (IPPNW). I was not used to taking turns speaking with an interpreter, but I spoke with my whole heart. It was the first time I had ever spoken through an interpreter. Everyone listened to my story responded enthusiastically. My sister Harue was still alive at that time, and when I said, "Harue is over 90 years old and is in good health," the whole audience stood up, cheering and clapping their hands. I was deeply moved by the warm, sweet treatment I received from the Italians, who were delighted by the fact that Harue had lived through that tragic experience.

Nobel Peace Prize laureate Betty Williams encouraged me saying, "Thank you very much for coming all this way." After my speech, people came to meet me. One hugged me and said, "I was touched. Grazie." Another shook my hand and said, "I have read Dr. Hachiya's book." I had to get up some courage to go to Italy, but I was extremely happy I did, and I feel that I did the right thing.

I hope to see the world filled with the smiles of our children and grandchildren.

Human beings do not need atomic bombs.

[Document 1] Shigeru Nonoyama

to Hiroshima looking for family members and were exposed to radiation. They had no other injury, but they tired easily and soon became feverish.

Doctors would say, "I wonder if you have pneumonia." After a while, they developed red spots on their bodies. They would think, "What's happening to me?" They lost their hair and vomited blood. Many died without any understanding of what had happened. Corpses quickly decomposed in the summer heat and attracted maggots— turning the bodies white. The stench of the burning bodies filled the town. The dead were cremated on the ridges of rice fields. There were no coffins available. We covered the corpses with firewood and burned them in the fields every day.

Shigeru married when he was 40. His wife, Kimie, was also a survivor. She was in Funairi-machi (now, Funairi-machi, Naka-ku), two kilometers away from the hypocenter. Before Kimie met him, she was engaged to someone else. However, the wedding was canceled because the fiancé's family did not want their son to marry an A-bomb survivor.

Since we were both survivors of the bomb, some said, "It's OK, they won't have healthy children anyway." We were fortunate to have three healthy children. I now have five grandchildren. Three of them are about the age Hideaki was when we were swimming in the river. What if my grandchildren suffer an atomic bombing? Just imagining it makes me shudder.

But I fear not only for my grandchildren. No one deserves to be bombed such a horrific weapon. The human family does not need nuclear weapons. When I drink sake, my burnt upper body becomes bright red. Even now, when I think of my mother, who lost so many

Hiroshima August 6, 1945

Even though the bomb burns healed, they were often covered by thick scar tissue known as keloids. Even decades later, my name was called in a streetcar by someone whose face was unknown to me. It turned out that he was an old friend, but with a keloid scar. That was an everyday occurrence in Hiroshima after the war. For years I saw many people with keloids in the public baths.

However, I developed no keloids and no scars anywhere on my body. All that remains is a faint line between my upper body, which was above water and exposed to the heat ray, and my lower body, which was in the water while I was in the Tenma River. I believe my unscarred skin is a gift from my mother, who so tenaciously did her best to save her son.

I recovered and returned to work at the Telegraph Bureau in November. I received a medical checkup at the Hiroshima Communications Hospital at the same time. The director of the hospital, Dr. Michihiko Hachiya, who performed the checkup, said, "You're probably the only person who survived the bomb in the river. Your skin is clean enough. Take care and don't overdo it." Dr. Hachiya was also a survivor. He was injured but he examined and treated survivors in the wreckage of his hospital building.

On the way to work to Fukuro-machi (now, Fukuro-machi, Naka-ku), a wooden sign announced, "Navy Officers Burial Site". Around the sign lay a thin layer of dirt. When I dug in the ground there, I found dead bodies with rotten skin peeling off. Many wooden signs like that could be seen throughout the city.

I simply thought the atomic bomb was a "new type of bomb". None of us knew anything about radiation. Many people came

[Document 1] Shigeru Nonoyama

August 6 and was exposed to the bomb. He passed away at the end of August. Tsuneko, Hideaki, Hiromi, Hirotaka and Masako—my mother's children and grandchildren departed one after another.

Maybe she couldn't afford to lament each time. I, myself, was on the brink of death and have little memory of that time. Glass shards filled Harue's face. Little purple spots like adzuki beans appeared on her face and body after about a week. When these spots appeared from face to chest, a person's hair would fall out bunch by bunch within a week. Although we didn't talk about this, we all thought that she would die soon.

She started throwing up jelly-like clumps of blood, enough to fill a bowl quickly. While my mother dumped one bowl of this chunky blood, she filled another one. My mother dug a hole in the garden and buried the blood day after day.

Harue miraculously recovered. She later said it was because she threw up all the bad blood. She lived to the age of 96 and passed away on February 6, 2013.

I hovered between life and death for three month from August to October. When a fly landed on a festering wound, it would bleed white maggots in a few days. My mother shooed the flies away with a fan through the night. She must have desperately determined not to lose any more sons or daughters. My dangling skin dried and turned hard like paper. My mother picked off the dry skin. She made a cream of straw ash mixed with cooking oil and applied it to my burnt head, face, chest and fingertips, turning me black. It stung at first but soon the hurt went away. When the wounds dried, they were covered by scabs. She soaked the scabs in cucumber juice and removed them. She applied the black cream again, and removed the scabs again, and kept repeating the process.

to look for his family. The black rain turned his white shirt black. His daughters were so transfigured he couldn't recognize them.

Nor was he himself. His face so swollen he couldn't see. Fortunately, he recognized his unscathed wife and the family was reunited.

Tsuneko, known for being kind and caring, and was loved by many. One who loved her was a farmer named Tamura in Furuichi, Asa-gun (now, Furuichi, Asa Minami-ku) 8 kilometers away from the hypocenter. The Tamura family offered to take us in. They were not even our relatives. It was mostly because of Tsuneko that our large family of 14 was able to take refuge with the Tamuras.

We thought that we might be attacked by enemy planes during the day so we waited to move in the night. Our mother borrowed a cart from a farm in Yamate-cho. Tsuneko, with an open chest wound, on the verge of death. Harue had blood all over her face. Hideaki had severe burns on his torso. Tsuneko's two-year-old child, Hiromi, these 4 were carried in the cart. We pushed the cart all night and reached the farm around daybreak.

Hideaki, who always hung around me like a little brother, passed away that day. A neighbor came to tell us that Tsuneko, who was staying at her parents-in-laws' house in Imuro, died on August 15 after a great deal of suffering. My mother was probably in shock. She just groaned and shed no tears.

Tsuneko's third daughter, Masako, a student at Shintoku Girl's School, remains missing. She was supposed to be on her way to school at 8:15 when the bomb exploded over Hiroshima. Harue's husband, Hirotaka, worked at the Army Munition Depot in Nagoya. He had taken a few days off work to see his family in Hiroshima as it had been a while since he saw them last. He arrived in Hiroshima on

[Document 1] Shigeru Nonoyama

We decided to escape to a safe place on a hill. We saw people with melted ears stuck to their cheeks, chins glued to shoulders, heads facing awkward positions, arms stuck to bodies, five fingers joined together and grab nothing. Those were the people fleeing. Not merely a hundred or two, the whole town was in chaos.

I saw that the noodle shop's wife's leg was caught under a fallen pole, and a fire was approaching. She was screaming "Help me! Help me!" There were no soldiers, no firefighters. I later heard her husband had cut his wife's leg off with a hatchet to save her.

Each and every scene was hell itself. I couldn't tell the difference between the men and the women. Everybody had scorched hair, burned clothes, and terrible burns. I thought I saw a doll floating in a fire cistern, but it was a dead baby.

A wife trapped under her fallen house was crying, "Dear, please help me, help me!" Her husband had no choice but to leave her in tears.

My family fled with my mother leading the way. Hirose Kita Bridge where we had been playing had been knocked down by the blast. Half the bridge was in water. It was low tide now, so we were able to slide down the bridge and cross the river. After walking about a kilometer and just before we reached Aki Higher Girls School in Yamate-cho (now, Yamate-cho, Nishi-ku), I could walk no further. I was laid down between two ridges in a potato field. The sky grew darker and darker, and then suddenly big black drops of rain started to fall. The rain grew so strong that my body was soon submerged in water with my face just barely above the surface.

Shigeru's father was on his way to work in Misasa (now, Misasa-cho, Nishi-ku) when the bomb was dropped. The heat ray came from behind, leaving his neck badly burned, but he was determined

Hiroshima August 6, 1945

I felt danger and quickly ducked into the water. The pressure from above was so great I couldn't swim or even move. Several times I swallowed water full of sand coming up from the river bottom.

I used all my strength to get to the surface and put my face into the air. The sun that had been blazing above us just moments before had vanished.

It was pitch dark. "What was that flash? Why is it so dark?"

Not being able to comprehend what had happened, I stood in the middle of the river.

After a while it gradually grew light.

I heard Hideaki's voice.

"Shigeru, what happened to you?"

I looked at him and saw his hair burned shriveled. The skin on his face and chest above the water had peeled off and was dangling like seaweed from his chest. The skin from his hand was dangling from his fingernails like rubber gloves. He and I stared at each other. Both of us had been utterly transformed. Hideaki and I looked just the same, but neither was aware that it had happened to us.

We scurried up the bank and stood stunned. No house was standing normally. Hijiyama Hill to the distant east was usually hidden from view by houses, but it was right there in front of our eyes. Our houses were crushed. The house was built on a riverbank so the sloped area was like a basement, which we used as a kitchen. My mother was there and unharmed.

I found Tsuneko with blood spurting out of an open chest wound. I tied my loincloth around her wound like a bandage.

Harue's face was bleeding from shattered glass. Harue's two daughters were miraculously unhurt. They were both under a cow pulling wagon that had come to clean out waste from the toilets.

People crawling out from the crumbled houses started to flee.

[Document 1] Shigeru Nonoyama

Nagoya, where there are no rivers, I wasn't used to playing in the water. Not being able to swim, the local kids made fun of me, calling me "Nagoya". I was so humiliated I sneaked out to the river at night and practiced swimming between the piers. Soon, I was able to swim.

That was about when I graduated from the Communications Staff Training Center and started working at the Hiroshima Telegraph Bureau. We worked in three shifts. On August 6, my shift was from 2 pm to 10 pm, so I was at home that morning. Tsuneko's first son Hideaki was with me. He was a sixth grader and had evacuated with his school to Imuro (Asa-cho, Asa Kita-ku) until the previous day. He had just come back to Hiroshima.

"Let's go swimming!"

Just when we took off our clothes, the yellow alert sounded. The tide was high but starting to go out. We could only jump from the bridge when the tide was high, so we waited impatiently.

Finally, the alert was lifted. We rushed out wearing nothing but loincloths and jumped from the handrail of the Kita Hirose Bridge.

We found some driftwood trapped between the bridge girders. Yoshiaki and I got it loose and pushed it upstream. The river was deep, and Hideaki couldn't stand on the bottom. He clung to the log as I was pushing it upstream.

The roar of B-29s came from nowhere.

"Let's not get shot! Hide under the water!" I shouted, but looked up the sky. At that instant, I saw a bright flash, like lightning.

At the same time, Hirose Elementary School, which had been standing by the river, was blown away in pieces. People also flew through the air. I saw countless hot water balls of various sizes like baseballs or ping pong balls running across the surface of the river, as if a blacksmith had put the red blade of a sword from a forge into cold water. The surface of the river grew hot.

Hiroshima August 6, 1945

Document 1

I spoke about the bomb in Rome and Florence

Shigeru Nonoyama
Born in January 1930. Exposed to the bomb in the Tenma River at Hirose Kita-machi (now, Hirose Kita-machi, Naka-ku), 1.1 km from the hypocenter when he was 15 years old. Married when he was 40. Started to talk about his A-bomb experience recently after his grandchildren asked him about it. He went overseas to share his experience in 2011. Eighty-four years old, resides in Asa Kita-ku, Hiroshima.

Exposed while swimming
Countless hot water balls raced across the surface of the river.

Shigeru was born in Nagoya, Aichi Prefecture, the youngest child of three siblings. His two sisters were married and lived in Hiroshima by the time he reached the age of remembering memories. After 1945, major cities throughout Japan were being hit by air raids one after another, but Hiroshima was spared. More people moved to Hiroshima. Shigeru and his parents moved to Hiroshima, depending on his two sisters and their families. His eldest sister, Tsuneko, had six children; his second eldest sister, Harue, had two. Fifteen family members from three families lived in two houses across an alley from each other.

Our house stood on the bank of the Tenma River. We caught goby, river shrimp, and crabs at low tide. At high tide, we would plunge into the water from a bridge. I was 15 years old. Coming from

CONTENTS

Introduction *4*

Document 1	Shigeru Nonoyama	*8*
Document 2	Katsuyuki Shimoi	*17*
Document 3	Senji Kawai	*28*
Document 4	Kazunori Nishmura	*39*
Document 5	Kazukuni Yamada	*49*
Document 6	Tadashi Kihara	*59*
Document 7	Yoshiharu Nakamura	*67*
Document 8	Toshio Morimoto	*76*
Document 9	Hiroatsu Taniguchi	*83*
Document 10	Kaoru Hashimoto	*94*
Document 11	Takanobu Hirano	*101*
Document 12	Shoso Kawamoto	*112*
Document 13	Kiyoshi Ito	*123*
Document 14	Tadayoshi Tashima	*129*

Acknowledgements *136*

Memorial Park. Often times we have been shocked by the lack of awareness people have, both inside and outside Japan, about the reality of the sufferings the atomic bomb victims have endured and how that continues to this day. This realization has inspired the members of the Hiroshima Peace Committee to come up with a project to collect the testimonies of the men who lived through the seventy years after the atomic bomb was dropped.

The members of the committee created a list of men who would be willing to share their experiences and interviewed them one by one. This process has helped each of us to come to unexpected realizations. The vivid and harrowing account of what these men went through was truly eye-opening and led us to deepen our desire and prayer for world peace. With the passage of time, the memory of the bombing is gradually diminishing in people's minds. The publishing of this book has been driven by our profound sense of responsibility to pass on people's actual experiences of the atomic bomb to the future generations.

We sincerely hope that many people as possible will come to read the stories of these men. It would be truly rewarding for us if this book will help the readers to deepen their understanding of the inhumane consequences of nuclear weapons and inspire them to take action in their own way to make sure that these weapons are never used again.

Daisaku Shiode
Chairman
Soka Gakkai Hiroshima Peace Committee

March 2014

possession of these weapons represents an outright negation of the dignity of life. He stated in his declaration, "Although a movement calling for a ban on the testing of atomic or nuclear weapons has arisen around the world, it is my wish to go further, to attack the problem at its root. I want to expose and rip out the claws that lie hidden in the very depths of such thoughts." He stressed that the fundamental answer to this problem is that we challenge the root thinking that justifies possession of nuclear weapons as necessary evil.

Determined to realize his mentor's initiative, Ikeda continued to engage in dialogue with world leaders over the course of many years and called for the abolition of nuclear weapons in his peace proposal issued every year. The reason why Ikeda continues to remind people about the atomic bombings of Hiroshima and Nagasaki is because this tragic history symbolizes the ultimate denial of human dignity, respect for life, and people's right to their limitless potentiality. For this reason, we believe that Hiroshima and Nagasaki shoulder an important role and mission to become a peace hub from which efforts to eliminate nuclear weapons must spread worldwide.

In December 2009, the Hiroshima Peace Committee was established within Soka Gakkai Hiroshima Peace Conference. It is the first one of its kind nationally that was formed by men's division members. The committee met once a month led by Yasuo Kubo, chairman of Hiroshima Peace Conference. During these meetings, active discussions took place regarding our organization's direction and future efforts toward the seventieth anniversary of the atomic bombings of Hiroshima and Nagasaki. We all agreed that the end to the nuclear age will not come unless we strengthen the world public opinion in support of nuclear abolition. Every year, we accompany many visitors from both Japan and abroad to the Hiroshima Peace

Introduction

On January 26, 2013, commemorating the 38th anniversary of the SGI Day, Daisaku Ikeda, President of Soka Gakkai International, issued his annual peace proposal titled, "Compassion, Wisdom and Courage: Building a Global Society of Peace and Creative Coexistence," looking toward the year 2030. In his proposal, Ikeda called for the holding of "an expanded summit for a nuclear-weapon-free world" in 2015, the year which marks the seventieth anniversary of the atomic bombings of Hiroshima and Nagasaki. He further proposed that this summit be convened in Hiroshima and Nagasaki with the participation of representatives of the United Nations, nuclear weapon states and leaders of the nuclear-weapon-free-zones. In his past proposals, Ikeda has suggested that the 2015 NPT Review Conference be held in Hiroshima and Nagasaki as a vehicle for realizing a nuclear abolition summit. His proposal for an expanded summit received wide endorsement and support from around the world. His emphasis on the involvement of youth in various countries is also reiterated in this year's proposal.

The key message of his peace proposals stress that "respect for life's inherent dignity" is the spiritual framework needed to realize a global society of peace and creative coexistence. "Respect for the dignity of life" is an unwavering belief that has consistently underpinned our peace movement since the second Soka Gakkai president, Josei Toda called for the abolition of nuclear weapons in 1957, at the height of the Cold War when the arms race between the two superpowers was intensifying. Toda's uncompromising stance to abolish all nuclear weapons was based on the notion that the very

Hiroshima
August 6, 1945

A Silence Broken

DAISANBUNMEI-SHA
TOKYO